A LETHAL LEGACY

A. L. JAMBOR

Woofie

ISBN-10: 0-9964373-5-5

ISBN-13: 978-0-9964373-5-6

Copyright©2017 A.L. Jambor

AUTHOR'S NOTE

This is a work of fiction. Names, characters, places, and scenes are either the product of the author's imagination or are used fictitiously, and any resemblance to actual persons, living or dead, business establishments, events or locales is entirely unintentional.

Cover design by: Amy Jambor; Photo credit: Period Images and ianwool@canstockphoto.com

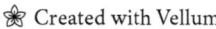 Created with Vellum

To my daughters-in-law, Danelle and Laurie, two glorious, strong women. I'm so glad you came into my life.

PROLOGUE

January 1882

*L*ord Harold Winston sat behind a large, ornate oak desk holding a fountain pen. He examined the document before him, and, satisfied it would set right a great wrong, he put down his pen.

Oliver, his new butler, knocked on the library door and entered the room to announce that his visitor had arrived.

"Thank you, Oliver. You may bring him up here."

A few moments later, Oliver led a tall, gaunt man into the room, and closed the door before leaving.

"McKenzie," Lord Harold said. "It's good to see you."

"I must admit this was most unexpected. I thought we had put the subject of your will to rest last year."

"Please take a seat."

Lord Harold went to one of the overstuffed chairs near the fireplace, and Errol McKenzie sat in the other. He had been Lord Harold's solicitor for thirty years.

"So, you've decided to change your will," McKenzie said.

"I've had a change of heart regarding the matter we discussed."

"I read that her stepmother died and left her in dire straights."

Lord Harold nodded. "It's not unlike Armstrong. He never thought of the future."

"I never met the man." McKenzie crossed his legs. "Are you acknowledging the relationship?"

Lord Harold sighed and shook his head.

"It will be as a bequest to my goddaughter."

"Are you her godfather?"

Lord Harold shook his head, and then stared at the fire.

"She was the love of my life," he said with a quiver in his voice. "I was heartbroken when she died."

McKenzie squirmed in his chair. Such displays of emotion were anathema to him.

"So you said when you told me you were changing your will."

Lord Harold took his handkerchief from the pocket of his smoking jacket and wiped his eyes.

"I can't stop thinking about the girl. She's an orphan now."

"She's an eighteen-year-old woman, milord. The best thing for her would be a solid marriage."

McKenzie put his head back and watched Lord Harold shift in his seat, and tap his finger on the arm of his chair.

"Her stepmother deprived her of opportunities to make such a marriage. Lady Felicia was a selfish, spoiled girl." He leaned forward. "But I will not speak ill of the dead. At least she provided the girl with an income, no matter how paltry."

"It's barely enough to keep a roof over her head." McKenzie flicked some lint off his trousers. "What will Dudley think when he finds out?"

Lord Harold gritted his teeth. His eldest boy, Roland, had died in India, the victim of an accidental discharge from his pistol. His death had led to Lord Harold's physical decline, and made his brother, Dudley, the heir to Lord Harold's title and his fortune.

As Lord Harold thought of Dudley, he got up, went went to his liquor cabinet, and opened the door. He took a decanter of brandy from the shelf, filled a snifter, and held it up to McKenzie, who shook his head. He took a large swallow, and then returned to his seat and kept the snifter in his hand.

"He will have the bulk of my fortune."

"He will, but he will want to know why you left her anything at all."

"I will explain to him that I promised her mother...no, her father, that I would see to it that she was properly cared for."

"But he will not be pleased."

McKenzie thought of Dudley and cringed. There was something odd about the man. He didn't like the way Dudley looked at him, as if he were a spider assessing his prey.

"I will deal with Dudley," Lord Harold said.

"I brought my clerk as you requested," McKenzie said. "He can witness your signature."

Lord Harold was still holding the snifter when he got up and went to his desk. The changes he'd made to his will were outlined on a single piece of paper. He sat behind his desk, and McKenzie came to read the codicil.

"It's well written," he said. "It will stand up in court should Dudley decide to take it that far."

"He won't. He'll be too concerned about his reputation to do anything about it."

Lord Harold turned to the bell pull and summoned Oliver, who appeared at the door within seconds.

"Oliver, fetch Mr. McKenzie's clerk."

"Yes, milord."

A few minutes later, the clerk arrived and witnessed Lord Harold signing the new codicil to his will. After the clerk signed it, McKenzie placed it in his case, and then turned to Lord Harold.

"I will see to it that a copy is delivered by the end of the week."

A. L. JAMBOR

He nodded to the clerk, who left them alone. "My advice is that you tell Dudley about this."

Lord Harold stood, and then drained the contents of the snifter into his glass. `McKenzie wondered how much brandy had been consumed since Roland's death.

"I will talk to him when he returns from Paris," Lord Harold said.

"Thank you," McKenzie said. He went to the door and paused before opening it. "Are you sure you want to leave her that amount?"

"I am."

McKenzie sighed. "Very well." He looked at Lord Harold, whose cheeks bore an alcoholic blush. "Please take care of yourself."

Lord Harold didn't reply. He waved as McKenzie walked away, and then he went to the window. He took out his pocket watch and tapped the side. It opened, and looked upon the face of his dear Phillipa. Time had faded the miniature portrait, but hadn't dulled the twinkle in her eye or the roses in her cheeks. He had fallen in love with her at first sight when Lord Michael Armstrong introduced her to him.

"What do you think?" Lord Michael asked. "I know she's young, and perhaps a bit naïve for her age, but she's lovely, don't you think?"

"Yes, lovely indeed," Lord Harold said.

Michael took Harold to the garden and they walked down the flagstone path to a gazebo at the center. They sat, and Harold noticed that Michael seemed distracted. He had crossed his legs and was shaking his foot.

"What is it, Michael?" he asked.

"I don't know if this life suits me," Michael said. "I find myself longing to roam around Europe as I did before I married." He looked into Harold's eyes. "I find the desire impossible to ignore."

"Well, then, take her along. You haven't had a honeymoon, have you?"

"No, but when I imagine the journey, I don't see her by my side."

Michael went on to confess that their couplings were less pleasant than he'd expected. He missed the passion of his French mistress, with whom he had spent many enjoyable hours in bed, and missed her terribly.

"So you can see why I can't bring Phillipa with me," he said.

Harold thought of his own mistress in London, a woman he had left two months before when she began hinting that she wanted to be his wife. He had his solicitor settle the matter with five thousand pounds and an introduction to an eligible bachelor. Michael's attachment to this other woman was nonsense, but Harold knew that no amount of talk would change the mind of a man in love. Michael was a fool.

"Is Millicent going to stay here this summer?" Michael asked.

"No. She's going to her mother's estate in Essex. She's taking the boys with her."

Michael tilted his head.

"Are *you* staying here this summer?"

"I am. I relish the idea of being here on my own. No chattering female or rowdy boys to disturb my peace will suit me nicely."

"So, should I decide to go to Paris, then perhaps you would look after Phillipa for me. Keep her company at dinner, things like that." He bit his lower lip. "She hasn't read many books, but she does listen well."

Harold thought of the beautiful young woman he'd just met and anger rose from his gut. What was wrong with the man?

Harold was old enough to know that should he agree to "look after her," one thing might lead to another, but despite this, his desire to see her again overruled his wisdom.

"I will check on her from time to time, but you must return by the end of summer. You are a husband now."

Michael agreed, and Harold began visiting Phillipa several times a week. He would arrive in the late afternoon, and they would walk in the garden before dinner. She told him how she had been coerced into marrying Michael, that he had been in dire financial straits and her father had offered a large dowry.

"I am eighteen," she said. "I found it difficult to feign interest in a gentlemen I'd met during the season last year. When I returned home without a promise of marriage, my father was eager to give my hand to Michael."

One evening, they were flirting over dinner when a thunderstorm sent a huge bolt of lightning into a tree outside the dining room window. It split the tree in half, and shook Phillipa to her core. Yet somehow, as they stood close to each other and watched the tree burn, her fear became desire, and the passion they felt could not be denied.

Their affair was born of love, and despite his promise to return in two months Michael stayed away for a year, and had no plans to return, until he was told that his lovely wife had died in childbirth. The baby, a sweet, brown-eyed girl, was small, but the housekeeper assured Michael that the child was merely petite, like her mother, when in fact the infant was only a month old. Harold mourned in private, unable to share his heartbreak with anyone.

The servants at Rosendale, the Armstrong manor house, were saddened by the loss of their young mistress, and Phillipa's personal maid, Hedda, accepted the responsibility of raising Felicity with the assistance of a nanny, and the butler, Mr. Conway, also watched over her whenever Lord Michael traveled abroad.

Harold would drop by from time to time to see young Felicity, and would often take her for walks in the garden, but the terrible sadness over losing Phillipa forced him to curtail his visits.

Twelve years passed before Harold saw Felicity again. One day, Michael wrote to him and asked if he would come to Rosendale for luncheon, as he was eager to renew their acquaintance. Harold read the note several times before agreeing to come, and when he went to Rosendale, he brought his son, Dudley, a cheeky youth of seventeen, who found the humdrum life of a gentleman farmer tedious beyond measure.

Harold enjoyed seeing his old friend, but felt awkward when introduced to Michael's lovely daughter. She resembled Harold's mother, and had the same cleft in her chin as he. While she took a reluctant Dudley to the garden, he and Michael shared details of their lives and drank brandy. By the time lunch was served, Harold was inebriated, and during the meal, let his deepest secret slip.

The girl seemed unaware of what he had said since she was quite enamored with Dudley, but as understanding dawned on Michael, his congenial smile faded, and he glared at Harold. He chose not to cause a scene in front of his daughter, whom he now knew was not his. Dudley was focused on his meal and his own thoughts, so he was unaware of his father's revelations.

After they finished eating, Michael rang for Mr. Conway and asked him to show Lord Harold and his son to the door. Harold, who, even in his drunken state, realized he had broken his old friend's heart, didn't object as he was led out of the dining room. He kept looking back at Felicity, and longing to hold her.

It was the last time he saw Michael or his daughter. She was now eighteen and left in an impoverished state she did not deserve. He was responsible for her existence, and it was his duty to see that she was well cared for.

Then he thought of his son, Dudley. His eldest son, Roland, had been the apple of his eye. The boy understood his duty to his family and his country. Harold had never gotten over his untimely death. If only Roland had lived, then perhaps, as the heir to the family fortune, he would have made sure his half-sister was cared for, but not Dudley. He wouldn't share a farthing with anyone.

Harold opened a new bottle and poured himself a brandy before he sat in front of the fireplace. He remembered the day Roland left for India, and how proud he had been to see the man his son had become. Roland had a good heart and the soul of a true gentleman. He was always looking after their mother, and she, like Harold, adored him.

But Dudley was another matter. He could turn on a charming façade when it suited him, or fall into a rage over the jam served at breakfast because it wasn't the one he fancied. His mood swings had been nearly impossible to endure during his adolescence, which led to his expulsion from the finest schools, until Harold hired a tutor so he could finish his education at home.

Now, at the age of twenty-five, Dudley was the sole heir to his father's fortune, and an eligible bachelor. His reputation among the ton was that of a rogue, but many believed he would change, and mothers intent upon finding their daughters husbands tended to overlook rumors of a dalliance with the wife of the Earl of Kingsbury.

Lord Harold looked at the glass in his hand. It was almost empty. He'd been cautioned by his physician to limit his brandy to one a day, but at his age, he dismissed the warning. As long as he had his affairs in order, he would do as he pleased.

He thought of Dudley again, for no amount of brandy seemed to banish him from Harold's mind. Dudley had begun to stop by the library and inquire after Harold's health, to which Harold would reply that he was feeling well. Harold understood that the lad's attentions were not born of any concern for his father's health, but rather a measure of the time the old man had left on earth.

Dudley was craving his inheritance, and Harold wasn't the

only one who noticed his new attitude toward his father's condition; Oliver was aware of it, too, and had taken to appearing by surprise whenever father and son were alone together.

As he sipped his brandy, Lord Harold recalled McKenzie's words.

"What will Dudley think when he finds out?"

Harold's hand began to shake, and the brandy rose on the walls of his glass like waves attempting to wash away his sin. The specter of illegitimacy was like a cancer on the heart of their society, one so evil it drove otherwise respectable people to do unmentionable things to hide the truth.

He thought of the adolescent girl, his own seed, and knew that if Dudley found out she was his half-sister, he might do anything to keep others from finding out about her. Anything.

Fear gripped Harold. He could never tell Dudley the truth. As far as he was concerned, Felicity was Harold's goddaughter, and nothing more.

He drained his brandy and went to bed. Tomorrow he would tell Dudley about the will and his bequest to Felicity.

CHAPTER 1

Lady Felicity Armstrong

Spring 1884

*L*ady Felicity Armstrong held the spyglass aloft and peered at the horizon. It had been two years since her ship set sail for the North China Sea, and one year since Captain Fowler's last letter, but Felicity hadn't wavered in her belief that the Captain would return. He had given his word, and unless she learned otherwise, she would stand by it.

She let the spyglass drift over the seascape and saw birds being lifted by the wind. Her childhood fantasy of joining them in flight returned as she longed to escape the harsh realities of life. She let herself enjoy the moment as the wind off the ocean blew against her, and she held out her arms.

Lost in her reverie, she allowed the spyglass to slip from her hand. She plucked it from the ground and inspected it for damage. The glass was still intact, but the moment of joy had passed. Felicity would never fly, and if the ship failed to return, she would also lose her dream of financial freedom.

"I refuse to let you spoil my day," she said aloud.

"Did you say something, milady?"

Millie O'Malley, a twelve-year-old girl from town who lived with Felicity and helped her with her chores, was standing near the front door of the stone-walled cottage. She admired Felicity; so much, in fact, that she had worked hard at mimicking her mistress's manner of speech.

"I was speaking to myself, Millie," Felicity said.

She looked at Millie and noted her slender frame, pale blue eyes, and lank, dirty blonde hair, all the result of a recent bout of influenza. Felicity's heart filled with compassion as she looked at Millie's sallow complexion.

"It's a lovely day. Why don't we have tea in the garden?"

"As you wish, milady."

"You get the cups and saucers, and I'll put the kettle on."

"I've already started the kettle, milady."

"As usual, you are two steps ahead of me." Felicity went to the girl, touched her cheek, and then put her arm around Millie's shoulders. "And what shall we have with our tea?"

"There's a bit of cake in the pantry," Millie said.

Ah, the cake. The day before, Felicity had walked to town to buy bread, but when she saw the chocolate cake dusted with a delicate ring of powdered sugar, an impulse overtook her. The cake was dear, but she thought of Millie, and before she knew it the cake was wrapped and placed inside her basket. On her way home, she looked at the coins in her purse and sighed. She had barely enough for next week's bread.

For two years, Felicity had lived in the town of Tolwich on the east coast of England. Romans inhabited the town two thousand years ago, and remnants of their occupation still littered the meadow that lay between her cottage and the town. A stone road leading from the end of town remained, though stones were missing, having been stolen by settlers to build their homes when they arrived.

The shops in town had been laid end to end, with an inn at its center. The inn had been a popular destination during the reign of Charles the Third as stagecoach travel grew, and London lured country folk with dreams of riches to its new industrial centers. Next to the inn was the livery. A pub, a bakery, and a mercantile also served the population of Tolwich, who were adapting to the new brick police station as they kept a wary eye on what many called "government spies."

Felicity's home was built on a bluff two miles from town. It had belonged to Felicity's father, Lord Michael Armstrong, and when she was a child, Felicity found a beehive in a large bush at the edge of the back yard. She had called it a bee's nest, and rather than correct her, her father and Mrs. Muir, their housekeeper, had christened the stone structure Bee's Nest Cottage, and had a sign placed near the front door.

Felicity loved taking walks to town and fantasizing about those who had walked on the stone road two thousand years ago. It helped to keep her own past at bay, though sometimes, when she went to town alone, memories were hard to suppress. Her gown was old, her hands rough from labor, and her purse contained but a few coins, and as she contemplated how to stretch those coins, her thoughts turned to Rosendale.

* * *

1882

ROSENDALE HAD BEEN in the Armstrong family for over two hundred years. Lord Michael Armstrong was the only son and heir of Lord Herbert Armstrong, whose wealth had come from a tin mine in Tolwich. By 1870, the tin was gone, and the Armstrong fortunes were dwindling.

Lord Michael inherited land, the manor house known as Rosendale, and farms manned by tenant farmers that provided a nominal income. That, paired with Lord Michael's inept financial decisions, had left him in a financial bind that forced him to marry one Lady Felicia Bremington, a girl who was not much older than his twelve-year-old daughter, Felicity.

Lady Felicia was the spoiled daughter of a Marquis who was eager to have her wed. Felicia's follies were often the subject of dinner conversations, and they had earned her the reputation of being a strumpet. The Marquis learned that Lord Armstrong was searching for a bride, and after a brief discussion over cognac at a gentlemen's club in London, a deal was struck that included a large dowry.

His daughter always wondered what had prompted him to make such a rash decision, for Lord Michael had never talked about marriage. When he announced his intentions at dinner one evening, Felicity was shocked, and she worried that his new wife would steal what little attention she had from her father. Her concerns were real, for Lord Michael often left his estate and traveled to France, where he'd kept a mistress for years. He would explain his absences as his need to "tend his businesses."

The money squandered on his travels left little to pay for servants. Many had come and gone, but Mrs. Muir, the housekeeper, and Mr. Conway, the head butler, remained faithful for years. Together, they raised Felicity, whose mother had died in childbirth.

When his plan to wed was announced, Mrs. Muir and Mr. Conway surmised that Lord Michael was eager to have another child, a male heir. When they met Lady Felicia, they felt that perhaps the lord had acted under duress for it was obvious she had no interest in running the household, or being a "wife." She loved fashion, cosmetics, and dinners with other members of the ton.

Though he promptly set about to impregnate her, Felicia proved to be as barren as the Arabian Desert. After months of unproductive couplings, Lord Michael went to France to tend to business, and took his mistress to Milan. In accordance with his many bad decisions, he arrived at the height of a cholera epidemic, and succumbed to the deadly disease soon after his arrival.

Felicia, in a rare display of kindness, tried to fill the void left by Lord Michael's death. She began by hiring a male tutor, a handsome rogue, whose duties more often called for tending the needs of Lady Felicia than teaching a morose adolescent girl. When Felicia grew weary of him, she replaced him with another, and then another, as Felicity spent most of her time reading the books in her father's library.

One evening, as she dined with the Marquess of Dolman, Felicia cast her eye on a Spanish matador named Fernando. He was a passionate but jealous paramour, and Felicia fell in love for the first time. She had always been in control of her relationships, but she soon found herself under *his* control. He enjoyed demeaning her, and would often strike her if she spoke out of turn. Her face was often bruised, and she would shake off inquiries by saying she had fallen.

Mrs. Muir did her best to shield Felicity from the harsh truth of her stepmother's relationship and would invite the girl to her quarters on the third floor. She had two rooms – a parlor with a fireplace and a bedroom. Felicity would go there in the evening after dinner to sit with Mrs. Muir. They sat on discarded wing chairs, one on each side of the fireplace, and they would share cocoa and cookies as Felicity shared her dreams with Mrs. Muir.

Felicity was frightened of Fernando, and the looks he gave her as she passed him in the hallway on her way downstairs. Sometimes, he would stand near Felicia's bedroom door and leer at Felicity, sending shivers up her spine. She confided to Mrs. Muir that she hated him, and Mrs. Muir told her that she had good reason to feel as she did, but to keep her feelings to herself whenever she encountered him.

"Don't give him any reason to raise his hand to you," she said.

The battles between Felicia and Fernando became more frequent as time wore on. Their shouting could be heard on the second floor, causing Felicity to run to Mrs. Muir's room for comfort.

One night, a row started as they were in the parlor. Felicia drank too much champagne and taunted Fernando about his prowess as a lover. She was too drunk to stop herself from whipping him into a rage, and then tried to run when she saw the look in his eye. She'd fallen several times as she ran to the library hoping to get the pistol out of Lord Michael's desk. Fernando followed her, yelling in Spanish, calling her horrible names, and threatening to kill her.

Felicia didn't get to the pistol. As she fumbled with the lock on the drawer, Fernando went to the shield and swords on the wall over the fireplace. He took one of the swords from behind the shield, grabbed it by its gold-plated hilt, and held it in front of him as he would in the arena.

"Toro!" he cried, and Felicia, caught between the desk and the drawer, was unable to run.

She fell to her knees with her hands clasped as if in prayer. She begged him to stop, but Fernando was unmoved. He came toward her with the precision of a man who understood his prey. As he brandished the sword, he kept his eyes on her, and she began to cry.

Mr. Conway discovered Felicia's body the next morning. He found her head in the library on the mantel under the shield. One sword was missing.

Fernando was captured a few days later. He had tried to board a ship for Spain after he pawned the sword. The police arrested him and he was tried, found guilty, and duly hanged.

CHAPTER 2

1882

*A*t eighteen, Felicity was an innocent. She had been protected by Mrs. Muir and Mr. Conway all her life, and had no idea how to run a household or manage money. She was totally dependent on others for everything, and the skills she had been taught would serve her only if she married an aristocrat.

She had never been to London for the season, had never been introduced to eligible young men, and had no idea what it cost to run a manor house.

A few days after she died, Felicia's solicitors, Mr. Handy and Mr. Conner, arrived at the manor house to read her will.

"Lady Armstrong established a trust for you after your father died," Mr. Handy said. His dour expression reflected the tone of his voice. "Of course, she had planned to deposit more, but failed to do so before her untimely death. I'm sorry to say that Lady Armstrong lived beyond her means, and there are outstanding debts that require payment. As a result, we will have to sell the estate and its contents to pay those debts."

Felicity was still in shock over Felicia's death and didn't say a word, not even when he mentioned the size of her yearly income, a pittance that would barely cover food and rent.

"Fortunately, Lord Michael had retained the cottage in Tolwich known as Bee's Nest Cottage, and out of compassion for your situation, the judge has decreed that it shall not be sold, but that the deed shall be given to you."

She recalled the cottage with fondness and was grateful to her father for keeping the property.

"I realize your income is small, but you might consider supplementing it by working as a companion, or perhaps a governess."

She had read the Bronte sisters' books. She didn't want to be a companion or a governess – she wanted to be who she was now. She didn't want her life to change, and while she watched the men assigned to take inventory of her family home wander from room to room, she kept denying the truth that she would have to leave it forever.

One day, Mrs. Muir took her aside and invited her to her room. Felicity sat in her chair by the fireplace, and Mrs. Muir sat in hers.

"My dear, you will have to consider finding a position. Your income will not support you, and I'm afraid your place in society offers you little choice. You told me Mr. Handy offered you suggestions as to …"

"I will not do it," she said.

Felicity got up and went to the window. She wore a navy blue mourning gown with a small bustle. She folded her arms across her chest and set her mouth in a hard line. Mrs. Muir continued.

"You would live in a house like this, or travel all over Europe. Wouldn't that be better than starving in a cottage by the sea?"

Felicity heard her say, "…cottage by the sea," and something awoke in her. She remembered running against the wind, and it seemed a fitting metaphor for what she was experiencing now. She thought of the garden behind the cottage where she and Mrs. Muir had planted vegetable seeds together. There were fruit trees and the hive in the garden, too.

"I'll grow food," she said.

Mrs. Muir sighed. The young seldom heed the wisdom of the old, and though she believed Felicity was strong, Mrs. Muir had soothed her many times in the night while the girl shivered in fear, and the idea of her living alone in that cottage made Mrs. Muir angry. Still, there was a time to let go of a child and hope that divine providence would guide them.

"Find a girl in town who can help you," Mrs. Muir said. "Let her stay with you and teach you how to take care of your house." Mrs. Muir went to the old armoire that held small gifts Felicity had given her over the years and picked up a small card. "This is where I will be if you need me." It was an address in Whitley. "I bought a small home there, and the solicitors are letting me take the furniture in my room." She bit her lower lip. "You are always welcome."

Felicity looked at her and smiled. She took the card and hugged Mrs. Muir.

"My dear, dear Mrs. Muir," she said as she pulled away. "And you are always welcome, too."

"Find a girl. It's unseemly for a woman to live alone."

"I understand. I will find a girl who will work for room and board."

"I shall miss you, milady," she said.

"And I you."

Handy and Conner, Esquires, paid for the carriages to take her to Tolwich. One held her and a valise, and the other held the things she'd been allowed to take with her. As she rode away, she waved at Mrs. Muir and Mr. Conway, and wiped a tear away with a gloved hand. She didn't cry for long, though, for Felicity had a secret, and as the carriage rumbled over the dirt road, she patted her purse and smiled.

* * *

AS SOON AS Felicity arrived in Tolwich, she asked the owner of the mercantile, Mr. Tompkins, if he knew how she might find a girl to help her clean her cottage. Mr. Tompkins raised his eyebrows and looked at her fine clothes. He remembered Lord Michael for he had delivered goods to Bee's Nest Cottage, and he, like so many others in the small village, had read the accounts of Lady Felicia's murder.

"Young Millie O'Malley," he said. "She lives in the shed behind the last house on King's Highway."

"Will she work for room and board?" she asked.

"You'll have to take that up with her mum."

Felicity found the shed on her way home and recoiled when Mrs. O'Malley answered the door. Her appearance and odor caused Felicity to back away as the woman glared at her.

"Well, what'd you want?"

"Mr. Tompkins said you have a daughter who might be willing to work for me."

Mrs. O'Malley ran her hand over her head and then smoothed her stained skirt. She thrust out her chin and smiled, revealing several blackened teeth.

"That's my Millie," she said.

"She could stay with me, if that's agreeable. I have a place for her to sleep, and would provide her meals."

"Aye, but how much would you pay?" Felicity blushed, and Mrs. O'Malley put her hands on her hips. "Well?"

"I can't pay her money," Felicity said. "But she would be well taken care of."

"Don't give a fig if she's taken care of. I can take care of her. What I need is ten shillings a week."

Felicity's shoulders drooped.

"I see, well then, I am sorry to have bothered you."

She turned to leave and a thin, dirty girl in a tattered dress ran out the door and grabbed the edge of Felicity's skirt.

"I don't eat much," she said, "and I work hard."

Her mother came out of the hovel and grabbed the girl by her hair.

"Get yourself back inside!" Mrs. O'Malley cried.

Felicity was at a loss. Her desire was to rescue the girl, but fear held her back as Mrs. O'Malley pushed the girl into the house.

"Ten shillings, that's the price," she said before slamming the door.

* * *

THE NEXT MORNING, Felicity heard a knock on her front door and went to look out her parlor window. She saw the waif who had grabbed the edge of her skirt. Felicity opened the door and saw that the child had washed her face.

"I want to work for you," she said. "Don't care what me mum says."

"But I can't let you stay without her permission."

"Don't need her permission."

"Why not?"

"I know things she don't want me to talk about."

The girl could be no more than ten years of age, but the darkness in her eyes, in her soul, was ageless. She reminded Felicity of the urchins in Mr. Dickens' novels.

"Does she know you're here?"

Millie looked at the ground, and then up at Felicity's face.

"I told her."

It was then that Felicity noticed that one of Millie's cheeks was tinged with a pink hue.

"Did she hit you?"

"It's nothing, miss." She smiled. "Will you let me work for you?"

Felicity thought of her empty pantry and looked at Millie's thin arms. The garden needed tending and it would be a long while before they saw any edibles, but the trees were blossoming, and she had made the acquaintance of her neighbor, Mr. Brewer, a farmer who told her she could have eggs once a week if she taught his son how to read, so she stood tall and held her hand out to Millie.

"I will, but if your mother comes to fetch you, I will have to let you go."

"Like I said, miss, she don't want me talking. She won't come 'round."

The first thing she did was to ask Millie to help her move the large brass tub out from under the sink so Millie could take a proper bath. The girl objected, screaming that she didn't want to get sick, but Felicity insisted, and soon, she was scrubbing the girl from head to foot while Millie whined about the temperature of the water.

Felicity gave Millie one of her camisoles, and when she put it on, its hem reached the girl's calf. She then found a belt that required extra holes and used a pair of scissors from the sewing box to poke them out. She stood back, looked at Millie, and sighed.

"It will have to due until we can find something more suitable."

Millie ran her hand over the soft silk camisole and sighed.

"It's heavenly, miss."

"You must call me milady. It's my proper title."

"Milady."

Millie smiled again. She was beaming, and her joy was infectious. Felicity was sure that having her would be a blessing.

Millie taught Felicity how to clean and cook, and they never had trouble falling asleep at the end of the day.

Over time, Felicity was able to get hay from Mr. Brewer for a pallet, and Millie covered the hay with a thin blanket Felicity found in an old armoire in the bedroom. When they harvested the apples, Felicity brought a basketful to Mr. Brewer.

CHAPTER 3

1884

*M*illie waited at the table in the garden. Her dress had been made from the curtains in the bedroom the year before and was too short, but she didn't complain.

"I used the last of the tea," Felicity said as she carried the tray across the yard. She put it in the center of the table.

The round table and four chairs had been there since Lord Michael brought them from Rosendale. Years of rain had worn away the varnish, but they were still quite sturdy, and just the right size for a garden.

"And we're out of sugar. Do you think Mr. Brewer would let us milk one of his cows for cream?"

She was smiling as she sat, for Millie had already told her she couldn't milk a cow, but her smiled faded when she saw the look on Millie's face.

"Is there something wrong?" she asked.

Millie was lost in thought and didn't reply, so Felicity put her hand on Millie's arm.

"What, milady?"

"I asked if there was anything wrong."

"No, milady. Everything is good."

Felicity poured the tea, but despite her words, Millie seemed distracted. Something was bothering her, but as Felicity had learned over the time they were together, Millie had secrets. There were things she would never share and no amount of coaxing would break her down. She chose to leave this discussion for another time and sipped her tea.

Millie was twelve now, but still thin, which made her look younger. Every morning, Felicity helped tie her hair back, but it was so straight, it would always come loose from the rubber band. Felicity looked at it and the dress she wore, and felt sad. Her income was too small to clothe either one of them, and they'd run out of curtains, but somehow she vowed she would save enough to buy a length of cloth from the mercantile, enough to make Millie a new dress.

"This is so good," Millie said when she took a bite of cake.

She smiled, and her eyes looked brighter. She smiled as she sipped her tea. The color was returning to her cheeks and her appetite was growing, too.

When she'd fallen ill, Felicity asked if she wanted to go home, but Millie had recoiled at the suggestion. She insisted on staying at Bee's Nest Cottage, and Felicity made her stay in the bedroom. After two days of worrying, Felicity felt Millie's forehead and found it cool. Since then, Millie's strength had grown, but she still fell asleep in the afternoon. She was looking a bit drowsy as she took another bite of cake.

"I think it's almost time for your nap."

"I'm not sleepy, milady." She looked at her cake and put her hands around the plate. "Please don't take my cake."

Felicity was vexed.

"I'd never do that, Millie."

Millie looked forlorn.

"I know. I'm sorry."

"There's no need to apologize. You still aren't yourself."

"I love chocolate," Millie said with a smile.

Felicity laughed at the bits of brown cake outlining Millie's two front teeth.

"I can see how much you love chocolate," she said.

A bird flew from the white picket fence surrounding the back yard to the branch of a tree and began preening itself, taking special care with each wing. Felicity watched it, and again felt the desire to fly.

"I wish I were a bird," she said softly.

"Aye, milady," Millie said. "I would fly so high no one would ever find me."

"And sleep in the tallest tree."

"Oh yes, milady, but I don't think I would like worms."

Millie emphasized each word. She wanted so much to be a lady like Felicity and hoped one day that her posh accent would help her find a job in a fancy shop in London.

"I quite agree," Felicity said. "Perhaps we could survive on berries."

They both laughed, and then Millie ate the last bite of her cake. Felicity had yet to touch hers.

"Why haven't you eaten your cake?" Millie asked.

Felicity looked at it, and then pushed it across the table.

"I'm not hungry. You may have it."

"Do you mean it?"

"Yes, you eat it. You have to get all your strength back."

She watched Millie as she ate the cake and wished she could be that young again. While she was only twenty, she felt years older, and thought of Mrs. Muir, who had been the one feeding her chocolate cake when she was Millie's age. She wondered if she would ever see her again and sighed.

"I'm going to take the tray inside," she said.

"But you haven't finished your tea?"

Millie was right. She couldn't waste tea. It cost money, and

Felicity had gained an appreciation of its value. She drank her tea while Millie scraped bits of chocolate cake off her plate, and then they got up, cleared the table, and went inside the house.

"I'll wash the dishes," Millie said.

"I'll help you."

"No. I'll do them. It's my job."

Millie was resolute as she blocked Felicity from going to the sink. Felicity put her hands on her hips and held her head high.

"You've been sick. I want to help you."

"And I want to do my job. Go take a walk on the beach."

Felicity's eyebrows rose at the tone of Millie's voice. She suppressed a smile as the girl's disobedience should be frowned upon, but it was so unlike Millie to act this way that she wondered what had gotten into the girl. Rather than argue with her, Felicity gave in and left the kitchen.

The cottage had been built in the 18th century by one of her ancestors. It had one bedroom, a parlor, a kitchen, and a pantry. The walls inside were whitewashed, and when her father came there, he had the floor covered in wooden planks. He had also replaced the gabled, worn thatched roof with a new one. He'd also had a small room attached to the bedroom and installed a water closet to replace the outdoor privy.

The parlor window faced the meadow, her bedroom window faced the sea, and the kitchen window faced the garden. Her father had also replaced the mullioned windows with casement windows and latticed panes, but the shutters remained outside and could be closed if the weather grew fierce.

Her father always said he liked the idea of "roughing it," so the cottage had been furnished with castoffs from the manor house. A settee in desperate need of new upholstery sat against the wall dividing the parlor and the kitchen, and a large, stuffed chair sat next to the fireplace. An oval, braided rag rug lay in the center of the floor. The settee had two end tables with brass lamps, and the walls were adorned with rustic scenes one of her ancestors had painted. There was a double bed in her bedroom with a lumpy mattress, an armoire, and a small dresser with a mirror. They were sad remnants of grandeur, rather like Felicity herself.

Felicity tried hard to keep her spirits from sinking, but she was always in danger of falling into a melancholy mood. Her poverty had tested her mettle since the day she arrived at the cottage, but now, after two years of scraping by, she was losing her battle against the dark, gloomy specter. She longed to wrap herself in its warm cocoon, as she had following Felicia's death. She had slept for days and refused to eat, but Mrs. Muir had coaxed her out of it with gentle kindness.

Felicity walked outside and took a deep breath. Besides a dress, Millie needed shoes, and the edges of Felicity's sleeves were threadbare. Thank God she had Millie. She had to be all right, for Millie's sake, and not give into temptation.

She walked to the edge of the yard, closed her eyes, and threw out her arms. The wind blew against her and she reveled in the sensation. The dark mood retreated and she opened her eyes, and then she saw someone walking across the meadow toward the bluff.

Her heart skipped a beat. The only visitor she and Millie ever had was Mr. Tompkins, who would bring her important letters. He always came in a wagon, though, never on foot, so who could it be?

Her heart pounded and a thought so wonderful struck her that she almost began to run down the hill. Could it be? Had he finally returned?

She pressed her lips together tightly and pinched her cheeks. Now, instead of running toward him, she wanted to run away. She wasn't ready to see him. She wasn't dressed, and she hadn't done her hair. Oh, what would Captain Fowler think of her?

CHAPTER 4

1882

*W*hen Felicity learned she would have to leave the manor house, she was devastated. It was home, the only one she'd ever known, and Mrs. Muir knew it was time to share a secret she'd been keeping since Felicity was born. They were in her room having tea shortly after Felicity had learned she would be leaving Rosendale.

"Those men are still taking inventory on the first floor," Mrs. Muir said. "Have you ever wondered about your mother's room?"

Felicity pondered her words, and then her eyes grew wide. After her mother, Phillipa, died, Lord Michael had ordered her room sealed. Not even Felicia had opened it, for she believed in ghosts, and was loath to disturb the spirit of her husband's first wife.

"They can't go in there," Felicity said.

"Oh, yes they can, my dear. They have the right, but they don't have the key." She held up a brass key. "They shouldn't be the ones to break the seal."

She held it out to Felicity, who reached for it, but stopped her hand in midair.

"I can't."

"But you must. It was your mother's room, and there are things in there they shouldn't touch."

Felicity thought of the men touching her mother's lingerie and winced. Mrs. Muir was right – it was something *she* had to do.

As she took the key from Mrs. Muir's hand, she was filled with excitement, but then recalled how her father had refused to even talk about Phillipa, and how angry he grew whenever she asked him why. Now she grew angry.

"He wouldn't talk about her," she said, her voice quivering. "He sealed that door as if to banish her existence."

Her hands were shaking and her heart pounding. She gripped the key as she looked at Mrs. Muir.

"He always felt responsible for her death," Mrs. Muir said.

"I understand, but he should have shared her with me. I know nothing about her."

"Then you must go to her room. It was her sanctuary."

Felicity left Mrs. Muir's rooms and went to the second floor. As she approached her mother's room, some long ago fear surfaced, a fear that had kept her from coming to this side of the manor house since she was a child. Many times, she had stood at the edge of the staircase and look down the hall, longing to look through the keyhole of her mother's room, but she never did. Her feet wouldn't move until she abandoned those ideas and went downstairs.

Felicity pushed through the fear and went to the door. She put her hands on it and laid her forehead against the cool wood. She listened for sounds of someone coming to stop her, but it was Sunday, and the men wouldn't return until the next day. The silence was comforting and gave her courage as she slipped the key into the lock and opened the door.

The door hinges creaked from disuse and the room was dark. As her eyes adjusted to the dim light coming from behind the closed drapes, she saw outlines of furniture. She entered as if a phantom were ready to strike, and wrapped her arms around her waist. The room was cold, and it smelled of dust and desertion.

She went to the window and opened the drapes. Dust filled the air and daylight flooded the room as the particles danced on a stream of sunlight. She sneezed, and then looked around the room.

Elaborate cobwebs decorated the ceiling, walls, and posters of the bed. As she walked to the other side of the room, she saw an armoire similar to the one in Mrs. Muir's room. She opened it and saw several gowns. She pulled one out and took it to the window. The fabric was like new, as if Phillipa had never worn it, and Felicity held the silk to her cheek and smelled a hint of lavender. The soft sensation was like a mother's kiss, and she began to weep.

She sank to her knees and clutched the dress as if Phillipa would materialize to embrace her. She rocked back and forth as years of anger and frustration fell from her heart, breaking off the hardened shell that had protected her in childhood.

After her tears were spent, she returned the gown to the armoire and went to the end table next to her mother's bed. The drawer contained a Bible and a rosary, and Felicity gazed at it trying to understand why her mother would have had a rosary. She had been raised a Protestant. Had Phillipa been a Catholic?

Felicity seethed as she thought of her father and all he had withheld from her.

She ran her hand over the satin duvet and more dust rose in the air. It was pink, made to complement the roses on the wallpaper, and the pillows were edged in lace. Felicity had been born in this bed, and her mother had died there.

"Mama," she said softly.

A warm stirring in the air surrounded her and she closed her eyes as a warm, comforting sensation surrounded her. When she opened her eyes, she was looking at the dressing table.

Her heart began to beat faster as she walked to it and sat on the velvet-cushioned bench. Felicity picked up her mother's brush, saw strands of dark brown hair, and a shiver went up her spine. This was her mother's hair. She had been a real living, breathing person, not a specter to be exorcized by her father's grief.

Felicity looked at the mirror. The frame was painted white and carved with ribbons. A garland of silk roses was draped around the edges. It was a lovely, fragile thing, much like Phillipa herself, and as Felicity looked at her reflection, she recalled her father telling her that she had her mother's eyes.

At the time of her death, Phillipa had been eighteen. Though she tried to imagine what her mother must have felt as she was about to give birth, Felicity's limited experience and chastity prohibited her from knowing what went on in the marriage bed, and in her naiveté, she had concluded that it was marriage itself that brought about the creation of life. She wouldn't learn of the physical relations necessary to commence procreation until the day she went to visit Mr. Brewer's farm and saw a bull mounting a cow.

She picked up a bottle of perfume and touched it to her nose. Roses, a scent she herself favored, filled the air around her, and brought a memory of her sitting on her father's lap in the library. He would read tales of King Arthur and he always smelled of roses. Perhaps he had been sneaking into Phillipa's room to sit at her dressing table, too.

There were three drawers on the left side of the table and Felicity opened each. The first two were filled with cosmetics, but the last held something that would change the course of Felicity's life.

She lifted the large, red velvet pouch and put it on the table-top. It was heavy, and the items within it rattled. She untied the drawstrings and looked inside, but she couldn't see what it was. She put her hand in and felt smooth surfaces, like glass, and grabbed one. As she pulled it out, she saw that the stone was one of many held together by gold links to form a necklace. Rubies glittered in the light from the window, and a large diamond swung from a golden pendulum at the center. Felicity was so surprised that she hadn't noticed she'd been holding her breath, and began to gulp for air.

She put her hand in the pouch again and pulled out another necklace, three bracelets, and several rings. She looked at them laid out on the tabletop and tried to calculate their worth, but again, her lack of experience left her unable to even fathom it, and she shook as she placed them back into the pouch.

A wicked thought ran through her mind as she held the pouch on her lap. The room had been sealed for years, and these jewels had been in the drawer since her mother died. Had her father known about them? If not, where had they come from? If he had known, would he have married Felicia?

The questions mounted as she left the room with the pouch and went directly to Mrs. Muir's room. She was about to knock when she stopped, and then went to her room instead. She put the pouch into her trunk and locked it before heading to Mrs. Muir's room. They talked about the past, how Phillipa had hired Mrs. Muir, and how she had elevated Mrs. Muir to lady's maid, passing over other maids who deserved the promotion.

"She liked me," Mrs. Muir said. "She trusted me, and I kept her secrets."

"What sort of secrets?"

"Oh, she often spoke of being lonely, and of her disappointment in her marriage. Your father left her shortly after they married, and she never understood his choice to travel without her." Mrs. Muir paused. "I don't want to sound disloyal to Lord Armstrong, but I must admit, he was an odd duck."

"Was he here when she died?" Felicity asked.

"No, but when he came home, he marveled at your beauty. I believe he rather liked being a father more than being a husband."

Felicity thought of the jewelry in her trunk and thought of sharing the find with Mrs. Muir, but something told her not to, that it was better if no one else knew about them.

As the weeks passed and the men concluded the inventory, it was time for Felicity to leave Rosendale forever. She wandered the hallways and looked into each room so that she would remember them all. She stopped at the door of her mother's room, and then went inside. She opened the armoire and took a handkerchief from a drawer, slipped it into her sleeve, and then left the room.

Handy and Conner never mentioned the missing jewelry. As she went to climb into the carriage that would take her to Tolwich, Felicity carried a valise and her purse, which was filled with her mother's legacy.

CHAPTER 5

1884

Felicity watched the stranger walk across the lawn. Alas, it was not Captain Fowler. The tall man wore a top hat, a dark suit, a plaid vest, and gloves. There was something familiar about him, though she couldn't recall if she'd met him before, but she found him somewhat attractive. A thin, blonde mustache hovered over his lip, and his dark blond hair was trimmed to his collar. When he took off his hat, she saw that his hair was pomaded and parted on the right side of his head. His pale blue eyes focused on her in a way that made her blush.

"Lady Felicity Armstrong," he said.

"Yes," she replied.

"Lord Dudley Winston," he said. He tipped his hat. "Mr. Handy told me where to find you."

"And pray, sir, why were you looking for me?"

He smiled, and his eyes twinkled.

"I was hoping you would remember me, but perhaps too many years have passed. I am Lord Harold Winston's son. We visited your home many years ago and you showed me your garden."

The scent of the garden – her adolescent fantasy of love and a young man running ahead of her emerged from a secret place she'd tucked away long ago. She had followed him through the garden to a small, intimate enclave Felicia used for her rendezvous with Felicity's tutors, and he'd teased her about her dress, which had grown too short. Felicity had had so few acquaintances that when Dudley came to visit, she was overjoyed. He promised to write to her, but as happens with most young men, he forgot his promise as soon as he and his father left Rosendale.

"I was hoping you'd remember me, but I see that I left no impression on you."

"Quite the contrary," she said. "It's good to see you, Lord Winston. How is your father?"

"I'm sorry to report that he passed away."

"Oh." She blushed. "I am so sorry for your loss." An awkward silence followed as she thought of inviting him into the sad little cottage. "Why don't we have tea in the garden?"

"I don't want to cause a fuss."

"It's no fuss at all."

She led him around the cottage to the table in the garden.

"It's lovely here," he said.

"It is. I am quite happy here." She looked toward the back door. "I must go and speak to my maid."

She left him and went to the kitchen where Millie was drying the silver teapot.

"Do you see the stranger?" she asked.

Millie looked out the window.

"Yes, milady."

"I've offered him tea. Please put the kettle on to boil."

"But there is no tea, milady."

Felicity blanched as she recalled using the last of the tea.

"What have you done with the leaves?" she asked. Millie nodded at the wet leaves in a pile on the counter next to the sink. "We'll use them again."

Felicity was irritated with her guest. He had come to her house without issuing a calling card or giving prior notice, leaving her with nothing to offer him. It was especially rude considering she had no husband or chaperone. He must know of her situation as he had asked Mr. Handy where she was, so he should have understood not to come unannounced.

She was fuming as she went to her tiny bedroom and looked at her reflection in the mirror. Anger made her cheeks too rosy, and her hair, banded and pulled back in a tightly wrapped bun, made her look like an irate schoolmarm. She released the pins, wrapped it into a loose chignon, and added a snood.

She looked at her clothes and sighed. The white blouse had faded to a dingy gray, and the red velvet skirt, once so smart, was now out of fashion. It had no bustle and was worn at the pleats, leaving small, naked patches that looked like stains. She took them off and went to the armoire to search for something else.

Felicity had three daytime outfits and a traveling ensemble she'd been allowed to take from Rosendale. She chose the brown day outfit, looked in the mirror again, ran her hand over her skirt, and then noticed that her face looked drawn. She had no makeup or rouge to conceal her flaws. She bit her lips , took a few deep breaths, and then went to the kitchen to check on Millie.

"Do you think you can carry the tea tray?" she asked.

"I can, milady."

"If it's too heavy, leave the tea pot behind and bring it after."

"Yes, milady."

Felicity walked to the back door and put her hand on the knob.

"Who is he?" Millie asked.

"He's an old acquaintance." She looked at Millie with a weak smile. "I knew him when I was a child."

"What does he want?"

"I have no idea."

Felicity felt his eyes on her as she walked across the yard to the table. She had never entertained someone from the upper classes, but as she walked, she recalled the etiquette lessons taught by Mrs. Muir, and she smiled. She caught a whiff of his elegant cologne as he stood and held her chair as she sat.

"It's quite charming here," he said. "Perhaps I should consider a home by the sea."

"I highly recommend it."

He was studying her face. He knew her story; most of their acquaintances in London were familiar with her descent and pitied her. Dudley did not. He found her situation appalling, and wondered why she hadn't found some old widower to marry. He looked away and to the sea, pretending he was sitting at a table in the south of France.

"I imagine you are wondering what brought me here," he said.

"I won't deny my curiosity."

She was comely, but not beautiful. His memory of her features had embellished them over time, erasing the point of her nose and widening the shape of her eyes. He wouldn't have recognized her had they passed on the street. She looked like a common shop girl.

"I heard of your misfortune when I returned from Munich. I recalled our brief encounter as children and wondered if you might enjoy a bit of company."

"You came to offer me your company?"

Her voice rose, hinting at sarcasm. He smiled.

"It was my intention, though now it sounds rather foolish."

Why did she sense he was lying?

"No, on the contrary. It was kind of you to think of me."

He watched Millie wobble across the yard with the tea tray and rose to reach her before she dropped it to the ground.

"Let me carry this," he said. The girl looked at his face and frowned as he took the tray from her hands.

"Yes, sir," Millie said softly.

He brought the tray to the table and set it in the center before taking his seat. Millie watched him and thought she had never met a man who smelled so good. Still, there was something about him that made her uneasy.

"Millie," Felicity said. "You are dismissed."

"Yes, milady."

The girl scurried back to the kitchen as Felicity looked at Dudley.

"Thank you for helping her." She poured the tea, and Dudley watched her hand shake as she handed him his cup and saucer. "I apologize for the lack of cream. I didn't go to town this morning."

"No apology necessary," he said.

Felicity's income had been the subject of a dinner he'd attended shortly after Felicia was murdered. The scandal was so delicious he could barely contain his desire to hear every detail, so he knew how much she had to live on. He couldn't imagine making excuses for the lack of cream, and trying to maintain his dignity in clothes that had been out of fashion for two years.

The next hour passed in pleasant chitchat. He took one sip of tea and then left the rest in his cup. Dudley brought her up-to-date on the latest news from London, and she listened while trying to think of something she could add to the conversation. Dudley didn't seem to notice her lack of enthusiasm when he talked about this lady or that lord, for they were people she had never known, and were of no importance to her. When it was clear they had exhausted every topic they might have in common, he took out his pocket watch, put on his gloves, and smiled at her.

"Well, I must be heading back to town. The last train to London leaves in an hour."

She hadn't thought much about the method of his arrival, but now she remembered him walking across the meadow and found it odd. Normally, a man like Dudley would have hired a horse or carriage.

"It's been lovely to see you," she said.

She hoped she sounded sincere, and from the smile on his face, it appeared she had succeeded.

She walked him to the edge of her front yard and he bade her goodbye. She watched him as he made his way across the meadow and shook her head. Despite his telling her he simply wished to offer her some company that, in his arrogant way of thinking, she was sure to welcome, she found the whole visit unnerving. She didn't believe he had come to offer her company, but since she could find no other reason for it, she decided to accept his reason and let go of her misgivings for now.

She returned to the cottage and saw Millie cleaning the teapot for a second time. She went to her and picked up the dishtowel.

"He's gone," she said.

"I didn't like him," Millie said.

"Why not?" Felicity asked.

"Because he smelled too good."

"That's hardly a reason not to like him," Felicity said.

Millie stopped washing and looked at her.

"He has mean eyes."

Felicity saw the sad look on Millie's face and thought about Dudley's eyes. After thinking about it for a while, she had to agree. Dudley had mean eyes, but a clever tongue that softened their effect. She thought about him coming all the way from London without knowing anything about her, and wondered if he expected to find her alone. The thought made her tremble in fear the way she had when Fernando would corner her in the hallway near her bedroom at Rosendale.

CHAPTER 6

1884

That evening after Millie went to her pallet, Felicity lay on the settee with her feet up and opened one of her father's books. She tried to read, but she couldn't stop thinking about Dudley. Noble people rarely did anything out of the ordinary, and it was considered bad form to arrive at someone's home without advance warning, even if that home was a tiny cottage by the sea. Despite her poverty, Felicity was still a lady, and Dudley should have sent word that he was on his way, especially since she hadn't seen nor heard from him in eight years.

She closed the book and tried to remember his father, Lord Harold Winston, who had been one of their nearest neighbors when she lived in Rosendale. With his death, Dudley would inherit the manor house and a townhouse in London, along with Lord Harold's title.

She had paid little attention to Lord Harold during their visit. She couldn't recall whether he had a wife. Was Dudley his only son? At his age, which she guessed to be around twenty-five, he should have been accepting invitations to the grand balls and soirées of the season, not visiting her, unless he had thoughts of marrying her.

She tried to read her book again, but was unable to concentrate on the words. Quiet evenings often brought memories, and Dudley's appearance had triggered thoughts of her father. The older she grew, the more she resented the way he'd handled her trust, and the way he'd left her with Felicia. She laid the book on her lap and sighed.

During her youth, Felicity's love for her father was unquestionable, but now she saw the cracks in his character. Why hadn't he made a new will after he married Felicia?

As she sat with Dudley that afternoon, Felicity remembered her feelings for him. He was the only boy she'd ever met, and at the time, his presence was enthralling. All the burgeoning sensations of her pubescent body had focused on him, and as they sat down to lunch with their fathers, she sat across from him, trying in vain to catch his eye, but Dudley was more interested in the large Canadian moose head hanging over the entrance to the dining room.

What had their fathers discussed during the meal?

She closed her eyes and willed herself to remember. She recalled the sound of her father's voice, but little else. They were probably discussing some law that Lord Winston was proposing in Parliament, or one of her father's business trips abroad.

Had he already met Felicia? Was she the subject of their discussion?

As she thought about Felicia, Felicity thought of Mrs. Muir, too. They had written to each other several times over the last two years, but Felicity hadn't been to see her, nor had Mrs. Muir ventured to Tolwich.

Would Mrs. Muir recall the day the Winstons visited Rosendale?

Perhaps Mrs. Muir had heard the conversation, or Mr. Conway had shared something with her.

Excitement rose in her chest. Felicity had always enjoyed a good mystery, and the thrill of investigation filled her with anticipation. She went to her writing desk and took out a piece of her precious stationery.

As she wrote the letter at the kitchen table, she wiggled in her seat. This was the most exciting thing to happen to her in years! She held her pen to her lips and smiled, but then grew sad as she realized it truly *was* the most exciting thing to happen to her in years.

* * *

A LETTER from Mrs. Muir arrived one week after Felicity posted hers. She was walking home from town and read the letter as she made her way across the meadow. The envelope also contained two banknotes, each worth one pound.

Mrs. Muir wrote that she was thrilled to hear from Felicity, and told her to come to Whitley.

"There are things I should have told you before you departed Rosendale. Please come to Whitley. I have enclosed your fare and look forward to seeing you soon."

She folded the letter and placed it back into its envelope, but put the banknotes in her purse.

Wildflowers were in full bloom and butterflies fought the gusts of wind that came from the sea. They would enter her path, only to be caught and sent far from her across the meadow. It was a welcome distraction from her thoughts, which kept echoing the phrase, "There are things I should have told you…"

What things had she kept from Felicity? Was Mrs. Muir ill? Was she afraid she would go to her grave before sharing what she knew with Felicity?

She held her head up and tried to enjoy the spring weather, but her heart was troubled. Being poor had given her insight into the harsh realities of life she would never have understood if she'd continued to live in Rosendale. She had taken so much for granted like the food on the table, the cleanliness of the house, and the love of her father, whom she had adored. Now, though, as she looked at the tiny cottage in the distance, she questioned his feelings for her.

She summoned a memory of her sitting in his lap by the fireplace as they read a book he'd recently acquired from London. She loved the cadence of his voice as he emphasized words and passages, and she closed her eyes so she could enter the story as more than an observer. It was a sweet memory, but lately, whenever she thought of him, the sweetness would fade and resentment would return.

When had he stopped reading to her, or taking walks, or coming to her room to say goodnight?

At the center of the meadow, she stopped and fell to her knees. She began to cry, sobbing as if she had just received the news of his death. She wrapped her arms around her waist and rocked back and forth until she spent all her tears.

"You stupid, wicked man!" she cried. "Why didn't you take care of me!" The questions rose on the wind and she felt drained. Then, from deep inside, a question rose that was always hiding underneath her resentment and anger. "Why didn't you love me?"

Felicity stayed on her knees for a long time. She sat back and let her arms fall to her sides. She was alone in the world. There was no knight coming over the hill to save her, and no rich uncle who would leave her his fortune. She had ignored the prospect of being a governess or companion because she wanted so much more.

Gazing at the sea, she thought of Captain Fowler. Had she been fooled? Had he taken advantage of her inexperience? Was he just another man who had betrayed her?

CHAPTER 7

1882

*S*hortly after she arrived in Tolwich, Felicity took the red velvet pouch containing her mother's jewels and boarded a train to London. It felt heavy as she walked from the train to a neighborhood where fine shops and elegant town-houses sat side by side. Felicity had seen a box bearing the address of the shop while the men were taking inventory and had written it down. She took a piece of paper from her purse and checked the address before going down the street to a small jewelry shop.

When she entered the store, the owner, an elderly jeweler named Morris Greenbaum, kept a wary eye on her. Felicity had chosen Mr. Greenbaum's shop because she had often heard Felicia praise his creations, and Felicity respected her stepmother's knowledge of precious stones. She also told Felicity something that she hoped was true.

"He knows how to keep a secret," Felicia said.

The elegant showroom was much larger than it appeared to be on the outside. It resembled a drawing room in a fine townhouse, and the jewelry was nowhere in sight. An elderly man with a goatee and wearing a monocle smiled at her.

"Sir," she said. "Are you Mr. Greenbaum?"

"I am."

"I am Lady Felicity Armstrong. My stepmother was Lady Felicia Bremington Armstrong."

Morris Greenbaum had known Felicia for a long time. Her mother had brought her to the store when she was a girl and she'd been entranced by the colorful stones he would show her mother. He was saddened when he heard of her death, and believed it was his duty to treat her stepdaughter with kindness.

"I am so sorry for your loss," he said.

He had a slight German accent.

"Thank you. It has been very difficult."

He also knew that Felicia had left the girl very little money. He studied Felicity's face and her posture. She was uneasy.

"How may I help you?" he asked.

"Is there somewhere we can talk in private?"

"Of course."

He tilted his head and gestured for her to follow him. He led her to a private room with no windows, red velvet seats, and a large desk with two chairs. When she sat, Felicity noticed a jewelry loupe sitting near the inkwell.

She took the pouch from her purse and slid it across the desk. Morris looked at it for a moment, and then opened it and dumped its contents on the desk.

"These are fine pieces," he said. "They don't look familiar."

"They belonged to my mother," she said. "I thought perhaps you would buy them from me."

Morris sat back and put his thumbs in the pockets of his vest. She was young, perhaps eighteen or nineteen, and she was twisting a handkerchief around her fingers.

His wife always complained that his heart was too big, and that he always fell for a sad story. He had promised her he would be more cautious in the future, but this girl looked so sad, and she was, after all, dear Felicia's stepdaughter.

"These pieces are worth far more than I can pay you," he said. "I suggest you allow me to find buyers that will offer you more."

Felicity's lip trembled as she continued to twist the handkerchief. She couldn't tell a soul where the jewels had come from. Would he want proof that they were hers to sell?

She looked at the paisley wallpaper and red velvet drapes that never revealed the light of day. The tasseled tiebacks and the marble mantel over the fireplace reminded her of home, and she began to weep. He looked away as he waited for her to compose herself.

"You have been through a terrible ordeal," he said.

"Yes, but you don't understand."

He sighed.

"I can assure you, Lady Armstrong, that I understand many things."

She shook her head.

She looked at him as a tear rolled down her cheek.

"No one knows they exist, and if my trustees were to find out…"

He put his hand out in front of him.

"Don't say another word."

He got up and went to the door, opened it, and then closed it before turning the lock. He returned to his chair and clasped his hands on the desk.

"Where do they come from?"

"They belonged to my mother. I found them in her dressing table."

He ran his hand over his goatee.

"Let me take a look." He pulled the pouch toward him and reached inside. He pulled out the ruby and diamond necklace.

"How do I know you haven't stolen these jewels?"

"I swear to you I found them in my mother's dressing table drawer."

"Why weren't they in a safe?"

"I don't know. The room had been closed since she died, and I can only assume she didn't want anyone to know about them."

He looked at the jewels and sighed.

"There are people who would take this apart and sell it piece by piece. It will take time, though."

She brought the handkerchief to her face and wiped a tear away.

"How long?" she asked.

"Months, if not a year."

She shook her head, and then looked at him.

"Does this mean you won't buy them from me now?"

He pulled out the rest of the jewelry and sighed again.

"My wife will not be pleased." He brought the loupe to his eye and inspected the diamond. It would garner a hefty price. "I can only offer you ten thousand pounds for the lot."

"Ten thousand pounds!" she cried. She looked into his eyes. "But you will make more than that, won't you?"

"Yes, Lady Armstrong."

"A lot more?"

"Yes."

Felicity tried to hide her excitement as she thought about the money. It was more than she imagined he'd give her, and she was sure it would be enough to finance her dream, and Handy and Conner would never find out about her mother's legacy.

"I'll take it," she said.

He opened a safe near the desk, took out a small metal box, and counted out the hundred pound notes. He put them into a plain envelope and slid it across the desk before closing the safe.

"If you change your mind, I will deny you were ever here," he said.

"I will not change my mind, Mr. Greenbaum."

She put the envelope into her purse. It stuck out of the top, making it impossible to tie the drawstrings.

"You must be careful with that. Are you taking it to the bank?"

"I was going to take it home."

"Then I'll have one of my clerks escort you." He smiled. "What are you going to do with the money?"

"I am going to buy a ship to sail to China and bring back goods to sell."

"You want to be an entrepreneur," he said. "Well, then, milady, I wish you a fair wind and a calm sea."

He got up and went to the door.

"May I have a moment please?" she said.

He nodded, and left her alone. She took the envelope from her purse and put it inside her corset.

* * *

EVERY WEDNESDAY, Felicity would walk to town to buy a newspaper so she could search the ads for investment opportunities. One day, she saw an advertisement for an investor "willing to take a chance on a seafaring man with twenty years experience." She read it and went onto the next advertisement, but kept coming back to the seafaring man's ad. There was something about it that made her believe he might be willing to accept a woman as a partner. Still, when she responded to his ad, she masked her gender by calling herself Lord Michael Armstrong.

Her heart skipped a beat when she received a reply the following week. The seafaring man was Captain Henry Fowler. He suggested they meet at a pub in Hampstead. She wrote back to him and agreed to meet him *outside* the pub at noon the following Saturday. That way, if he didn't want to partner with her, they could part company as if they'd never met.

Felicity took care to dress that day, wearing her navy blue mourning gown, and asked Millie to help dress her hair. When she stepped off the train her heart began to pound. Captain Fowler was expecting a man, so she had to be prepared in case he became angry. She held her head high as she walked to the pub, and when she saw a man dressed in an older suit and sailor's cap standing outside the pub, she stopped and took a deep breath.

He looked to be in his mid-thirties, and Felicity thought he was handsome. As she got closer to him, she noticed that his hair, unlike that of the men of her class, was not pomaded, but fell in small waves that covered his ears and neck. It was brown, as was his beard.

She walked to him and stopped a few feet away. He looked at her with pale blue eyes and smiled, nodded his head politely, and then looked away.

"Captain Fowler," she said. He looked at her again. "My name is Lady Felicity Armstrong."

"I'm waiting for Lord Michael Armstrong," he said. "Is he on his way?"

He thought it odd that a lady would arrive alone, and to a business meeting nonetheless, and he saw the roses in her cheeks pale.

"I wrote to you," she said. "I used my father's name."

A woman had duped Captain Henry Fowler!

He began to pace as his anger grew, and then he stopped and looked at her. She looked so vulnerable as she waited for him to speak. Twenty years at sea should have turned him into a crusty seadog, but Henry still had a kind heart, and thought Lady Felicity looked like an angel.

"Does he know you're using his good name to meet strange men in front of pubs?"

Now she blushed bright red, and he suppressed a smile. Henry had been searching for a hard-nosed businessman who could afford to lose a few pounds, not this slip of a girl whose innocence was written all over her face.

"I think you misunderstood my ad," he said. "I'm looking for a business*man*."

"And I want to invest in a business."

"Milady, please, I can't do business with you. I'd never feel right taking your money."

"Does it lose its value in the hands of a woman?"

"No, of course not..."

"And it will buy whatever a man's money buys."

"Yes, but it's not about the money," he said. "It's...you." Now he leaned forward. "Don't you have a guardian?"

Yes, I do, she thought, *but they must never know about this money.*

Anger she had held in for a long time rose in her, and she thrust out her chin.

"Blast!" she cried.

People on the street looked at her and frowned, and now Henry's cheeks reddened. He took her by the arm and steered her toward a café a few feet away.

"I'll talk to you," he said, "but you must act like a lady."

She stopped and wrenched her arm from his hand.

"It's obvious you have no intention of letting me finance your venture, so I think our business is concluded."

She walked away, leaving him standing alone in front of the café. As she walked, she wept, and frustration caused her to stomp rather than walk. The rules of society, while necessary to keep order, were also unfair to women, and despite the fact that single women could handle their own bank accounts and have their own businesses, it was expected that they would lose that independence once they married.

Felicity was still learning the ways of the world, and had never felt so limited by her gender. Captain Fowler was not a cruel man; he was simply a man who had been raised to believe that a woman was the heart of the *home*, not the workplace. Only middle-class spinsters worked to support themselves.

Her title was also an impediment to her success in business.

Society expected her to do what they deemed appropriate, which allowed her to be a governess or a companion, and Felicity had already decided she would rather live in poverty. As she entered the rail station, she pondered the idea of relinquishing her title, for the truth was that any change she desired would be impossible for her without a man in her life.

She sat in the rail station while she waited for the next train and fought off the dark forebodings that threatened to immobilize her. She didn't see Henry enter the station.

He had wondered why she was alone, and his curiosity made him follow her. A young woman like her usually had some sort of chaperone who would limit her ability to travel about the city alone. He began to fear for her safety, and to imagine all sorts of evil besetting her as she walked the streets of London.

He saw her sitting on a bench and sat beside her. She glanced at him and tried to hide her surprise by adopting a hard expression.

"What do you want?" she asked.

"I want to know why you're here alone," he said.

"My father died when I was young, and my stepmother a few months ago. I have no one else in my life."

"But you're a lady. Surely someone is handling your money."

"I have a small allowance, which barely covers my yearly expenses."

"Then how were you going to invest in me?"

He spoke softly. She looked into his eyes and saw kindness. Could she trust him with her secret? He didn't know the names of her solicitors, and unless she told him, he never would.

"My mother died when I was born. She left me some...money. It isn't part of my trust."

Henry had been at sea since he was thirteen. The men he worked with were hardened by years of distrust and fear, so he recognized that she was sharing something clandestine, a secret that was difficult for her to share. He felt honored that she would trust him.

They sat there for a long time as he thought about partnering with a woman. It just might be the most foolish thing a man would ever do, but despite his misgivings, he decided to do what he hoped he wouldn't regret.

"I must be mad," he said. He exhaled loudly and put his hands on his knees. "Does anyone know you were coming here today?" She shook her head, and he smiled. "You shouldn't have told me that."

"But you asked."

"And you should have said yes, people know. Don't you see I could have taken you to an alley and done terrible things to you?"

"I'm sorry."

"The first thing you must remember is to keep certain facts to yourself no matter what."

"I will."

Her voice was so soft, and he thought she had lovely eyes.

"And you must never trust anyone. Never tell them how much money you have, or where you keep it."

"I won't."

He looked to heaven and sighed.

"You're like a lost lamb," he said. "And if I don't agree to take your money, I'm sure you'll lose it before the month is out."

She was about to admonish him when she realized what he was saying.

"You'll let me invest in you."

"Aye, but I have conditions."

"And they are?" she asked.

"That we sign a proper contract and keep our association private."

"Because you're embarrassed to have me as a partner."

"No, because people have no business knowing what we're doing." He looked at his hands. "I had a partner once. I'd known him for years, since I was a boy swabbing the decks on my first ship, and I thought I knew him. One day I woke to find myself in an alley, my pockets empty, with no idea where he was. He had gotten me drunk and taken our boat. I never saw him or it again."

She put her gloved hand on his.

"I'm so sorry."

His confession helped form a bond between them. When her train arrived, they agreed to meet at a solicitor's office the following Wednesday, and he waited until her train left the station before walking back to his room.

That night, he sat on his bed with his legs stretched out in front of him, and drew her face on a piece of paper. He folded it so there would be no crease in her face, and put it in the pocket of his jacket.

When she arrived on Wednesday, he was there to greet her, and they walked to a townhouse a few blocks away. The sign on the door read "Beecham and Carstairs, Esquires." She hesitated as they walked up the steps to the front door and he looked at her.

"What is it?" he asked.

"They might know my name," she said. "They might know my solicitors."

"Do you have a middle name?"

"Phillipa, after my mother."

"Then you are Miss F.P. Armstrong."

As they sat in front of Mr. Beecham's desk, she watched his face when he heard her name, but there wasn't a hint of recognition. She signed the contract, "F. P. Armstrong, a single woman" and after Henry signed, they bid Mr. Beecham adieu. When they left his office, Henry was beaming.

"I can't believe this is really going to happen."

"I know. I feel positively giddy!"

He smiled. "You're glowing, Lady Armstrong."

"Please call me Felicity."

Captain Fowler looked at her brown eyes, her straight nose,

and her thin lips. She was no Lily Langtry, but she had a sweet face, a face he found himself thinking about long after they parted that afternoon. When he got home, he wrote her address on the back of the paper on which he'd drawn her face and now he pinned it to his jacket pocket.

* * *

OVER THE NEXT FEW MONTHS, they met several times at the café. The waiter would take them to the same table, and always smiled for he believed the gentleman was going to pop the question any day. Henry would regale her with stories of his adventures, and she would watch his eyes. They were at once soft and hard, which made it difficult for others to tell exactly what he was thinking, except when he was thinking about her, and then his eyes would sparkle.

They searched for a month and found a ship she could afford. When it was ready to sail, Henry hired a crew and planned to leave while the weather was still favorable. When he saw her stepping off the train that last day, his heart began to pound, and Felicity had to restrain herself from throwing her arms around him. They went to the ship and he brought her on board to see what her money had bought. She saw her name written on the bow and her eyes widened in surprise.

"You've named it after me," she said.

"Aye."

"You've named it after *me*."

"I looked it up and your name means happy, lucky, and prosperous. It seemed like a proper name for your vessel."

She smiled and felt warmth rising from her stomach. She followed him to his cabin and he let her go in alone. It was nice, but lacked the frilly touches of a woman.

"You need something colorful in here," she said.

"I like it just fine."

He smirked when he saw her narrowed eyes, and suppressed the desire to throw her on his berth. He led her back upstairs and they stood on the dock looking out to sea. He gave her a gift, a brass spyglass with her name inscribed on it and the words, "May the wind always be at your back."

"My dear, Irish mother blessed me with that the day I went to sea. She died before I returned."

Felicity wanted to cry, for she had not bought him a gift, and the kind words touched her.

"I've nothing for you," she said.

"What do you mean you've got nothing for me? You believed in me!"

She stood on her tiptoes and kissed his cheek.

"I just wish I had some token you could take with you."

He reached into his pocket, unpinned the piece of paper with his drawing, and showed it to her.

"You'll be going with me."

She stared at the drawing and was dumbstruck, for she recognized how lovingly he had rendered her countenance. She looked at his eyes and saw tears.

"Take me," she said. "I want to go with you."

He took her hands in his and kissed them.

"You must stay here where I know you'll be safe."

"But how shall I live until you return?"

Now he put his arms around her and hugged her. She pressed her face against his chest and wept.

"You must live," he said. "You're my north star. I need you to guide me home." His words brought sobs that were hard to stop, and he held her tighter and whispered, "Please, Felicity, you must send me off with a smile."

She pulled away and looked into his eyes as she memorized his face.

"I'm sorry."

"There's no need to apologize. I shall return, and when I do, I'll bring us a bounty so big that you'll be swimming in gold."

She smiled and touched his face.

"I'm going to hold you to that."

He searched her eyes for a hint of doubt, but saw none.

"No regrets," he said.

"No regrets."

He feared she would stand on the dock and watch him go, and he didn't think he could bear to see her left so alone. He walked her to the rail station and made sure she was safely aboard the train when it left the station. He promised to write to her through their solicitor, and she did the same.

Felicity would often stand in her yard, look at the moon rising over the sea as stars dotted the navy blue sky, and imagine what he was doing. She hoped that he was thinking of her, too, as he used those stars to navigate his ship.

CHAPTER 8

1884

She walked into the cottage waving the letter, and smelled supper cooking.

"I got a letter from Mrs. Muir," she shouted. "She sent me money so I can go to Whitley."

Felicity walked into the kitchen where Millie was cooking their supper of carrots and potatoes. Millie looked over her shoulder as Felicity took off her hat and gloves.

"She sent you money?" she said.

"Yes, she sent me money." Felicity walked to the cupboard over the sink and held up a tin of tea. "I've also bought some Earl Grey."

She put the tin in the cupboard, and then went to the bedroom and looked at herself in the mirror. She didn't think she looked like the picture Captain Henry drew anymore. There were circles under her eyes now, and her face was pale.

She left the room and got the dishes from the breakfront to set the table. She had something on her mind. She waited until they were seated, and after saying grace, she folded her hands on the table.

"When I go to Whitley, I think you should stay with your mum."

Millie's face grew hard.

"Yes, milady."

Millie's voice quivered, and Felicity noticed her shoulders slump.

"I wouldn't feel comfortable leaving you alone."

"I don't mind, milady. I like being alone."

"You wouldn't be afraid?" Felicity asked, recalling her first nights at the cottage when every sound made her cringe.

Millie smiled. "Oh, no, milady. I wouldn't be afraid at all."

"You are quite sure?"

"Oh yes, milady."

Felicity began to eat her supper but still felt uneasy about leaving Millie alone. In the two years since she had moved in, Millie hadn't gone home once, not even for holidays, and went to church with Felicity. They never saw her mother or brothers at church, but on occasion had seen them in town. Millie never acknowledged them, which Felicity found odd, but she felt it wasn't her place to interfere.

Sometimes Millie would recoil when she saw her brothers, and Felicity noticed she would change from a smiling girl to a cringing waif who walked behind her as if she wanted Felicity to shield her from their sight. As long as she was in the cottage, Millie was fine. She barred the door at night, and Felicity knew she kept a kitchen knife under her pallet. She had never asked Millie about it, but its presence added to the puzzle that was Millie O'Malley.

"Very well. You can stay here while I'm gone, but you must promise to bar the door at sunset."

"I always do, milady."

"And make sure the ashes in the stove are cold before you go to bed."

"Yes, milady."

Felicity sighed again.

"I promise I will return as soon as possible."

"Yes, milady."

Felicity reached across the table for Millie's hand.

"Then it is settled. I will hold you to your word."

Millie took her hand and squeezed it. The girl's joy was palpable. She even began to hum as she ate, spreading joy to Felicity's heart. It took so little to make the girl happy, and Felicity hoped Millie would retain the ability to embrace happiness.

"I haven't been on a train in a long time," Felicity said.

"Mrs. Muir was your housekeeper," Millie said.

"She was like a mother to me. I love her dearly."

"Why do you have to go?"

"Do you remember that gentleman who called on me?" Millie nodded again. "Well, I want to ask Mrs. Muir about him. He and his father came to our house when I was young."

"He had mean eyes."

"So you said, and he should have known better than to arrive at my door unannounced."

"Because we didn't have any tea left."

"Yes, that, too. I don't believe he came because I needed company."

"Maybe he's in love with you."

Felicity laughed, and then saw the red patches on Millie's cheeks.

"I don't think he's in love with me," she said. "Besides, I looked dreadful that day."

"I thought you looked beautiful."

Now Felicity blushed.

"Why, thank you, Millie. It is always good to hear that someone thinks you are beautiful."

They finished their meal and Millie took the plates from the table while Felicity went to the bedroom to search the armoire for her traveling gown. She pulled the brown outfit off the hangers and laid the pieces on the bed. Unlike her everyday clothes, these looked new, though out of style.

She thought of wearing it on the train where she would be with other women who might notice her. For two years, she hadn't given them a thought, but now, faced with a long journey outside her small town she was again assaulted by feelings of inadequacy.

"No," she said. "Not this time."

What difference did it make if she wore a dress that had been out of style for two years? Was there a rule keeper who kept score, following men and women about with a tally of do's and don'ts?

The dress was lovely and comfortable, and she fully intended to enjoy wearing it. If anyone dare give her a condescending look, she would give one right back!

She smiled at her arrogance. Sweet, docile Felicity felt a thrill go up her spine. Perhaps it was time to test her mettle by acting upon her instincts rather than a set of arbitrary rules written by people with more money than she. It was the rules that wore you down and kept you in your place. Perhaps wearing yesterday's fashion with pride would escalate her quest to find peace with her station in life.

CHAPTER 9

The morning she was to depart for Whitley, Felicity rose early, washed her face and hands, and donned her traveling clothes. Millie had the kettle on when Felicity brought her valise to the parlor, and a pot of oats boiling on the stove.

"This is wonderful," Felicity said as she sat.

"You need a good breakfast for your journey."

Millie sounded so much older than her twelve years. She brought a cup of tea and a bowl of oats to Felicity, and then brought the same for herself. They ate in silence as each contemplated the day ahead, and realized how much they would miss each other.

"Don't forget to bar the door when it gets dark," Felicity reminded her.

"I promise. And be careful, milady."

"I will come back, Millie."

Millie smiled, and Felicity laughed at the oats caught in her teeth.

"Oh, I shall miss you, my girl."

When they finished eating, Felicity put on her jacket, hat, and gloves, and looked at Millie.

"How do I look?"

"You look like a lady," Millie said.

"Then I pass muster?"

Millie nodded.

"Well, then, I must be going or I shall miss my train."

She grabbed the handle of her valise and looked at Millie. The girl looked so small and frail that Felicity wavered in her decision to go, but Millie had a backbone of steel. She went to the door, took the umbrella from the stand, handed it to Felicity, and then held the door open wide.

"Thank you," Felicity said, "and remember to bar the door."

"I *will*," Millie said.

"I shall see you in three days."

"Yes, milady."

Felicity looked back once to wave to Millie before descending the hill. The meadow was wet with dew as the sun rose over the sea, and the drifting scent of honeysuckle met her at the bottom of the hill. The memory of her first summer two years before brought a smile to her face. The beauty of the meadow had helped diminish her sadness.

As she walked, she switched the valise and umbrella from one hand to the other as she made her way to town. It was times like this she missed having a horse and carriage, and promised herself that one day she would have them again.

The platform was empty when she arrived at the station. She still felt uneasy about leaving Millie alone, so when she saw Constable O'Toole patrolling the rail station, she went to him and asked him to keep an eye on Millie.

"I'll be gone for three days," she said. "I'd feel better if someone was watching over her."

"I'll be glad to take a ride out there, milady. You go and have a lovely time."

She sat on a bench on the platform and listened for the

whistle announcing the arrival of the train. She tapped her foot as she strained her neck to see down the tracks.

The train rumbled into the station a few minutes before eight, so Felicity grabbed her valise and umbrella before heading to the queue lining up in front of the entrance to the "Ladies Only" car. Felicity didn't notice the stranger in a bowler hat eyeing her intently as she boarded. He was leaning against a column and reading the Times, and after she was safely aboard, he folded his paper and boarded the train, too.

* * *

FELICITY CHOSE a seat near the front and sat next to the window. She wanted to avoid looking at her fellow passengers, especially the young women who wore the latest fashions. She kept her eyes on the platform as people waved goodbye to her fellow travelers, and when she stole a peek at those around her, she was happy to see that the car was half-empty, and that her fellow travelers were women with children.

When the conductor announced the next stop was Whitley, Felicity grabbed her things and waited for the train to slow down before getting up. She looked at the rail station and decided it looked just like the one in Tolwich. She stepped off the train, went to a porter, and asked for directions to Mrs. Muir's house.

Whitley was an ancient town. The stone road that ran from the rail station to the market at its center spoke of the town's Roman origins, but the buildings had been rebuilt during the reign of Henry the Eighth. The pub had a Tudor style façade and a thatched roof, and sat by itself on a small incline. The police station, on the other hand, looked as if it had been carved from an immense boulder. Other medieval era shops sat along the main road, and followed the line of the road as it curved here and there, leading to a small cul-de-sac.

Three cottages had been built on the horseshoe-shaped clearing; one at the head and two facing each other. The one at the head was empty, roofless, and crumbling, while the other two showed signs of occupation, particularly the one on the left, which was bright with a fresh coat of whitewash. It was surrounded by a white picket fence complete with a trellis of blue morning glories that had been growing out-of-control for years. The front of the house was covered in ivy, which framed a red front door. A large, latticed casement window faced the street.

Felicity walked to the cottage on the left and knocked on the door. Mrs. Muir opened it at once while tears formed in her eyes. Pure joy was etched on her face. She embraced Felicity and held her tightly as they stood at the doorway, for neither wanted to break the embrace, but soon Mrs. Muir's lumbago forced them to part.

"Lady Felicity, I can't believe you're here."

Mrs. Muir led her into the parlor and they both sat on the faded brocade settee that had been in Mrs. Muir's room at Rosendale. A low table sat in front of it, and as Felicity looked around, she saw the old armoire, the end tables that had come from Mr. Conway's room, and a large, stuffed chair covered in navy blue chintz near the window. The navy blue fabric was faded where the late morning sun had bleached the color away. A hearth was on the right wall, and the mantel held a small portrait of an adolescent Felicity and a clock.

Mrs. Muir had stitched pillows and crocheted blankets with bright colors in stark contrast to the white walls. Unlike Felicity's sad little cottage, this one felt like a home.

"I adore this cottage," Felicity said.

"It was rather run down when I bought it, but I'm quite happy with it now."

"I noticed that the one across the way is quite run down."

"That's Roger's house. He's a good lad."

Mrs. Muir looked older. She had abandoned her white servant's cap for a lacey snood, which held her long gray hair in place at the nape of her neck, and ringlets surrounded her face. Her blue eyes sparkled in the daylight like those of a younger woman.

"It is so good to see you, milady" she said.

"I've missed you terribly," Felicity said. "But I wasn't aware of how much. Seeing you again…I just missed you so much."

She laid her head on Mrs. Muir's shoulder and the old woman put her arm around Felicity's shoulders.

"And I you," Mrs. Muir said. "I've been praying for you every day."

The doors had been taken off the old armoire, and Mrs. Muir used it to display the gifts Felicity had given her when she was a girl. Felicity saw them and smiled.

"You still have the nest." She got up and went to the armoire to touch the delicately woven robin's nest. She looked at the other items on the shelf and felt a tug at her heart. "And my baby slippers." She looked at Mrs. Muir and smiled. "I always felt loved with you."

"You were loved, milady, and still are."

Felicity walked to the window.

"Are you happy here?" she asked.

"Most happy, my dear. I can easily walk to town, and I'm not alone." Mrs. Muir got up and joined her. "The sun rises over Roger's house every morning. He often sits outside and keeps an eye on things. I'm grateful to have him there."

"Do you ever miss having a husband and children?"

Mrs. Muir shook her head.

"You were my child. From the moment you were born, I cared for you. Your father had engaged a nanny, but as you grew, it soon became apparent that you preferred me to her. I persuaded your father that I was capable of caring for you and still attending to my other duties." She put her hand on Felicity's arm. "I will admit now that Mr. Conway would often take you on his knee when I had duties to tend to, but you were never a burden."

"He was a good man."

"As good a man as ever lived." Mrs. Muir took a deep breath. "Are you hungry?"

"I am."

A wall separated the kitchen and the parlor, and it had an arched doorway on each side. A round table and four chairs sat in the center of the kitchen, and Mrs. Muir had installed a stove in the old fireplace. She had a pump put in the kitchen so she wouldn't have to go to the back yard for water. A tin-lined sink and counter had been built under the kitchen window, and Felicity gasped when she saw the modern oak icebox next to a tall cabinet.

"You have an icebox!" she cried.

"Aye, and an indoor privy, too. I'm not ashamed to admit that I indulged myself when I moved here."

Felicity fought the envious feelings that rose inside her. She focused, instead, on the peace of Mrs. Muir's presence. She sat at the table set for two while Mrs. Muir put on the kettle. The scent of lavender wafted over her head, and Felicity saw bunches of the fragrant herb hanging on a string in front of the window.

"Do you have a garden?" she asked.

"Aye, a large garden. I grow the herbs I use for cooking." She pointed to the breakfront and Felicity saw rows of jars filled with dried herbs, each labeled, and in alphabetical order. "Also vegetables and chickens. I like to keep busy."

"Do you ever hear from the other servants?"

"I'm afraid not."

"Not even Mr. Conway?"

Mrs. Muir smiled. "I heard from him once. He said he had been offered a position in London."

"I always thought he was quite intimidating."

"Aye, but his bark was worse than his bite."

The kettle whistled and Mrs. Muir made a pot of jasmine tea. She took a loaf of bread out of a box on the counter and cut it into thin slices. She fetched a round of cheese from the pantry, put it on a cutting board, and brought everything to the table on a tray. She observed Felicity as they made their sandwiches and noticed how thin she looked. Her heart ached for her former charge, and she was glad that she had bought a leg of mutton for their supper.

As Felicity sipped her tea, Mrs. Muir wondered if, perhaps, Felicity might consider moving to Whitley. Their combined incomes would give the girl a better quality of life, and quell the occasional loneliness of living without companionship.

"How are you doing, milady? Are you happy?"

Felicity tried to smile, but there was nary a hint of pleasure on her face.

"I have food and shelter, and a companion." She looked into Mrs. Muir's eyes. "A girl from the village whom I hired to help me has become a friend."

"Oh, I'm so happy to hear you are not alone. Tell me about her."

"She is young, not yet thirteen, but she has the eyes of an old soul. I have taught her how to speak with what she calls a "posh" accent, and she has taught me how to cook and clean."

A shadow passed over Mrs. Muir's face as she thought of Lady Felicity cooking and cleaning. She looked at her hands and saw the red roughness of the skin. Mrs. Muir almost began to cry again.

"I wish I could meet her."

"I would have brought her with me, but..."

"I didn't send enough money."

Now, Mrs. Muir wiped her eye and looked away. She got up, grabbed the teapot, went to the counter, and made more tea. She let the tears roll down her cheeks while she measured the tea, and again wiped her eyes before returning to the table. Felicity was smiling in an effort to keep her own tears at bay.

"We have a garden and fruit trees, and a farmer who is generous with his eggs, so we're not starving," Felicity said.

Mrs. Muir smiled, too, for pity was not going to change her dire situation. Felicity needed hope.

"And you don't mind the work?"

"No. Millie and I work together. We get it done in no time at all."

"I must admit I was heartbroken when I saw you leave Rosendale. I feared you'd be all alone on that hill, and shivering in terror after sunset."

Felicity looked at her teacup.

"It was awful the first night, and for several nights after, but it made me realize that I was not helpless."

"Do you still grow sad?"

Mrs. Muir remembered Felicity's mother and the bouts of melancholia she had endured before Felicity was born. She noticed the affliction in her charge and tried to help her overcome it by showing her lots of love and affection, but it didn't always work. Sometimes, Felicity would avoid Mrs. Muir for she knew her sad spirit made her loving caretaker sad, too.

"Sometimes I feel it coming on and fight the urge to give in. Other times, I let it take over, but thankfully, it doesn't last long."

"That's good to hear. I suppose the girl helps you focus on something other than your sadness."

"She is quite determined to keep me well." Felicity sat back in her chair. "She is the best thing that's ever happened to me." Mrs. Muir noticed a subtle change to the look on her face as Felicity thought of Captain Fowler, but then Felicity cleared her throat and looked in Mrs. Muir's eyes. "I don't know what I would do without her."

"And what are your plans for the future, milady?"

Felicity sighed. "Right now, all I want to do is keep body and soul together." She looked at Mrs. Muir. "And the truth be told, I am too old and too poor to be considered a prize by any man, so I don't think I shall marry."

Mrs. Muir reached across the table and squeezed her hand. "Pay no heed to those who say you're too old to find a husband. There are good men aplenty who will see your worth."

"But how do I meet them, that's the rub. I'm too old for the season, and I've no father to offer a large dowry in exchange for my hand."

Mrs. Muir's eyes grew misty as a memory from long ago rose in her heart.

"Well, I'm a poor one to give advice on marriage," she said. "But you mustn't give up. I believe you were meant to have all the good things life has to offer."

"From your lips to God's ears," Felicity said.

They sat for a moment, each lost in her thoughts, and then Felicity remembered what had brought her to Mrs. Muir's door.

"Mrs. Muir, do you remember when Lord Winston came to the manor? I remember I was twelve, and he had his son Dudley with him, but I can't recall why they came to see us."

A strange look passed over Mrs. Muir's face.

"I do recall their visit."

Felicity waited for her to continue, and when she didn't, Felicity did.

"Do you remember why they visited?"

"Aye, I do recall Mr. Conway talking about it."

Mrs. Muir's eyes went to her hands. She had hoped this day would never come. She had hoped to shield Felicity from the harsh truth forever, but the sins of the father are always visited upon their offspring, or in this case, the sins of the mother on her lovely, innocent daughter.

CHAPTER 10

The room was quiet but for the ticking of the parlor clock as Mrs. Muir considered how to share a secret she'd sworn to keep as Phillipa lay dying. Now she would have to break it, and she hoped her words wouldn't destroy Felicity.

"Your father and Lord Winston where friends. He was our closest neighbor, and a frequent guest." She paused. "I had not joined the staff until your mother married your father, but Mr. Conway, who was a footman at the time, would often share his lunch with me. We would talk about the household."

"Didn't you tell me my mother hired you?"

Mrs. Muir nodded.

"Yes, your mother engaged me. She was eighteen years when your father married her." She paused again. "Her father had agreed to the match after your father suggested it." She took a deep breath. "She was an obedient daughter. After they wed, Lord Armstrong tried to show her affection, but his attempt at being a proper husband ended when he grew restless." She looked in Felicity's eyes. "You remember father's wanderlust." She put her hands around her teacup. "A few months after they wed, he told her he had to go to France to tend to one of his enterprises, but Mr. Conway knew that your father…had a woman in Paris."

Felicity's eyes widened.

"He had another woman?"

"Aye. Like most men of his class, he kept her even after he married. Before he left, he asked Lord Winston to look after the manor house and his new bride, and Lord Winston agreed."

Mrs. Muir took another deep breath and looked at Felicity.

"He would often arrive in time for dinner, and Mr. Conway, who had been promoted to under-butler, overheard their conversations." She blushed. "I'm embarrassed to say that he shared what he heard with me."

She hesitated, and Felicity, who was focusing on every word, touched her hand.

"It doesn't matter now," Felicity said. "Please go on."

"They became…enamored, your mother and Lord Winston. They grew close, and over time, she fell in love with him."

"And all this time, my father was with another woman in Paris."

Mrs. Muir nodded.

"Lord Winston was very handsome when he was a young man, and your mother felt abandoned. She was alone in that house, tending to her duties, and longing for companionship."

Felicity sat back and wrapped her arms around her waist. Mrs. Muir hesitated for a few moments as she observed the similarities between Felicity and her mother. Felicity had her eyes.

"I was promoted, too, and became your mother's maid. I liked her, and she trusted me. She told me things she wouldn't share with anyone else."

"Did Lord Harold make her happy?"

"Blissfully so, but she was young and innocent, and he was a married man with two sons. They could never marry." She took a deep breath. "One day, I found her in bed. She was as white as the bed sheet she clung to, and she told me she felt ill every morning."

"Poor thing."

"She was with child, Felicity, Lord Harold's child."

Felicity stared at Mrs. Muir as the color drained from her face. Shock and revulsion drew her hand to her mouth, as she understood what Mrs. Muir was saying. She shook her head.

"No!" she cried.

"She didn't understand what was wrong, and the doctor confirmed that she was with child. Your father had been gone for so long, and she feared he would turn her out if he found out the truth." Mrs. Muir's eyes were glassy. "Your mother died shortly after you were born. The staff chose to protect her and we agreed to tell your father that you had been born three months before his return. That way, he would believe you had been conceived before he left."

Felicity kept shaking her head.

"No one outside of Rosendale ever knew she'd been with Lord Winston. Lord Michael always believed you were his daughter until…"

Felicity looked into her eyes.

"Until what?"

"Until the day Lord Winston and his son visited Rosendale."

Felicity remembered looking at Dudley across the dining table as their fathers talked. She could still hear Lord Harold's slurred words, but she'd never connected the words with their true meaning.

"I was in the kitchen when Mr. Conway came to find me." Mrs. Muir got up and went to Felicity. "He told me Lord Winston had been drinking. He started talking about Phillipa and began to cry. He kept going on about how much he cared for Phillipa. He kept saying over and over that you were so lovely, just like your mother, but that you had your father's cleft chin."

She reached for Felicity's hand.

"Mr. Conway held his breath as Lord Michael looked from you to Lord Winston. He must have recalled the time he'd spent in Paris, about his request that Lord Harold watch over Phillipa, and he knew."

Felicity's eyes filled with tears that rolled down her cheeks.

"Lord Harold has that tiny cleft in his chin, too." Mrs. Muir hesitated, and then went on. "Your father asked for more brandy, but he didn't say another word. After Lord Winston and his son left, your father asked Mr. Jones, the butler, how often the lord had visited while he was away. Mr. Jones was an honest man, God rest his soul, and he answered him truthfully."

"His heart must have been broken," Felicity said, her lips trembling.

"He married Lady Bremington shortly after that. Mr. Conway said he believed it was because he wanted…"

Felicity looked at her.

"He wanted what?"

"He wanted a son."

Felicity's eyes glistened.

"Of course. He wanted a legitimate heir."

Mrs. Muir held Felicity's hand tightly.

"He loved you, Felicity, even after he knew your weren't his own."

Felicity shook her head.

"No, he didn't." She got up and went to the kitchen window. "I remember when he married Felicia. He was always gone, always on some trip to the 'continent,' and I rarely saw him anymore."

The memory of that meal with Lord Winston sharpened, and Felicity remembered the way he'd looked at her, and how uncomfortable it made her feel.

"Did he ever see Lord Winston again?" she asked.

"Not that I recall," Mrs. Muir said.

Felicity went to Mrs. Muir, put her hands on the back of her chair, leaned over, and pressed her cheek against Mrs. Muir's.

"You're the only one I ever had," she said softly.

"And I was glad to be."

Felicity stood but kept her hands on the chair.

"Is there anything else I need to know?"

"No." Mrs. Muir got up. "I have something that might help you understand the choices your mother made."

"What is it?"

"A packet of letters she wrote, but never sent, to Lord Winston. They're in the top drawer of the armoire."

Mrs. Muir went to the icebox and got the leg of mutton while Felicity went to the armoire and opened the top drawer. The packet of letters was tied in a red ribbon. She withdrew them and went to the settee.

* * *

FELICITY SPENT the next hour reading her mother's letters. They read like passages from a diary, containing all her hopes and dreams, and professions of love that caused Felicity to blush. The naked emotions displayed on each page created the portrait of a woman who had been forced into a life she never wanted, and when she gave in to her impulsive passions, she fell into a knot that she couldn't untie.

Felicity's judgment of her mother's infidelity changed to empathy, as she understood what it was like to be thrust into a world without guidance or support. Phillipa had loved Lord Harold, and their time together was memorialized in flowery prose that emphasized their intimacy. As she wrote, Phillipa abandoned all inhibitions, describing Lord Harold's "manly chest," with fervor, forcing Felicity to push the packet of letters aside to save them for another time if she chose to read them at all.

She went to Mrs. Muir, who was at the stove, and put her arms around her.

"Did you read them?"

"No. I knew she had written them and thought they might contain things she wouldn't want her husband to see, so I retrieved them the night she died and put them in my room. I thought when you were ready that I would give them to you."

"I'm not ready," Felicity said.

"I'm sorry, my dear, but sometimes fate has other plans for us."

Felicity saw the colander of washed potatoes on the counter and picked up the paring knife next to them. She sat at the table and cut them, and then Mrs. Muir put the pieces in the pan with the leg of mutton so the grease would brown them.

"She really loved him," Felicity said.

"Aye, she did."

"Do you think that's why Dudley came to see me?"

Mrs. Muir stopped putting the potatoes in the pan and looked at Felicity. She shook her head as she thought about him coming to Felicity's cottage unannounced, and an evil thought entered her mind. Had he expected her to be alone?

"That was unacceptable," she said.

"He's my brother," she said. She looked at Mrs. Muir, her eyes wide. "I'm a bastard."

Mrs. Muir came to her and took her hands.

"You must never say that." She bit her lower lip. "You must never tell a living soul. The world is unforgiving, Felicity. You would be reviled. You would never live it down."

"He must know I'm a bastard, and if anyone were to find out, it would be as hard on him as on me."

Bastardy bore a social stigma so heinous that even highborn ladies and gentlemen were not immune from the dishonor associated with illegitimate children. Both mother and child were viewed as an affront to decency, and as such, orphanages rejected the children. Those born out-of-wedlock often met a horrible fate as desperate mothers, rich and poor alike, sought ways to shield themselves from public disgrace by giving their child to a babyfarmer.

Veiled ads placed in newspapers advertised widows with small incomes willing to care for young or sickly children in exchange for 15 shillings a month. They would also adopt the child for 12 pounds.

The mother agreed to meet a third party in public where the transaction would take place. These farms were the last resort for desperate mothers who most likely knew they would never see their child again. Babyfarmers preferred sickly children, or babies under two months, for their deaths would avoid scrutiny.

Laws were introduced that addressed the issue of baby farms, which spoke to the mortality rate and neglect associated with unscrupulous caregivers, but they would languish for years until another shocking story appeared in the papers, renewing the public's outrage.

One particular story about a Mrs. Waters was particularly egregious. She had drugged and starved over 16 children to death, and then abandoned their bodies on deserted streets. Her actions prompted the Infant Life Protections bill in 1871, which failed to pass due to a clause that required nurses to be registered and supervised. Suffragettes claimed the clause would put a financial strain on employers, which might hinder the employment of nurses, and they also objected to the registration and supervision being handled by men.

As a member of the ton, Dudley understood how society viewed illegitimacy, and if he knew Felicity was his half-sister, it might explain why he came to see her. Her existence could affect his suitability for marriage. But why not just tell her the truth?

As she and Mrs. Muir ate their supper, Felicity picked at her food, and Mrs. Muir worried about Dudley Winston. She had not seen him the day of the visit, but Mr. Conway said he was an insufferable youth who taunted Felicity, who was too naïve to know he was mocking her, and now that he was an adult with a reason to fear a scandal, she worried that he might be driven to desperate measures to keep his secret.

You're being foolish, she thought. *He's not a boy anymore. He's a gentleman.*

But Mrs. Muir had known many gentlemen in her time, and she knew his title was no insurance against ill intentions. Still, it was all she had to assuage her fears, so she kept her thoughts to herself. She did, however, warn Felicity to guard the letters and keep them in a safe place.

* * *

THE NEXT MORNING, they ate their breakfast, and made plans to go to the market. The eggs from Mrs. Muir's chickens tasted so good that Felicity vowed she would learn how to make a coop for her back yard, and buy a chicken and a rooster from Mr. Brewer so she and Millie could have fresh eggs, too.

"I had to learn how to care for them," Mrs. Muir said. "I was too busy caring for you to learn while I was your housekeeper."

"And you didn't have them when you were young?" Mrs. Muir's wistful expression made Felicity smile. "What are you thinking?"

"I came to your house when I was a young woman," she began. "I was hired as a scullery maid, but I knew nothing about cleaning. I had been a spoiled girl."

"You never told me this before."

"No. I didn't tell Mr. Conway, either. I was always afraid it would change his opinion of me. That's how it was back then."

"It's not much changed now," Felicity said.

Mrs. Muir winked at her.

"Indeed. I was twenty-four when I came to Rosendale. Much like yours, my circumstances had taken a turn." Mrs. Muir's shoulder's dropped. "I was born Lady Hedda Muir."

Felicity raised an eyebrow.

"Yes, and much like you, my father had died and left me with such a small yearly income that I was forced to look for work." She looked at Felicity. "I'd tried to find work as a paid companion, but...there was a scandal, you see, involving my father, and ladies were unwilling to take me on, as if I wore the taint of his misdeeds.

"Your mother's good grace saved me, milady. She knew who I was, but instead of turning me away as other households had, she took me in. She fed me and gave me a room. She brought me into her house without judgment. I worked hard and she rewarded my diligence many times over."

"And you made peace with your station in life?"

Mrs. Muir smiled. "Oh, yes, milady. I've been able to forgive my father and those ladies who spurned me, and now I have a peaceful home and a quiet neighbor."

"But you're alone."

Mrs. Muir sighed. "I live alone, yes, but I'm not alone. Roger is fine company whenever I feel lonely. It's enough for me."

Felicity frowned. "I want children."

"And so you shall have them. I've heard of women who married in their thirties, milady. If this is your heart's desire, you should never give up hope."

"I fear I've already given up hope." She looked at Mrs. Muir. "I live in a cottage by the sea. Single gentlemen are scarce."

And I'm in love with a man I haven't seen in two years.

Mrs. Muir smiled. "Then perhaps you should consider selling that cottage and moving."

"The thought has crossed my mind." She looked into Mrs. Muir's eyes. "But then I think, what if I'm wrong? I could lose what little I have."

"What if you take the risk and find a wonderful life awaiting you?"

Felicity sighed and shook her head.

"I'd feel better knowing what awaits me."

"Oh, young people!" Mrs. Muir threw up her hands. "No one ever knows what awaits them. You have to be brave enough to take that first step. It's not luck that brings success; it's bravery."

"But I'm a single woman."

"And single you will stay if you keep waiting for your prince to arrive before the stroke of midnight."

Felicity blushed. She was waiting for a phantom ship to appear on the horizon.

She got up, took their plates to the sink, and looked out the kitchen window. A man in a bowler hat was standing near the fence looking at the house.

"How old is Roger?" she asked.

"He's near my age."

The man looked to be in his forties, but it was hard to tell because his hat hid his hairline.

"There's an odd man out there looking at this house."

Mrs. Muir went to Felicity and looked at the man.

"Well, that is not Roger. I wonder who he is."

"He looks a bit unseemly," Felicity said.

"I don't like the idea of strangers lurking about."

She went to the kitchen door and went outside.

"You there!" she cried, but the man was gone.

CHAPTER 11

*T*he market stalls were overflowing with goods. Fruits and smoked fish filled their baskets, and then Mrs. Muir spotted the man in the bowler hat lurking near the edge of the crowd.

"There he is," she said. "The man in the bowler hat."

Felicity followed Mrs. Muir's gaze and saw him. Chills ran up her spine.

"Do you think he's following us?"

"I can't imagine why." She took Felicity's arm. "Come. Let's go see the constable."

Mrs. Muir glanced behind them as they walked up the road, but the man had disappeared. They moved swiftly toward the ancient stone police station. The grim interior had a counter, and behind it, three empty cells. A man in a blue uniform sat behind the counter and looked up as they entered.

"'Morning, ladies." He had a handlebar mustache and a gleam in his eye. "How can I help you today?"

Mrs. Muir put her hands on the edge of the counter near his nameplate, which read, "Police Constable Woolsey."

"We believe a man has been following us," she said.

"A man you say."

"Yes," Felicity said. "He wears a bowler hat."

"And why do you think he's been following you?"

His mocking tone annoyed Mrs. Muir.

"We've seen him twice this morning. The first time he was looking in my kitchen window. The second time, he was watching us as we walked through the market."

Felicity saw the twinkle in his eye. He wasn't taking them seriously, and now she, too, was annoyed.

"I assure you he is quite real, and a nasty looking character," Felicity said. She thrust out her chin. "We would like an escort home."

The officer looked at the large clock on the wall.

"Very well, you wait here," he said.

He slid off his stool and disappeared through a door next to the last cell. Both ladies tapped their feet as they waited, their baskets growing heavy on their arms, and impatience mixed with fear causing them to bristle.

"What is taking him so long?" Mrs. Muir said.

"Would you like me to hold your basket?"

"No, milady, I am fine."

But she didn't look fine, and Felicity feared she might swoon. Her brow was covered in perspiration, and her cheeks looked pale. Felicity looked around for a chair and spied a wide windowsill that might accommodate Mrs. Muir's small frame.

"Why don't you sit down?" she said.

"I promise you I am fine. Now where is that man?"

P.C. Woolsey returned and climbed on the stool.

"Police Constable Leary will be right out," he said without looking at them.

"Your rudeness is beyond belief, young man."

He looked at Mrs. Muir, and once again, Felicity saw the twinkle in his eye. He found Mrs. Muir amusing, and his lack of respect was appalling. She wanted to say something to put him in his place, but before the words came to her, P.C. Leary came through the door behind him and came around the counter.

"Ladies," he said. "Woolsey here says you're being followed."

"We, Lady Armstrong and I, have noticed an unseemly gentleman watching us both at my home and at the market. We fear his intentions are less than honorable."

Felicity nodded her head.

"It's true," she said.

"Have you any idea why he'd be following you?" he asked.

"None whatsoever," Mrs. Muir said. "Which is why we are here. We don't wish to be accosted by a ruffian."

"Aye," he said. "Well, then, I'll see you home."

Leary walked around the counter and past the ladies, who followed him out the door.

"It's this way," Mrs. Muir said as she turned to her left.

Leary took the lead and walked at a brisk pace. As they walked, the ladies gave him a description of the man, who sounded like every other workingman in Whitley.

"Don't like strangers lurking about," he said.

When they reached Mrs. Muir's house, Leary went inside first, and when he was satisfied there was no one in the house, he allowed them to enter.

"Keep your doors locked," he said. "I'll take a look around the market. Don't you worry, ladies, we'll find him."

"And if you don't?" Mrs. Muir asked.

Leary put his hands behind his back and rocked on his heels. While he believed the ladies had seen a strange man, he doubted he was going to accost them in their home. He was probably planning to steal one of their purses, or grab a basket as they walked home. Still, with the surge of passengers using the new train route, he had arrested several "unseemly" characters in the last few weeks, and he decided it was better to accommodate the ladies than to leave their fate to chance.

"I'll ask one of my men to come 'round a few times to make sure you're all tucked in."

"Is that all you can do?" Mrs. Muir said.

"Strangers don't get by us for long, missus. If he's still here, we'll catch him."

"Perhaps we should cover the window," Felicity said.

"Now that's a sound idea," Leary said. "Well." He tipped his hat. "I'll be off."

He left them standing at the doorway. Mrs. Muir saw Roger sitting across the street and waved. He waved his pipe in return.

* * *

MRS. MUIR FROWNED.

"I know it's the right thing to do, but it is so unfair."

"What is, Mrs. Muir?"

"Covering the window. It will make the cottage feel so small."

"We only need to cover them until he's caught, and you heard what the constable said. He's a stranger. They will easily spot him if he's still here."

"But what if they don't? What then?" Mrs. Muir shook her head. "No. This is my home, and I won't be cowed into shutting myself away."

Felicity was vexed by Mrs. Muir's attitude. Nevertheless, she respected her and didn't mention covering the windows again. She did suggest they spend the evening in the kitchen, though, which had a curtained window. She closed those curtains, and Mrs. Muir frowned.

"You know, Mrs. Muir, I've never learned how to make a custard pie."

"Would you like me to teach you?"

"I'd be delighted if you would."

They spent the rest of the afternoon making egg custard and rolling dough. They talked about their past together, avoiding subjects that brought them pain, and focusing on the things that made them smile.

"It feels wrong to teach you how to make custard," Mrs. Muir said.

"But I helped you with our meal last night."

"Yes, and that felt wrong, too."

Felicity pursed her lips and put her hands on her hips.

"It's also wrong for a lady to die of starvation simply because she doesn't know the first thing about preparing food."

Mrs. Muir raised her eyebrows and smiled.

"You're right."

"And *you* worked as a scullery maid."

"I did." She sighed. "And I was grateful." She looked at Felicity. "Milady, you are still young. There is still hope that a gentleman will one day ask for your hand. You must maintain your dignity."

Felicity sat at the table.

"I don't think I want a gentleman," she said softly. "In truth, the only man I'm interested in, or have ever *been* interested in, is Captain Fowler."

"And who is Captain Fowler?"

Now Mrs. Muir sat at the table.

"He captains a ship I've invested in. I haven't heard from him in over a year."

Mrs. Muir wondered where Felicity had gotten money for such a venture.

"We signed a contract, and his solicitor was to send me his letters when they arrived at his office."

"Why didn't he write to you directly?"

"Because I was afraid Handy and Conner would find out." Felicity sat back in her chair letting her hands fall to her lap.

Mrs. Muir nodded her head.

"Where did you get the money?" she asked.

Felicity got up and began to pace the floor. Her guilt over pilfering her mother's jewels had been hidden under a sense of bravado that told her she had a right to them, but now, the reality of her ruse was made clear. She had stolen them from the estate. What would Mrs. Muir think of her?

"You didn't do something foolish, did you, milady?"

Felicity kept her eyes on the floor as she stopped.

"Yes," she said softly.

Mrs. Muir brought her hands to her mouth.

"Oh, milady."

"I sold my mother's jewelry."

Mrs. Muir's eyebrow rose, and a smile creased her lips as her fears were allayed.

"So, you found them."

Felicity looked vexed. Mrs. Muir got up, went to her, and took her hand.

"I tried so hard to retrieve them from her room, but your father sealed it and made it clear that no one was to enter it again."

"You knew they were there?" Felicity asked.

Mrs. Muir nodded.

"She told me about them before you were born. She said that if anything ever happened to her, I was to give them to you. She feared your father would marry again and give them to another woman. They were family jewels, and *you* were *her* family."

Felicity stared at Mrs. Muir.

"She didn't trust my father."

Mrs. Muir shook her head.

"Her mother had given them to her and told her that she was to keep them from your father." Mrs. Muir smiled. "She was wise, your grandmother. She understood the ways of men, and made provision for her daughter."

"And for me."

"Yes, but when you didn't mention finding them, I went to the room and looked into the drawer. I thought that perhaps your father or Felicia had found them." She squeezed Felicity's hand. "Oh, milady, I'm so happy it was you and not them."

"I remember feeling as if she were there, and I was drawn to the dressing table."

"She would be so proud of you." Mrs. Muir smiled broadly. "Oh, milady, you took a bold step and I admire you for it."

Felicity smiled, but it was tinged with sadness.

"But what if he's absconded? What if I never see him again?"

Mrs. Muir tilted her head and looked Felicity in the eye.

"Have you done something to be ashamed of?"

"No, never."

"Then I wouldn't worry. Things happen on long journeys, and he might be on his way home right this very minute."

"From your lips to God's ears."

"Amen," Mrs. Muir said.

"Still, I fear he might be in trouble."

Mrs. Muir looked at Felicity's pale complexion and downcast eyes.

"You said the only man you want is Captain Fowler."

Tears rolled down Felicity's cheeks as Mrs. Muir pondered her problem.

"Where is this solicitor?"

"His office is in London."

"Then you should stop there on your way home."

"But what can he tell me that he can't write in a letter?"

"Perhaps nothing, but it will be harder to keep something from you when you're standing in front of him."

Felicity agreed. If she saw his eyes, she'd know if he was telling her the truth, or hiding something Captain Fowler didn't want her to know.

Mrs. Muir sighed.

"I have to visit the privy again," she said. "It seems like that's all I do lately."

Felicity went to her bedroom and took the letters out of her purse. She was looking through them when she heard Mrs. Muir return to the kitchen. She glanced out the parlor window as she walked by and stopped.

"Mrs. Muir," she said, "please come here."

Mrs. Muir came to Felicity's side and looked out the window. She saw the small, dark-eyed man in a bowler hat standing in front of old Roger's yard.

"The lurker is back, and no constable in sight."

"Then perhaps we should go to the constable now," Mrs. Muir said. "We will take an umbrella with us in case he tries to stop us."

"That's exactly what we'll do."

The scent of baked pie reached them as they prepared to go to the police station, and Felicity ran to the kitchen and pulled the pie out just before it burned. She looked at the brown edges and sighed.

The older woman looked tired, and Felicity worried that she might be doing too much. She knew the windows were closed tightly and the door had a bolt, and she would keep a kitchen knife handy should the man decide to burst through the parlor window.

"Perhaps we should wait until morning," Felicity said. "If we go now, there's a good chance he will accost us."

Mrs. Muir *was* tired, and despite her earlier bravado, felt the strain of missing her nap for two days. She sighed as she looked at Felicity.

"Very well. We'll go in the morning." She sat on the settee and Felicity sat beside her. "So, tell me all about this Captain Fowler."

Felicity smiled. "He has blue eyes that sparkled in the sunlight. I still remember the way he smiled and laughed, and the way he looked at me." She looked up at Mrs. Muir, her eyes glistening. "If I never see him again, I don't know what I'll do."

"Nothing helps soothe the soul better than a cup of tea."

Mrs. Muir patted Felicity's hand, and then tried to get up off the settee, but Felicity's hand stopped her.

"I can do that," Felicity said. "You rest while I make the tea."

Sometimes decisions are contemplated for weeks or months, and sometimes they glow like a beacon in a storm, lighting the way to safety. As she placed the tea leaves in the pot, Felicity knew with unparalleled certainty that she didn't want to be Lady Felicity Armstrong any longer. When the kettle whistled, she filled the cups, and took them into the parlor.

"Mrs. Muir," she said.

"Yes, milady."

Felicity put Mrs. Muir's cup on the end table near her.

"I've decided I no longer what to be Lady Armstrong. I'm going to relinquish my title."

Mrs. Muir looked at her in horror.

"Don't talk that way," she said. "It is your birthright."

"You abandoned your birthright and you've been very happy," Felicity said. "I see you living here, walking to market, living a simple life, and I realize that the thing that is holding me back is the belief that someday I can have my old life back, but it isn't to be."

"You can't be certain of that. I was twenty-four when I made that decision."

"And I'm twenty, past my prime, and I don't want an old widower with four children. I want to choose my life."

"Milady, no one gets to choose their life. We are what we are. It's God's choice to make."

"Well, perhaps God has made this choice. I have been set adrift. Perhaps this is His will."

"I refuse to believe God would do such a thing."

"Why not?" Felicity sat next to her. "Why wouldn't he? I'm a far better person since I've had to fend for myself. I have more empathy, more understanding. It makes perfect sense to me."

Mrs. Muir couldn't argue with her reasoning. God often put obstacles in her path and the overcoming is what built her character. She thought about her own life, how she had to relinquish dreams of a noble life with a husband and children, and understood why Felicity had come to this conclusion.

"I suppose it does make sense," Mrs. Muir said. "Are you sure you are ready to let it all go?"

"I will probably contemplate it for a day or two, but my heart is telling me that it is the right decision."

"Very well then, *Miss* Armstrong, but I wager the smell of that pie wafting through the air just might fetch you a husband yet."

Mrs. Muir winked, and Felicity smiled.

a nightmare roused Felicity from a fitful sleep. Images of the man in the bowler hat had appeared in her dreams, causing her heart to pound and her hands to shake. He was following her and Mrs. Muir, and just as they neared the safety of the cottage, he grabbed Mrs. Muir, who screamed, and the scream woke Felicity. She opened her eyes, listened, and heard a faint "thump," but then all was quiet.

She got up and opened the door. She looked into the parlor and saw that the armoire drawers were open and their contents spilled to the floor.

"Mrs. Muir" she said.

The cushions on the settee had been turned over, and the lamp on the table beside it was missing.

"Mrs. Muir!" Felicity cried. "Mrs. Muir!"

She went to the kitchen and saw Mrs. Muir lying facedown on the floor with a pool of blood near her head. A cast iron skillet lay beside her, and small pieces of broken glass littered the floor around her head and hair.

"You must do something." A voice in her head brought Felicity back to reality. "Go and get the police."

She ran outside and began to scream for help. Roger, Mrs. Muir's elderly neighbor, was having a smoke in his yard when he saw Felicity run out of the house in her nightgown.

"Hey, there," he said as he crossed the street.

"Oh, please, you must help me. Something's happened to Mrs. Muir. I need the police."

Roger noticed how pale she was and nodded.

"I'll fetch them, miss," he said, and began hobbling down the road to the police station.

Felicity's legs wouldn't move, nor would her mind stop flashing images of the blood under Mrs. Muir's head. She kept her eyes open, for the images were worse when she closed them.

She fell to her knees and leaned on her hands. She changed the scenario in Mrs. Muir's kitchen to something she could handle.

"She has just taken a fall," she said, "and hit her head."

She thought about going back inside, to see if Mrs. Muir was breathing, but she felt frozen in place. Her emotions were shutting down, and a warm blanket of numbness was falling over her. She sat with her legs pulled up underneath her and pulled bits of grass from the yard as she waited for the police to arrive.

P.C. Leary came to the yard and saw Lady Felicity sitting near the kitchen door in her nightgown. He had little experience with titled ladies and gentlemen, but he doubted they would allow themselves to be seen thus unless something was terribly amiss.

"Are you all right, milady?"

She looked at him as if she were a lost child, and then looked at the kitchen door.

"It's Mrs. Muir," she said, barely above a whisper.

Leary walked through the kitchen door and stopped when he stepped on a piece of glass. He saw the body and the blood, and then examined the room. Mrs. Muir's head was facing the door as if she had been running toward it. There was a basket of herbs on the table – she must have been in the garden. Beside it was the base of the brass table lamp lying on its side. She still wore her shawl, and a skillet lay beside her, the obvious murder weapon. The perpetrator had hit her from behind when she brought the basket inside.

Leary went outside to find Roger helping Felicity get up off the ground. He thought about the ladies, who were fine when he left them at the house the day before. They hadn't shown signs of discord, but you never knew what lay beneath the surface. Perhaps they had fallen into an argument and feelings ran high. But when Leary looked at her slumped shoulders and quivering lips, he couldn't believe she had perpetrated the crime.

"Where were you when this happened, milady?"

"I was asleep," she said, her voice muddled with emotion. "I had a nightmare, and I heard a scream. It woke me."

Roger hobbled past Leary and went toward the kitchen door.

"Mind yourself, Roger," Leary said. "Don't go inside."

"I saw her outside this morning," he said. "She was in her garden. I said 'good morning,' and then I went in to make me coffee." Roger looked at Felicity, and then at Leary. "I'll bet it was him."

"Who?" Leary asked.

"The man what I saw lurking at the window."

Felicity roused from her stupor.

"You saw him?" she said.

"Aye, and I knew he was up to no good." When he saw he had their attention, he stood as tall as he could, pushed out his chest, and lifted his chin. "He was peeking in the window t'other night and I yelled for him to go before I shot him in the arse." He looked at Felicity. "Sorry, miss."

"We told you about him," Felicity said to Leary. "The man in the bowler hat."

"That's the one," Roger said.

Leary blushed. He'd promised to look for the man, but as soon as he'd left, he'd chalked it up to women's hysteria, made a note on the duty blackboard, and then spent the afternoon at the pub where he "kept the peace." He looked at Roger and hoped the old codger had gotten a good look at the man's face.

"Roger, you say you saw Mrs. Muir in the garden."

"I did."

"Did you see the man today?"

Roger shook his head. "But who else could it be? No one 'round here would want to hurt her."

"He went through the drawers in the parlor," Felicity said. "She must have found him inside the house."

Felicity trembled as she thought of Mrs. Muir finding the stranger in her home and trying to get away.

"He was looking for something," Leary said. "Did she have valuables?"

"Caw," Roger said. "She didn't have more than anyone else."

"Milady," Leary said. "Did she?"

Felicity shook her head.

"Nothing worth dying for."

"So you have no idea why he'd want to harm her?"

She shook her head again, and then looked up at Leary.

"She was the dearest soul," her voice quivered. "There was no reason anyone would want to harm her."

Felicity wasn't much bigger than the victim, but he'd seen tiny women leave large bumps on the heads of their husbands when they were enraged, but those moments were often preceded by years of abuse. Besides, he hadn't seen anything amiss between them. He looked at Roger. He was glad the old man had seen the stranger, too, for it lent credence to the women's story.

"Roger, do you think you could describe him?"

"I mostly saw him from behind."

"I can describe him," Felicity said.

"When you're dressed, I'd like you to come to the station." He leaned toward her and bent over so he could see her eyes. "We'll find him. That's a promise." He looked at Roger. "Stay out of the kitchen. I'll be back to photograph the scene."

They watched Leary as he headed down the road, and then Roger looked through the kitchen door. He saw the blood and turned away.

"She was a good lass, that one," he said. "Twern't right this happening to her."

"No, it was cruel," Felicity said.

"Awe, miss, the cruelest fate of all."

The blanket of numbness was still in place, protecting her from feeling too much. She had to go into the house to change her clothes, and would be able to do so by going through the front door.

"I must get dressed," she said softly.

"Do you want me to come with you to the police station?" he asked.

She looked at his rheumy brown eyes and managed a smile.

"Yes, please."

"I'll wait at me own house if you don't mind."

He stayed until she went to the front door, and then stayed when she couldn't open it. It was still bolted from the night before. She hesitated, and then walked to the kitchen door. She hesitated again, and then took a deep breath before going inside.

* * *

FELICITY KEPT pace with Roger's hobble as they walked to the police station. Few words were exchanged as the shock of Mrs. Muir's death settled in, and neither of them could stop thinking of her. Leary had returned with a doctor and a large camera, and they waited until Felicity had left with Roger before attending to their grim duties.

When Felicity and Roger arrived at the station, Woolsey opened the door beside his counter to let them in.

"We got a man here who can draw the suspect," he said. "He's this way."

They followed Woolsey to a large room containing several desks and blackboards. A man in a business suit was seated at a desk near a window. He cast a weary smile as they approached him, and stood to offer Felicity his seat.

"Are you Lady Armstrong?"

"Yes, and this is Roger."

The man nodded toward Roger. He wore a paisley vest under his suit jacket and his hair was short and pomaded. He was clean-shaven and wore wire-rimmed spectacles. Felicity caught a whiff of his sandalwood cologne as she sat in the chair next to the desk, and then saw a large sheet of paper and a pencil on the desk.

"My name is Sydney Barlow," the man said. "I'm an architect, but I often lend my skills to the police when something like this occurs."

"You're a real artist, Sydney?" Roger asked.

"Yes, I am." He looked at Felicity. "Shall we begin?"

Sidney sat at the desk, and Roger took a seat at another. Sidney held the pencil in his right hand, poised to begin.

"Now, if you can describe what the man looked like, I'll start sketching and I'll ask you for details as we go along."

Felicity recalled seeing him from the kitchen window.

"He wasn't tall," she said. "And he always wore a bowler hat."

"Can you recall what else he was wearing?"

"He wore a suit jacket that matched his trousers."

Sydney continued to ask questions and either Felicity or Roger would describe the man's eyes, nose, scruffy beard, and any other details that would help render a good likeness of the culprit. Sydney ran his pencil over the page, embellishing the details in accordance with normal human anatomy, and then held up the sketch for their approval.

"You must add the hat," Felicity said. "He always wore it."

"I'll make two, side by side; one with the hat, and one without."

It took him some time to make the second sketch, so while he worked, Roger got up and looked out the barred window on the other side of the room. Felicity watched him as she tried to keep her mind off Mrs. Muir, and soon Sydney held up his new sketch.

"How's this?"

Felicity shuddered as she looked at the picture, for the one with the hat looked just like the man she'd seen.

"That's him," she said, and she looked away.

"Then I'll prepare a poster that will be circulated throughout England." Sydney put his pencil down and got up. He looked at Felicity with sympathetic eyes. "I am so sorry for your loss, Lady Armstrong. Thank you for coming in so quickly." He held out his hand to Felicity and she shook it. "Would you like me to escort you home?"

"I'm walking her," Roger said as he thrust out his chin.

"Of course, well then, I will take care of this straight away."

"Thank you, Mr. Barlow," she said.

Leary was waiting for her when she and Roger emerged from the station.

"I'm to walk you home," he said.

"I'm walking her," Roger said again.

"Aye, Roger, you can walk her, too." He looked at Felicity. "The inquest is this afternoon. We've already sent word to the local chaps. I'll need you there to give testimony."

Felicity didn't want to talk, or think, or see anyone, but she knew that those men would determine whether Mrs. Muir had been murdered, allowing police to start an investigation. The sooner they made their decision, the sooner they would start looking for the man in the bowler hat.

"I'll be there," she said softly. "Where is it being held?"

"We're going to use the community hall behind the church." He hesitated a moment. "We've already taken her there."

Felicity's eyes misted and she put her hand to her mouth. Leary took her arm and gently guided her to the road while Roger hobbled behind.

CHAPTER 13

*A*s Felicity awaited the inquest, two women from the church came to clean up the mess while Vicar Stephens sat with Felicity in the parlor. They watched while the women picked up the things that had been strewn around the room. From time to time, the women would ask Felicity where to put the items. The vicar, a plain man with a balding head, was blessedly quiet.

When the women were done, the vicar rose and went to the kitchen to look at the floor. He was pleased to find that the blood had come off the wooden floor, though a slight pink stain was left behind. He looked around for a rug and spied one in front of the hearth.

"If you have no objections," he said to Felicity, "I'd like to move this rug to the kitchen."

Felicity didn't answer, nor did she gesture, so he took it upon himself to make the decision and dragged the rug to the kitchen. He moved the table and chairs to place it, and then put them back where they belonged, only now they were on top of the rug. Satisfied that would help obliterate the image of Mrs. Muir's body from Felicity's mind, he went back to the parlor, stood before her, and placed his hands behind his back.

"Would you like some tea?" he asked.

"No, thank you."

He began to rock on his heels as he waited for Felicity to release him from his duties, but she kept staring at her hands. He cleared his throat and she came to life.

"Thank you, Vicar Stephens," she said. She got up and walked to the front door.

"If you are able, I'd like to speak to you following the inquest."

"Will you be there?" she asked.

"I will be attending."

"Will you sit with me?"

He put his hand on her forearm.

"Of course. Would you like me to escort you to the church?"

"Roger has offered to come with me."

He opened the door and she watched him walk up the road. She closed the door and wrapped her arms around her waist. She avoided looking at the kitchen doorway and returned to the settee.

Felicity's belief in God had been fostered during her childhood when Mrs. Muir would take her to Sunday services at a small church near Rosendale. Her father's attendance was limited to holidays, marriages, christenings, and funerals, and Felicia had eschewed attendance altogether, but Mrs. Muir found peace in her faith, and hoped Felicity would be able to overcome her melancholy through faith in something greater than herself.

Mrs. Muir's hope had not been fulfilled, and Felicity hadn't found a home in church. She found more solace in a good book, a walk by the sea, or in the company of a kind and generous soul. She didn't mock those who believed, for from time to time, she had sensed the "presence" of something, such as when the voice guided her earlier that day, but she was still not convinced that it was anything more than her own mind guiding her out of the darkness. When she mentioned God, it was that voice she was referring to.

She went to the kitchen and looked at the rug on the floor. It looked out of place, and it was not where Mrs. Muir had kept it, so she took the table and chairs off the rug and pulled it back to the hearth.

* * *

THE CHURCH WAS a former Catholic Abbey that Henry the Eighth had confiscated in an effort to purge Catholicism from England. As Felicity and Roger walked into the narthex, she thought of the king, a man so powerful he could create a religion simply because it would allow him to divorce his first wife to marry another, younger woman.

Still, the church was a lovely representation of medieval architecture, with statues of Saint Peter and Saint Paul carved on each side of the entrance to the narthex. The arched ceiling beams enhanced the sanctuary, giving the feel of a much larger cathedral, and the stained glass windows told the story of the crucifixion and accession of the Christ.

Felicity was grateful for the beauty of the church for she was able to focus on it as Roger led her through the sanctuary to a large detached community room behind the church.

The austere room was in stark contrast to the elegant glory of the church. It held nothing but chairs for the attendees and a long table at the front. Mrs. Muir had been laid on the table, and when Felicity saw her, she almost swooned.

Roger caught her arm and led her to a chair. The room felt too hot, and she longed to open the button on the neck of her blouse. She held Roger's arm until he set her down, and after she assured him that she was all right, he left her to greet someone a few chairs away.

There were two rows of chairs for the panel of local men who would hear evidence and render a decision regarding the death of Hedda Muir. The men had done this many times before. They took their duty seriously, and asked pertinent questions.

The constable was there, and the vicar, who was talking with a man she didn't recognize. At one on the dot, the vicar called for everyone to take their seats, the unfamiliar man went to stand behind the table, and Vicar Stephens sat beside Felicity.

The unfamiliar man introduced himself as the town physician, and he described Mrs. Muir's wounds. He concluded that she had received a blow to the head by a hard object. Her skull had been fractured in such a way that her breathing stopped, and that led to her death. It was his opinion that her death was not natural.

The doctor stepped away and P.C. Leary stood to offer his description of the crime scene. The men asked him questions, too, and then Vicar Stephens looked at Felicity.

"They would like to hear from you now."

"May I stay here?"

She didn't think she could bear being close to Mrs. Muir's body.

"Yes, but please stand."

Leary looked at her and thought she looked older than when he left her that morning. He modulated the tone of his voice as he questioned her.

"Can you tell us about your relationship with Hedda Muir, Lady Armstrong?"

Felicity felt a warm sensation as if someone had put their arms around her.

"She was our housekeeper when I was a child."

"And why did you come to Whitley?"

"I hadn't seen her for two years. She invited me to come for a visit."

"And how did you get along with her?"

Felicity wiped her eye with her gloved fingers.

"Very well. I adored her."

"Did you ever have cross words?"

Leary moved from behind the body to stand closer to Felicity.

"We didn't argue. There was nothing to argue about."

"You and Hedda Muir came to the police station yesterday and told me that a man had been following you. When did you first notice him?"

"I saw him standing in the back yard. Mrs. Muir went outside to tell him to go, but he had already gone."

"Can you describe this man?"

As she had that morning for Sydney Barlow, she described the man in the bowler hat.

"And you saw him again in the market?" Leary asked.

"Yes. That's when we came to you."

He asked her about that morning, and she described how she'd come out of her room and seen that the parlor was in shambles.

"Do you have any idea what he was looking for?" a man asked.

Felicity shook her head.

"I do not."

The men asked her a few more questions, to clarify her relationship with Hedda Muir, and then Vicar Stephens told her she could sit.

Leary asked Roger to stand and give his testimony, and he told them how he had seen the man near the parlor window.

"He was on his knees peeking in the window, and I shouted at him that I would shoot him in the arse if he didn't move on."

The audience laughed, and Roger thrust out his chin.

When he was done, Roger sat.

The rest of the proceedings were a blur as Felicity wondered what had driven the man, who she was convinced had perpetrated the crime, to murder? Mrs. Muir was a former housekeeper. She had no money, or jewels, or gold. She believed P.C. Leary was right, that she had come inside and he attacked her from behind. She must have seen the disheveled parlor, and then seen him. Had he meant to kill her? Or had he thought to knock her out and escape?

"A verdict has been reached," Leary said. "The panel has concluded that Hedda Muir was murdered."

Having made their decision, the men were discharged from their duties. Some stopped and offered their condolences to Lady Armstrong before meeting their mates at the pub. Vicar Stephens waited until they had gone to take her to his office behind the sanctuary, but he wouldn't let Roger come in, so the old man hobbled to a pew and sat.

CHAPTER 14

The spacious office had a latticed window that distorted the light from the late afternoon sun. It cast shadows on Vicar Stephens as he sat behind his desk. X's covered his clothes and the left side of his face. It was a bit distracting as he was trying to assume an air of somber dignity. Felicity sat across from him and watched as he ran his hand over a document on the desk.

"I met Hedda Muir when she moved to Whitley," he said. "She spoke of you many times."

"She raised me."

"She had a great deal of respect for your father." Felicity remained silent. "Hedda took me into her confidence shortly after she arrived. She was a consistent attendee, and always had a kind word of praise for my sermons. She was a lovely lady." His last words were muffled by a sob. "Oh, dear, do forgive me." Tears now ran down his cheeks. "It's so unfair. Why should she die that way? Hedda never hurt a soul."

Felicity looked away as his clerical façade disintegrated, and he began to sob.

"She always had time for those in need," he said. "She would visit them and leave them feeling better than when she'd arrived." He wiped his eyes with his handkerchief. "Oh, dear, I must get a hold of myself."

He wiped his eyes again, put his handkerchief away, and again ran his hands over the document.

"Please forgive me," he said. "As I said before, Hedda Muir took me into her confidence and asked me to prepare a will. She also chose me as the executor of her estate."

He waited to see if she would ask any questions.

"Hedda was a frugal woman. She told me that she saved nearly every penny she'd earned as a housekeeper and she amassed a tidy sum. She left a small bequest to the church, and the rest of her estate, including her home, has been left to you."

Felicity stared at him in disbelief.

"Are you certain?" she asked.

"Quite certain, Lady Armstrong."

She began to sob, and Vicar Stephens went to her and put his hand on her shoulder.

"She was so dear," Felicity said. "So, very, very dear."

"That she was."

He began to cry again as she wept. When she settled down, he wiped his eyes and returned to his seat.

"Well, then, I shall continue. At this time, the money is in the bank. You will have to let me know where you would like me to send it."

Felicity looked at the document in front of him.

"Is it wrong to ask how much there is?"

"Not at all. You have decisions to make. If you put the money in a trust, you should see at least two hundred pounds a year. While this might seem a small sum, handled wisely, it should be enough to take care of the taxes on the house with some leftover. She told me you had a small allowance from your stepmother, so between the two, you should be able to handle your yearly expenses."

Two hundred pounds a year added to her current allowance meant the difference between abject poverty and a comfortable life. Mrs. Muir had given her more than an inheritance; she had given her freedom.

He looked at her as if for the first time. She was comely, but too old to make a good marriage. Still, if she put her mind to it, she might find a widower seeking a wife to handle the household duties. The unfairness of her situation did not occur to him, as he had been raised to believe that this is what women wanted; a good, steady husband, children, and to be cared for like the precious souls they were.

"I will write you as soon as I've talked to my solicitor," she said.

"Very well." He sighed. "Such a loss. Is there anything else I can do for you, Lady Armstrong?"

"No, and thank you for all you've done."

"Oh, dear, I almost forgot." He slid the document to her. "This is the deed to the house."

She looked at the deed, dated a little over two years before, and saw "Hedda Muir" as owner.

"The taxes have been paid for this year."

"I am overwhelmed," she said.

"It's to be expected." He tapped his fingers on the desk. "I have scheduled the funeral for ten tomorrow. I will prepare a eulogy and if you would like me to say anything, please don't hesitate to let me know."

She mustered a smile as she folded the deed and put it in her purse.

"I know Roger will want to attend with me," she said. "Thank you again for taking care of her."

As they walked into the sanctuary, Roger, and then Vicar Stephens walked them to the door. He watched them walk to the road before his eyes once again filled with tears.

* * *

THAT NIGHT, Felicity tossed and turned. She kept hearing noises, and things that wouldn't have caused alarm yesterday were now harbingers of death. When the clock struck three, she got out of bed and went to put the kettle on.

She lit every lamp in the house and the kitchen before lighting the stove. She focused on her tasks, and she disproved the old adage about a watched pot never boiling. She made her tea, took her cup to the big chair near the hearth, and sat.

As she laid her head back, she sighed. She'd cried so much the day before that her head ached, and her eyes were sore.

Around five, the first hint of a new day's dawning appeared over Roger's house. Black turned to navy blue, and then to light blue, pink, and yellow. Felicity had fallen asleep in the chair and was awakened by a light rapping on her door. She looked over her shoulder at the window, but she couldn't see who was there, and fear gave her pause. What if the man had returned?

Would he have knocked?

"No," she said.

She got up and went to the window. It was Roger, and he nodded when he saw her face.

"'Morning, milady."

"Hello, Roger."

She ran her hand over her hair and retied the sash on her dressing gown before opening the door.

"I've brought you some biscuits," he said with a slight smile.

He held out a tin of Huntley & Palmer's biscuits.

"Thank you. That's very sweet of you. Would you like some tea?"

"Oh, I don't want to be a bother."

"It's no bother at all, Roger."

She led him to the kitchen.

"Do you mind sitting in here?" he asked.

She held the handle on the teakettle.

"Perhaps we should sit in the parlor."

He put his hands on the back of the chair and leaned on them.

"These biscuits will do nicely with our tea," she said.

"Aye. They were Hedda's favorites."

"Did you spend a lot of time together?"

"She would come across the street in the afternoons and we would share biscuits. She'd make hers, but I would buy mine."

"Then I imagine you will miss her."

He looked at the table, and wiped his cheek.

"Aye."

After the kettle boiled, she put the cups, saucers, and tin of biscuits on a tray. Roger took it from her hands and followed her to the parlor. She sat on the settee and he put the tray on the low table in front of it, and then he sat in the blue chair.

It was odd sitting there without Mrs. Muir, and waiting for her to come around the corner. She opened the biscuit tin and offered them to him.

"You said that this room was a shambles. Did you set it right?"

"The ladies from church came and straightened it yesterday."

"They're good, them ladies. They bring me supper once a week." He kept looking toward the parlor. "What was he after?"

"I can't think of a thing." She looked him in the eye. "And why was he watching this house? It just doesn't make sense."

"Hedda didn't have a thing more 'n me."

"That's precisely why it's so strange."

"I told her to put up curtains on that window," he said. "The whole world could look right inside at her."

Felicity looked around the parlor.

"You said he was kneeling under the window."

"Indeed he was."

A shiver went up her spine.

"That is odd."

"Aye, and it was dark, but you had the lamp lit. Now, I've been standing out there smoking me pipe every night since she moved in, unless it's too cold, and I knew something was off. Then I saw something move, and I saw his outline in the window, so I figured he was peeking inside. That's when I shouted at him. These old eyes are still sharp. I knew something was off."

Roger kept talking, but Felicity's mind was elsewhere. There could be no doubt that the man had been watching them, but why? It was obvious to all that Mrs. Muir had nothing more than any other resident on the street, and she was elderly.

Perhaps he had seen her get off the train. Women traveling alone were often assaulted, hence the need for a "Ladies Only" train car, but there were other women in the car who looked more prosperous than she. It baffled Felicity, and not knowing what he had on his mind was making her angry.

"Why didn't he break in while we were at the market?" she asked. "He would have been gone before we returned."

"Was that when Constable Leary walked you home?"

"Yes, that was the day."

"That was the night I saw him."

She tried to remember what they'd been doing, and recalled the conversation they'd had in the kitchen while making the custard pie. They had talked about her mother's jewelry and her feelings for Captain Fowler. Perhaps he heard them talking about the jewelry and thought she still had a necklace or two.

It still made no sense. He had followed them about, had lingered at the cottage, and had been seen twice. If he was a thief, he wasn't a good one, but if he wasn't a thief...

"I can't understand any of this," she said.

"Then it's best to just let it be for a while. I find that if I stop thinking on something, it sorts itself out."

She smiled. She could see how Roger and Mrs. Muir had become friends.

"You said you've known Mrs. Muir since she moved in," Felicity said.

"Aye. Hedda bought this cottage from me. It belonged to me brother, but he passed."

"It must have been nice living so close to your brother."

"Well, not so nice as you'd think," he said. "He could be hard, my brother." Roger sipped his tea. "He didn't like sharing. He tried to keep the money me da left us all for himself, but me da saw to it I got my share."

"He made a will."

"Naw, no will, just buried a pot in the back yard and left me a note."

Felicity smiled broadly.

"I would imagine your brother didn't like that."

"He carried on like a drunken sailor! Cursing and shouting, why I never laughed so hard in me life."

"And you still lived across the street from each other?" she said.

"Aye. We made our peace, but for a while, I thought he was gonna kill me." His smile faded. "Sorry, miss." He sat back and laid his hands on the tabletop palms down. "Oh, he thought about it, I know he did. He even sent someone round to do me in, but one of me mates warned me and I took off for a few days. He was a right bastard, he was." He looked at her. "Sorry, miss."

She thought about something he said and she looked him in the eye.

"He sent someone round to kill you?"

"Aye. Some bloke he met at the pub. Just a drunken sod, but he had a pistol, and my brother offered him five quid to do me in."

She felt her chest tighten. If Dudley knew she was his father's bastard child and his half-sister, would he think she would try to claim an inheritance? Was he, like Roger's brother, so unwilling to share the money with her that he would rather see her dead?

She trembled as she thought about their conversation during his visit. He told her his father had died, and that he had heard about her situation and wanted to offer her some company. Even then it had seemed a feeble excuse, but she had no reason to think he had anything else on his mind. She tried to remember what he'd said, but she had been so fixated on his breach of etiquette that she might have missed something truly important.

"I can't believe your own brother plotted to kill you."

"Money will make a man do strange things. I've seen gamblers begging for their lives over debts owed, but a week later, they're at the tables, holding cards, and putting their X on a promise to pay."

"But murder seems such an extreme response to anything, let alone debt."

"But you have to understand the nature of mankind, milady. We're all craven beasts when you get right down to it."

"I don't see us as craven beasts, Roger. We all have the ability to restrain ourselves."

"Aye, and most of us abide by the law, but I tell you this, milady, when pushed to the limit, a man *will* kill to survive."

She shuddered, and Roger saw her tremble.

"What's wrong, miss?"

"What if the man in the bowler hat was here to kill me?"

"Caw," he said waving his hand. "Who'd have a reason to kill you?"

"Someone who might believe he has a very good reason."

"If that man wanted you dead, he would have done it that night. He'd have climbed into your bedroom window and slashed your throat."

She cringed as her hand went to her throat, and Roger blushed again.

"Sorry, milady."

"No, you're right. He ran off because you saw him, but he could have come back."

They sat in silence as they thought about the man's intentions, and Felicity closed her eyes and shook her head.

"Oh, God," she said. "If he was looking for me… Oh God, if I hadn't come here, she'd still be alive."

"You can't blame yourself, milady."

"But if he was sent here to kill me…"

He clasped his hands on the table and leaned toward her.

"You can't go blaming yourself for that. It was him what killed her, not you."

"But he wouldn't have been here if I'd stayed at home."

"And what? Got yourself killed?"

He reached for her hand.

"She was so happy you were coming to see her that she couldn't stop talking about it. I knew Hedda. She loved you. She wanted to see you more than anything." He looked into her eyes. "You made her last hours the happiest she'd ever had."

She thought back on the day she arrived and how happy Mrs. Muir looked.

"Oh, God, Millie."

"Who's Millie?" he asked.

"She's my friend, and my helper. She lives in my house, and she's there all alone." She got up. "You have to go, Roger. I have to go to the police station."

"Why don't you let me go? Tell me what to say, and then I'll fetch you when it's time for the funeral."

"That makes sense," she said. "Tell them to send a cable to Tolwich telling Constable O'Toole that Millie might be in danger. They have to send someone to the cottage right away."

CHAPTER 15

A sudden storm brought rain, and the dirt road was slippery. She held her umbrella close, but a gust of wind blew underneath and turned it inside out. She struggled to set it right as rain soaked her gown, and it seemed as if the weather had plotted against her, too.

It was still raining as they lowered Mrs. Muir's casket into the grave. Felicity and Roger stood side-by-side, each holding an umbrella over their heads, as they listened to Vicar Stephens' eulogy. The dirt beside the open grave was nothing but mud, and the gravedigger was none too pleased. He kept glaring at the vicar, who seemed unaware of the man's irritation, and the clergyman went on for several minutes.

When Vicar Stephens finished his eulogy, Felicity had wanted to spend a moment alone by the grave, but she was soaked through, and had to change before boarding the train home. She and Roger walked back to the cottage together. He waited as she hesitated at the door listened for the sound of someone lying in wait, but all she heard was the ticking of the clock. He bade her farewell before leaving, and she kissed him on the cheek.

Felicity stripped off her wet clothes, put on her everyday

blouse and skirt, and looked at her reflection in the mirror. She had been concerned about the age of her traveling gown before she came to Whitley; now, she didn't give a fig what anyone thought. She was too overwhelmed with grief.

She sat on the bed and wept. Her emotions were so jumbled that she didn't want to go, but with the prospect of a madman returning to finish what he started looming over her, she had no choice but to rally herself and go. She then thought of Mrs. Muir's bedroom armoire. She must have a traveling gown. Would it be wrong to wear it home?

She went to the armoire and looked at the gowns. A navy blue pinstripe was similar to her brown traveling gown, so Felicity took it out and tried it on. It fit, but was an inch shorter. Even so, it would do, and she hung her brown gown on the doorframe where it would stay if, and until, she returned.

The rain had stopped and as she walked to the station, she kept an eye out for the stranger. As she waited for the train, Felicity noticed the poster with his drawing affixed to one of the ticket windows.

Soon after it rumbled into the station, Felicity boarded the train and found another window seat in the "Ladies Only" car. This time, her fellow passengers were young women, traveling either alone or with a chaperone. She tried not to stare at the women who, like her, had no one to converse with, but she spent several minutes eyeing one sitting two seats in front of her on the opposite side.

The woman's face wasn't visible, but her clothes, like Felicity's, were worn, and her hair was pulled back and pinned up under a ghastly hat. Her tan, green, and black plaid woolen suit was dull and too hot for spring, and the woman used her hand-kerchief as she tried in vain to keep perspiration from running down her face.

She wore no gloves, had no fan or any luggage that Felicity

could see, and when she turned her head to look out the window on the other side of the car, Felicity saw the side of her face.

Her cheek was pale and her eyelids were puffy. Strands of hair that had escaped the pins were a mix of brown and gray, and her lips were pressed together so tightly that it looked as though they had disappeared. Felicity looked away.

Numbness as seductive as a siren's song at sea sat beside her, and as the motion of the train relaxed her she found it hard to resist its call. She thought of poor Mrs. Muir, who had always tried to coax her out of her moods, and she straightened her back. She would not succumb to its call this time.

The image of Captain Fowler appeared in her mind, and her words as she clung to him.

"Take me with you."

Why hadn't she gone with him, shared his bed, raised his children on some Caribbean island?

The idea shocked her, even as a part of her wished she had been brave enough to walk away from her life in England. Her cheeks grew hot and she looked around to see if anyone was watching her, as if her thoughts had been written above her head. She tried to cast away the image of them holding each other under a rough woolen blanket, but it wouldn't go, and soon she was patting her forehead with her handkerchief.

As the train pulled into the station in London, Felicity noticed that the woman she'd been staring at was standing. Her back was bent forward as if she'd spent years carrying a heavy burden. When the train came to a halt, the woman lurched forward, and then backward, but she didn't falter.

There's a lesson in that.

Felicity stood, grabbed her valise and umbrella, and left the train. The first thing she saw was the poster of the man in the bowler hat affixed to a column.

The solicitors, Messers Beecham and Carstairs, were located

several blocks away, and if she were to return to the train on time, she'd have to walk faster.

* * *

THE OFFICE WAS in a building on a sedate street lined with trees and elegant townhouses. Felicity remembered the first time she'd come there and recognized the building right away. She climbed the stairs of the red brick building and entered the foyer, which smelled of pipe tobacco and leather. It reminded her of the library at Rosendale.

Two large windows brightened the reception area, but the sunny atmosphere was dampened by the look she got from a young man sitting behind the desk. He hadn't been there two years ago, and he pursed his lips and tipped his head back as he looked at her. He didn't mask his disdain for her clothes, or the fact that she had arrived unaccompanied by a man.

"Good afternoon," she said. She paused as she waited for him to offer her a greeting, but he remained silent. She was going to tell him she was Miss Armstrong, but she didn't like his attitude. "I am Lady Felicity Armstrong and I'd like to speak to Mr. Beecham."

He sniffed loudly as he studied her face. She wore no makeup and her hat was outlandish.

Another noble on the skids, he thought, and derision laced with glee filled his head with wicked asides, which his position at Beecham and Carstairs forbade him to utter. He made a show of looking at his appointment ledger and then he looked up at her.

"You don't have an appointment," he said.

"I'm in London for the day. Mr. Beecham prepared an agreement between Captain Henry Fowler and me, and promised to keep me abreast of Captain Fowler's progress, though I haven't received a letter since December of last year." She tilted her head back and straightened her spine. "Since I haven't heard from Mr.

Beecham in several months, I would like to speak to him personally."

The man's devilish smile irritated her, but he sat up straight and wrote something on a piece of paper.

"Mr. Beecham is on holiday," he said. "I can make you an appointment." He looked up. "He will return in three months."

His attitude infuriated her. Her lip quivered as her anger grew, and she looked right into his eyes when she spoke.

"Is there someone else I can speak to?"

"I'll see if Mr. Benjamin will speak with you."

She watched him walk down a short corridor and enter an office. Felicity placed her valise and umbrella on the floor, sat in a large leather chair, and folded her gloved hands on her lap. It was the same chair Captain Fowler had occupied when they were there together, and sitting in it made her nostalgic.

Soon, she saw the young man come out of the office and stop at the entrance to the hallway.

"Mr. Benjamin has agreed to see you."

She got out of her seat, grabbed her things, and followed him to the office. At the door, she tried to look past him, but he filled the doorframe, so all she could see was the edge of a desk.

"*Lady* Armstrong," he said, his mocking tone raising her heckles, and she grasped her umbrella tightly lest she bash him over the head. He left before she could raise it in the air, and now she was looking at Mr. Benjamin.

"Lady Armstrong," he said. "I'm Noah Benjamin."

He was young, small, and resembled a mouse with dark brown hair and eyes. He was shorter than Felicity, but came around and held the chair in front of his desk for her as she sat. He even took her valise and umbrella and placed them on the floor near the door before sitting in his own chair.

"I understand you are here to inquire after Captain Henry Fowler."

"Yes. The captain and I signed an agreement executed by Mr.

Beecham. Captain Fowler was to report to Mr. Beecham, who, in turn, would send me a letter with the details of that report. The last letter came to me several months ago."

"This is the captain's file," Mr. Benjamin said. "Mr. Beecham gave it to me to handle when I joined the firm."

He opened it and saw the last letter on top of several documents. The letter was dated seven months ago. He passed it to Felicity, who nodded.

"That's the last letter I received," she said.

"It appears that we have been keeping you informed as per our agreement."

"And you've heard nothing from the captain since his last report?"

"I assure you, Lady Armstrong, if we had received a report, we would have sent you a letter."

She bit her lower lip and stared at her hands. Mr. Benjamin looked of her clothes and hair. It was obvious the lady had fallen on hard times, and he felt as if he was watching her hope vanish before his eyes. He had a compassionate heart and hoped she would not cry, and smiled as he tried to think of something he could do to brighten her spirits.

"Perhaps I can send an inquiry to the address on his last report," he said. Her face brightened. "However, I cannot guarantee we will receive a response."

"I understand, and I am grateful for your assistance."

Her eyes pleaded with him to stay true to his word, so Mr. Benjamin wrote a note for the file. He had a sensitive nose and found that when a noblewoman entered the building, her perfume would leave an irritating trail as she walked down the corridor. Lady Armstrong wasn't wearing perfume, yet another indication of her dire straits.

Mr. Benjamin recalled the newspaper stories about the murder of Lady Felicia Armstrong and had followed the trial of Fernando Dominguez with great interest. While Mr. Benjamin was not a nobleman, and not welcomed into gentlemen's clubs due to his Hebrew heritage, he had some connections that kept him abreast of the latest news regarding the upper classes.

At the time of her murder, Felicia Armstrong's life had been scrutinized ad nauseam and was the subject of unending gossip. He knew that the Armstrong family fortune had been decimated, and that Felicia's stepdaughter had been left a pittance.

"I remember when your stepmother died," he said. "And I know that Handy and Conner are representing you. Have they treated you well?"

The lines around her mouth tightened. She looked at Mr. Benjamin's eyes. He wasn't like Handy and Conner, nor was he like Mr. Beecham. He was kind, and his demeanor put her at ease and allowed her to tell the truth.

"No," she said. "I'm quite disappointed in them."

"I've heard they are not always attentive to the needs of their clients." He looked into her eyes. "Perhaps you would consider changing your representation?"

"Is that possible?" she asked.

"It is, and what's more, I would handle your trust without a fee, if you agree to let me invest it for you."

Her eyes narrowed. "Why?"

"Because I believe they are taking advantage of you," he said. "And I can make you more money."

He stood and went to the door, opened it, and then shut it before returning to his seat. He leaned forward and spoke in a low tone.

"I graduated from university two years ago. Shortly after, I was hired to handle the small cases brought to the firm by less fortunate clients who wouldn't balk at being represented by a Hebrew."

He waited for a reaction, but her gaze remained steady.

"I want to do something much bigger." His eyes glowed with excitement. "I have a talent for investment, but Beecham and

Carstairs have no intention of letting me work for their clients." He looked at the door and leaned toward her again. "I don't mind telling you, Lady Armstrong, writing contracts is as dull as dishwater, especially for the middle-class. Sometimes I feel as if I shall die at this desk and no one will find me for weeks."

She liked him. His dilemma was similar to hers. He had little control over his circumstances, but unlike her, he seemed to know how to make his dreams come true.

"Lady Armstrong, if you let me manage your money, I will double it inside of a year." He opened a desk drawer and withdrew a small, locked box. He took a twenty-pound note from it and held it up. "Further, to win your trust, I will take this twenty-pound note and invest it in your name. All proceeds over twenty pounds will go into your account. If I fail, you can return to Handy and Conner with your income intact."

She looked at the money and blushed as the urge to grab it and run overtook her. Her eyes widened and she swallowed hard.

"You believe you can double it in a year?" she said.

"Or even triple it. I've done it before."

She looked at his earnest expression, but doubt left her wondering why he would do this for her. He said it was to win her trust, and he was willing to use his own money. So far, she hadn't fared well when it came to investing money, but she liked Mr. Benjamin.

"If I transfer my funds to this office, can you promise I won't lose any of my income?"

"I'll handle it myself."

She thought of the agreement she'd signed with Captain Fowler. She needed something in writing as insurance in the event he should he fail.

"I want a written agreement," she said.

He smiled. "And you shall have one."

He withdrew a sheet of paper from the drawer and wrote down the details of their agreement. When he was done, she read it, and Mr. Benjamin went to fetch the secretary. The young man still looked at Felicity with contempt, but he witnessed their signatures without saying a word.

"I shall contact Handy and Conner to arrange the transfer of funds," Mr. Benjamin said after the secretary left. "And I will send you the details straightaway. "

She smiled broadly as she thought of her former solicitors. She wished she could see their faces when they learned that she had taken her money out of their hands, and then she wondered if they would contest her actions, as she had no male guardian.

"Will they honor this request if it comes from me alone?" she asked.

"Yes, milady. You are an unmarried woman. You have the right to do whatever you choose with your money."

She smiled again. She hadn't realized there was any benefit to being unmarried.

"I have just received a bequest from a dear friend. I will have the executor send that to you as well."

Mr. Benjamin beamed as he folded the contract, put it in an envelope, and handed it to her.

"Once I receive the funds, I will send you a letter," he said. "And I'll look into the Captain Fowler business as promised."

He went around the desk and picked up the valise and umbrella, and then led her down the corridor to the foyer.

"I will be in touch," he said as he handed the items to her. "I hope you have a safe trip home."

"Thank you, Mr. Benjamin. I look forward to hearing from you."

She arrived at the rail station with minutes to spare, and as she settled into her seat, she felt hopeful. She would write to Vicar Stephens to let him know that Mr. Benjamin would be handling her inheritance. The idea that the small solicitor could double her money was folly, but still, his enthusiasm was real, and she believed in his sincerity.

For now, the idea that she had twice the money she'd had before took some of the sting out of losing her investment money to Captain Fowler. She reminded herself not to judge him yet, but to wait until Mr. Benjamin found out what had happened. Until then, she would give Henry the benefit of the doubt and keep her eye on the horizon.

CHAPTER 16

The motion of the train soothed Felicity, and she woke to find a conductor tapping her shoulder.

"We're in Tolwich, miss," he said.

When she got off the train, Felicity cast a furtive glance to her left and right for the man in the bowler hat. She saw his poster on the ticket booth window and cringed at the sight of his face.

Her heart beat faster as she walked out of the station wondering if the man might be lurking nearby. She was eager to get home to Millie, but first, she stopped by the police station to ask if they'd sent a man to check on her.

A young man in a blue policeman's uniform smiled when she came in. Felicity guessed his age to be around eighteen, and he got off his stool to greet her.

"Aye, miss, how can I help you?"

"Did you receive a cable from the police in Whitley?" she asked.

"Yes, miss, it come this morning."

"Is Constable O'Toole here?" she asked.

"No, miss, he's off on patrol."

"Do you know if he went to Bee's Nest Cottage recently?"

The young man straightened.

"I went there, miss." He smiled broadly. "I'm Police Constable Edward Jones. I went to the cottage this morning and a young lady was working in the garden."

"How long did you stay?" she asked.

"I patrolled the area, and then left as I was instructed."

"And did another man take your place?"

"I don't think so, miss." He blushed when he saw the look on her face. She was not pleased. "But a man patrols the rail station whenever a train arrives."

Now she frowned. She hadn't seen an officer when she arrived.

"I didn't see anyone patrolling the rail station when I arrived."

"But Constable O'Toole just left to meet the train that arrived ten minutes ago."

"I just departed that train, and I can assure you he was not there."

Jones blushed. Had O'Toole checked the train, or had he gone to the pub?

"You might have missed him."

She pursed her lips and her cheeks reddened.

"Well, then, you tell Constable O'Toole…you tell him that I'm very disappointed, and that until they capture the man who murdered my dear friend, I will expect an officer to stay at the cottage night and day!"

"I will, miss. I promise I will tell him as soon as he returns."

She left the police station and walked past the pub. She almost went inside to look for O'Toole, but thoughts of Millie drove her past it and to the edge of town. She was tired from a lack of sleep, and fear kept her shoulders tight, so she tried not to think of the distance she still had to walk.

The meadow took on a surreal aspect as dusk cast a gloomy

pall over the two miles left between her and the bluff. A recent storm had turned the dirt to mud, and her shoes were no match for the mud that lay between the old Roman stones. By the time the cottage came into view, her shoes were caked in mud, she was exhausted, and the growing darkness had increased her anxiety.

She arrived at the bottom of the hill as the stars began to appear. She looked at the sky and almost cried, for the thought of climbing to the cottage was worse than the act itself. She gripped her valise and started up the hill, all the time thinking that she had to get home, that Millie was waiting for her.

When she reached the summit, she looked at the light in the window and smiled. It was good to have someone waiting for you, someone who cared. She went to the door and was pleased to find it locked.

"Millie!" she cried. "I'm home."

Felicity heard Millie's footsteps pounding as she ran to the door. She threw open the door and embraced Felicity.

"You're home, milady." Millie pulled away and looked at Felicity. A brilliant smile illuminated her face. "Oh, how I've missed you."

Felicity dropped her things and held Millie tightly.

"I've missed you, too."

"I've made supper. I knew you were coming. I just knew it." She took Felicity's hand and pulled her inside, and then retrieved the valise and umbrella before closing the door. "Eddie... Constable Jones, came 'round this morning and told me what happened to your friend. I'm so sorry, milady."

"How long did he stay?" Felicity asked.

"He was here for a while. He stood near the edge of the yard while I was tending the garden."

"There should be someone posted at the door now. I'm very disappointed in Constable O'Toole." Felicity took Millie's hand in hers. "Until we know he's been captured, we must keep the door bolted, and the windows locked. The man broke into Mrs. Muir's house, so we must be diligent."

"Yes, milady."

Felicity took the girl into her arms and held her. Millie felt her fear, and Felicity felt something in Millie's pocket.

"What's that?" she asked as she touched Millie's pocket.

"It's a knife. I put it in there after Constable Jones left this morning."

Felicity pulled off her gloves and took off her hat.

"Please be careful, Millie." She put the gloves into her hat. "He's stronger than you. He might take that knife and use it against you."

"I'll be careful." She bit her lower lip. "Are you hungry? I can put supper on the table."

"Yes, please do. I haven't eaten since this morning."

Felicity took her valise to the bedroom and removed her jacket before taking the pins out of her hair. It fell to its full length at her waist. As she began to brush it, she felt a pain in her arm. It had come from carrying her valise for so long. She looked at her reflection in the mirror and thought, *Why do I need such long hair?*

Women who lived in manor houses had maids to brush their hair, but for poor women, it was a burden, and Felicity felt she had burdens enough. She didn't see it as her "crowning glory," and didn't give a fig if men preferred it, for until she heard otherwise, the only man she wanted was nowhere in sight. Her hair was a nuisance, one that could be banished with a pair of scissors and an extra set of hands.

Felicity went into the kitchen and sat in her chair. Millie had put the food on the table and after they said grace, they ate with gusto. When they finished clearing the table and doing the dishes, Felicity got the shears from the drawer in the breakfront and handed them to Millie.

"I want you to cut my hair."

Millie looked vexed.

"What, milady?"

"I want you to cut my hair."

Millie's eyes widened.

"But your hair is your crowning glory, milady."

"So I've heard, but frankly, it's more of a bother than anything else. I'm tired of tending it all the time."

Millie thought Felicity's hair was the most beautiful thing she'd ever seen, and felt so uneasy about cutting it that the thought of feigning illness crossed her mind, but Felicity had been so good to her that if she wanted her hair cut, it was the least Millie could do for her.

"Yes, milady."

Millie took the shears from her hand. Felicity sat in her chair, and Millie laid Felicity's hair on the outside of the chair rungs.

"Just cut it straight across," Felicity said. "Near the center of my back."

Millie felt like crying.

"Are you sure, milady?"

"Completely sure."

Millie put the blades near the center of Felicity's back and opened them. She slid them under the hair, and cut off a large strand. As it fell to the floor, she looked at it and sighed.

She cut another large strand off, and then another, until she reached the other side. She stepped back and looked at the pile of hair on the floor.

"It's done, milady."

Felicity ran her hand through her hair and pulled it over her shoulder. The bottom brushed the edge of her breast, but she was still able to gather it into a ponytail.

"Thank you, Millie."

Millie went to the pantry to get the broom, and Felicity went to the bedroom mirror. She felt as if a weight had been lifted off her shoulders, and when she saw her reflection now, she was glad she had cut it off. She could still pin it up when she left the house, so as far as she was concerned, it was a good choice.

She heard Millie putting the dishes away and lit the lamp on the end table next to the settee. She looked at the window and thought of the man in the bowler hat, and then turned off the light.

CHAPTER 17

The next morning, Felicity glanced out the kitchen window. The gray sky threatened rain, which would water their vegetables and nourish the wildflowers in the meadow. This time, though, the wind was picking up and whistling through the cracks in the window. She went to the parlor window and looked for a constable, but saw none. Her irritation with Constable O'Toole grew, but if she wanted to chastise him, she'd have to walk to town.

Millie was finishing up the breakfast dishes as Felicity contemplated what to do if the man broke into the house, and decided it was time to carry her father's small, Remington pistol in her pocket.

"I'm going outside to close the shutters," she said.

"Yes, milady."

She went to the front door and as she stepped outside, she saw the figure of a man standing far off in the distance across the meadow. She trembled, and closed the shutters on all the windows before going back inside. She went to her bedroom and retrieved her father's pistol.

Once it was in her pocket, she went back outside and walked

to the edge of the yard. The figure was receding now as it headed toward town. Thunder cracked overhead and her skirt billowed in the wind, then rain pelted her as she ran back to the cottage. Millie was at the door.

"I saw him earlier," Millie said. Felicity's eyes exposed her fear. "I walked to Mr. Brewer's for some eggs and he was in the meadow."

"You aren't to go anywhere alone!" Felicity cried.

"I'm sorry, milady. I just wanted to make you a good breakfast."

The sad look on Millie's face turned Felicity's anger away. She put her arm around Millie's shoulder, and the girl thrust out her chin.

"I'm not afraid, milady. I know how to fight."

Felicity smiled. "Then you must teach me so that if anyone dares try and hurt us, we can work together to bring them to their knees."

Millie smiled broadly as she imagined them pummeling the stranger.

Rain hit the tin roof hard, and the sound of thunder was deafening, as it roared overhead. The ladies sat on the settee and held each other until the storm passed.

* * *

WHEN THE THUNDER STOPPED, they spent the rest of the afternoon cleaning the cottage. Millie dusted, and Felicity swept and mopped the floors. Millie took the quilts off the beds and replaced them with summer blankets, and when they had finished, they opened the shutters and windows to let in some fresh air, but as yet, no one from the police station had come to keep an eye on them.

The last two years had wrought changes in her, but the events of the past week had matured Felicity, and instead of suppressing anger, she was learning how to express it. When she saw that they were still alone, she gathered her hair into a snood, and told Millie they were going to town.

The clouds had gone and the sun was high in the sky. Its warmth, combined with the wind off the sea, had dried the earth. Felicity had been waiting for the right time to talk to Millie about moving to another house, and as they walked, she started by telling Millie about her visit to Whitley.

"I'm very fond of Tolwich," Felicity said. "It's a lovely town, but now that I've visited Whitley, I'm not sure which town I like better"

"Tell me what it's like," Millie said.

Felicity described the town in detail, and told her about Roger and Vicar Stephens, too. She also talked about Mrs. Muir's house.

"The house is nicer than ours," Felicity said, "but I don't think I could stand living there."

"I don't think I could live there either, not after your friend died there."

Felicity shuddered as she thought of Mrs. Muir lying on the kitchen floor.

"But it would be nice to live in a house like that, don't you agree?" Felicity said. "The town is larger. Perhaps it's best if we sell both houses and buy a new one."

Millie looked at the ground as she walked and didn't say a word.

"Would you want to go with me?" Felicity asked.

Millie looked at Felicity and smiled broadly.

"Oh, yes, milady."

As they entered town, Felicity kept her eye peeled for the man in the bowler hat.

"We're stopping at the police station," she said. "I'm going to give Constable O'Toole a piece of my mind."

Millie had never seen her so angry, and hoped Felicity wouldn't get arrested for yelling at the constable. When they reached the police station, they went inside and saw P.C. Edward Jones sitting behind the counter. When he saw Felicity's face, he got down off his stool and straightened his back.

"Where is Constable O'Toole?" she said.

"He's patrolling the rail station, miss."

"Milady," Millie said. "You call Lady Armstrong milady."

P.C. Jones swallowed hard.

"Milady."

"So, he's patrolling the rail station. I see. And who was sent to watch us last evening?"

P.C. Jones blushed a deep red. He couldn't tell her that O'Toole had come back to the station with rosy cheeks and beer on his breath. Jones would have gone to watch the cottage himself, but was sent out to patrol the town when O'Toole decided to go home early and left P.C. Larson in charge. Larson didn't like Jones because their family had been feuding for years, and he disregarded the younger man's protests concerning Lady Armstrong's protection.

"I'm sorry, milady."

She looked around the station and saw the wanted poster on the wall.

"Sorry won't keep that man," she pointed to it, "away from us. What if he kills us in our sleep?"

"Oh, that would be terrible."

"Of course it would be terrible."

Her voice was loud enough to be heard in the street, and passersby looked into the door. Jones was flummoxed. He couldn't leave the station unattended, but he had to find O'Toole before Lady Armstrong did. He got up, took a set of keys off the hook under the counter, and came to them.

"I will escort you home if you'd like, Lady Armstrong."

"We're going to the market. I will stop by before we go home. I suggest you find Constable O'Toole."

Jones followed them out the door and locked it as the ladies walked away.

The village was quiet and the market, which was usually bustling with patrons, was peaceful. The merchants wore dour expressions, so Felicity asked old Mrs. Perkins, the fishmonger's wife, what had happened to cast such a pall over the square.

"Prince Leopold has passed away."

His Royal Highness, Prince Leopold, the Duke of Albany, had been Victoria and Albert's eighth child. He was intelligent, thoughtful, and accomplished in a variety of subjects, but he was also afflicted with the bleeding disease. Despite his illness, he had attended university, served in the military, and fathered two children, one of which had yet to be born.

"That is sad news," she said.

"Aye."

"I feel sorry for the queen," Millie said.

"It must be devastating to lose your child," Felicity said.

Prompted by her own words, Felicity asked if Millie wanted to say hello to her mother before leaving town, but Millie just shook her head.

"She doesn't want to see me."

"Why do you think she doesn't want to see you?" Felicity had never understood the relationship between Millie and her mother. They lived in the same town, yet they hardly spoke if they saw each other in town.

"She doesn't care about me," Millie said as she looked over Felicity's shoulder. "I see Constable O'Toole."

Felicity turned and saw him coming toward them. His rosy cheeks could be attributed to his fast pace, but Felicity suspected he'd already been to the pub.

"You've returned, milady," he said. "I was sorry to hear about your friend." He looked at Millie and smiled. "I've been keeping an eye on Miss Millie here, but I'm sorry to say, we haven't heard anything regarding that fella."

"So, you've been to the cottage?" Felicity said. Millie looked at her, but remained silent. "Strange I didn't see you yesterday when I arrived home."

O'Toole rubbed his chin.

"Aye, well, P.C. Jones was supposed to keep watch last night. I've given him a piece of my mind, I have, and I guarantee he will be there tonight."

"I met P.C. Jones yesterday when I came into the police station. He said you were patrolling the rail station, but I didn't see you there when I got off my train."

He looked like a fox caught in the henhouse.

"So you've met P.C. Jones."

"Yes, I've met him, and he told me how vigilant you've been in your duties."

The look on her face cowed the big man, and he took a deep breath.

"Aye, well, why don't I have him walk you ladies home? He can even spend the night with you."

"Very well, and you will patrol the rail station? I've seen this man. He's a nasty character. He killed Mrs. Muir. You don't want him to kill again, do you, Constable O'Toole?"

"No, milady. I'll post a man there. He'll stay and keep an eye on every train."

"I also must tell you that Millie and I saw a strange man today," Felicity said.

He narrowed his eyes.

"Millie saw him on her way to Mr. Brewer's farm, and I saw him standing in the meadow."

"Well, then, let's fetch P.C. Jones so you can be on your way."

While she appreciated that Jones had been trained as an officer, she still worried that he was too young and inexperienced to protect them from a man who had killed someone. Still, he would be with them, and that would be three against one. She and Millie followed O'Toole to the police station and found P.C. Jones on his stool behind the counter.

"Jones!" he cried. The lad jumped. "Go fetch the carriage and take the ladies home. You'll be staying the night out there."

Jones slid off the stool and grabbed his hat from under the counter. He nodded to the ladies before going through a door at the back of the room.

"He'll meet you out front," O'Toole said. He looked at Felicity. "I'm sorry, Lady Armstrong. I'll see to it that you and Miss Millie are protected from now on."

She glared at him, but chose not to say anything. She needed their protection.

She and Millie waited in front of the station and Millie giggled when she was in the "carriage." It was a wagon the police used to transport prisoners. It opened at the back, and had barred windows.

"People will think we've been arrested," Millie said.

"Is this the best you have?" Felicity asked Jones.

"Aye, milady."

He got off the wagon and opened the back door so the ladies could climb in. Once they were seated, he secured the door and hopped back into his seat.

The ride was bumpy as they hit each rut in the road, and while Felicity fumed, Millie thought it was the most fun she'd ever had. They held onto the seats as the wagon rode over the Roman stones and were relieved when it finally came to a halt at the bottom of the hill.

"Please wait here," Jones said.

He took the horse off the wagon and led it up the hill with the ladies following close behind. When they reached the cottage, Jones tied the horse to a tree at the side of the house, and then went inside to inspect the cottage.

"You can come in now," he said.

Felicity and Millie carried their baskets to the kitchen and put away the things they'd bought, and then Millie began to prepare their supper.

"You are welcome to eat supper with us," Felicity told Jones.

"On, no, milady. I'm on duty. I've brought a sandwich." He held up a lunch tin and she nodded. "Well, then, I'll be outside if you need me."

Since the wind had died down, Felicity opened the shutters before going inside. She also wanted to see him and know that he was still there.

The ladies ate their supper of boiled potatoes and fish, and Felicity told Millie that she had learned how to make a custard pie.

"We'll have to try it sometime," Felicity said. "We must also buy a tin of biscuits."

"I like biscuits." Millie looked at the fish. "And I wouldn't mind if we had chicken now and then."

"Mrs. Muir had chickens. She had fresh eggs every day. Her neighbor promised to care for them."

"We could get a chicken from Mr. Brewer, but we have to make a place for it to stay."

"I'm sure we can find a coop in a catalogue. Perhaps Mr. Brewer could build it for us if we make him a custard pie."

After they'd cleaned their supper dishes, Millie went to the bedroom to take a book from Felicity's bookshelf, while Felicity took her mother's letters from her purse. Millie sat in the chair and Felicity on the settee, just as she had at Mrs. Muir's house. She read those letters she hadn't read, but her mind kept returning to what Roger said about his brother.

"Money will make a man do strange things."

His brother had wanted him dead, and all because their father left Roger some money his brother wanted. She didn't want to believe him, for if she did, she'd have to also believe that Dudley, a titled, educated man, would hire someone to end her life rather than share his inheritance. She was shocked that he would think so little of her that he would believe she'd risk her reputation, and his, for a bit of cash.

But try as she might, she couldn't think of another reason why the man in the bowler hat would be after her. She got up and went to the window. It was too dark to see him, but she heard Jones talking softly to himself. She worried that he might be taken by surprise and hurt by the man, so she opened the door and asked him to come inside.

"Sleep in the chair," she said. "And leave the lamp on so he can see you if he comes."

Jones felt odd staying in the chair, but he also felt less afraid.

"Thank you, milady."

She and Millie left him alone, each going to her own bed, and each slipping her weapon under her pillow.

CHAPTER 18

hen Felicity walked outside the following day, she went to the back yard and reveled in the glorious scenery. Wildflowers dotted the meadow, and in the garden, birds were feathering their nests. Nature was unaware of the turmoil in her heart. She took a few deep breaths, and then went back inside.

Any noise, any creak heard in the night had awoken Felicity, and she would grab the pistol lying under her pillow. Her stomach was in knots. She found Millie at the stove lighting the fire. Her drawn face indicated that she, too, had had a restless night.

Her stomach was in knots when Felicity found Millie at the stove lighting the fire. Her drawn face indicated that she, too, had had a restless night.

"I didn't sleep well, milady."

"I had a restless night, too. Did you hear Constable Jones leave this morning?"

"He came to the kitchen and saw me. I think it surprised him, and he blushed." She smiled. "He said he had to go and would send someone when he got to the station."

Felicity's stomach grumbled and she looked at the clock. She thought of walking to Mr. Brewer's farm for the eggs she got in exchange for reading lessons.

"Why don't we go to Mr. Brewer's for eggs?"

"I already got this week's eggs. That's when I saw the man."

"Oh, yes, you did."

Millie filled a pot with water and put it on to boil. Felicity had put the pistol in the pocket of her robe and felt its weight against her leg. Her back hurt, and her neck ached. It felt as if all her muscles were tight, and no words would sooth them until the man was captured.

They ate their meager breakfast and drank their tea, and then Felicity smiled.

"I think we should go and see Mr. Brewer anyway. I want to ask about his chickens."

After they dressed, they headed to Mr. Brewer's farm, and moved their eyes from side to side as if the man would jump out of the hedgerow that separated the farm from the meadow. The farm was large and spread out over acres of land, and she could see part of it from her hilltop cottage. The green patches reminded Felicity of a quilt, with each square placed in perfect symmetry. As they approached the farm, the scent of manure and mud filled the air.

They found Mr. Brewer in the loft of his barn pushing hay to the ground below. He tipped his cap when he saw them, and they waved.

"Mr. Brewer," Felicity said. "Do you mind if I ask you about your chickens?"

He laid his pitchfork aside and came down the ladder. He wiped the sweat from his brow with his handkerchief, and then walked outside. Mr. Brewer was in his fifties and had lived on the farm his whole life. He was tall and slender, and the lines in his face had been created by years of working under the sun.

"Aye, ladies," he said.

"I was wondering what you would charge me for a hen and a rooster?" Felicity asked.

"I'd say four quid," he said.

Felicity bit her lower lip. With Mrs. Muir's money, she might be able to afford the chickens, but not the coop. She would have to purchase that first, and wait until the next month to buy the chickens.

"I see, then we shall have to wait. Have you any idea what a coop would cost?"

"Well, you're talking about wood and wire, and labor to build it, so I'd say, 'round about five quid."

"That much," Felicity said.

"Aye. If you want it to weather the storms."

Millie left them to greet a pig named Ethel, who grunted when she saw her friend. Felicity thought about the cost and sighed.

"Well, then, we shall have to wait a bit longer," she said.

"When you're ready, I can have me son come by and set you up. He's a carpenter."

"Thank you, Mr. Brewer. I'm sorry we interrupted you."

"Not at all," he said. "I was needing a break."

She called Millie and they walked home. As they neared the hill, they saw that the beach was full of people enjoying the warm spring air.

"I think I'll work in the garden for a bit," Felicity said.

"I'm going to start lunch," Millie said.

Millie had done a wonderful job of weeding the garden, but the tall weeds by the fence had almost reached the top of the pickets. She went to the fence and started pulling the weeds, throwing them in a pile on the other side of the fence.

She was several yards from the cottage and the wind muffled any sounds therein. It was a good hour or more before she finished, and she was hungry. Millie would have made their lunch, so why hadn't she come to the kitchen door to call Felicity?

She wiped the dirt off her hands by rubbing them together as she walked to the back door. She heard Millie whimpering and ran inside. Millie was on the parlor floor holding her arm

"He came at me and knocked me down. I didn't have a chance to cut him."

"Oh, dear God," Felicity said. She touched Millie's arm, and the girl cried out in pain. "I fear it's broken."

The front door was open and Felicity saw a constable leading a horse into the yard.

"I'm P.C. O'Brien. Someone came to the station and reported seeing that man on the poster. P.C. O'Toole sent me straight away."

He saw Millie on the floor.

"He was here," Felicity said. "He attacked Millie. I think her arm is broken." She looked around the parlor and her anger flared. "I cannot believe you lost him again!" she cried. "And look what he's done. He could have killed her." She looked at him with hard eyes. "She needs the doctor."

The constable hesitated as he looked at the disheveled parlor.

"I can't leave you alone," he said.

"She needs a doctor!" Felicity was furious. She pulled the gun from her pocket and held it out for him to see. "If he returns, *I will shoot him.*"

"Yes, milady, of course. She needs a doctor."

He grabbed the horse's reins and took off. Felicity bolted the doors, and then went to tend to the injured girl. She helped Millie to her feet and over to the settee. Millie was trying to be brave, but Felicity saw the pain on her face.

"Let's put your legs up." Felicity picked up her legs one at a time and took off Millie's shoes. She then put a pillow under her head. "Would you like some tea?"

Millie shook her head. Felicity brought a kitchen chair to the parlor and sat beside her. The girl looked up at her and smiled.

"Thank you, milady."

"You were very brave, Millie," she said.

"It all happened so fast. I was making lunch and I thought I heard a noise. I went to the parlor and saw him in the bedroom. He had black eyes."

"Did you get a good look at him?"

Millie nodded.

"He looked dirty, and scared."

A half hour passed before O'Toole knocked on the door and called out to Felicity.

"I've brought the doctor," he said.

O'Toole stood in front of a middle-aged man wearing spectacles. The man tipped his top hat and smiled.

"I'm Dr. Miller."

"Please, come in. She's right here."

Millie was pale and shivering. The doctor looked at her and asked Felicity to fetch a blanket. She took the blanket off her bed and returned.

"Cover her and then get her some water," Dr. Miller said.

She got a glass of water and brought it to Millie. O'Toole was watching and shaking his head.

"I've got men looking all over town and on the beach. They'll check the farms, too."

"He must have broken in when we walked to Mr. Brewer's farm," Felicity said.

Frustration and anger reddened her cheeks. She looked at O'Toole for answers, and he had none.

"I had a man posted at the station," O'Toole said.

"Then why didn't he see him get off the train?"

Her voice was loud, and the doctor glared at them.

"Please mind the girl," he said.

"Let's go outside, milady," O'Toole said.

He tried to take her arm, but she shrugged off his hand. They stood at the edge of the yard and Felicity looked at the cottage with tears in her eyes.

"Have you any idea why this man might be after you?" O'Toole asked.

She shook her head, but thought about Roger. She couldn't tell O'Toole why she thought Dudley might be trying to hurt her unless she told him everything. To disclose her bastardy was risky as she was not sure she could trust the constable, who might let it slip one night after a few pints at the pub.

She thought of Millie lying on the settee in such pain. She heard her cry out, and O'Toole grabbed her arms.

"He'll call you if he needs you."

"She needs me now."

"Lady Armstrong, if you know anything, you have to tell me."

She took a deep breath.

"I can't."

She began to cry. He released his grip on her arms and waited for her to collect herself.

"So you do know something," he said. "You have to tell me."

She wrapped her arms around her waist and looked at the ground.

"You have to promise me you will keep what I tell you in confidence."

"You have my word."

"I had your word that we would be protected, Constable."

"You're right. I was remiss. I didn't think he would come here, but you were right, and I won't make that mistake again."

Her lower lip trembled. She had to trust him; she had to protect Millie.

"My mother had an affair with a man named Lord Harold Winston." She took a deep breath. "Lord Winston was my... father." She dropped her arms to her sides. "I believe his son has discovered the truth, and he might be afraid…that I will try to claim an inheritance."

O'Toole understood the social stigma attached to bastard children, and he also understood that the love of money drove men to desperate ends.

"And who is his son?"

"Lord Dudley Winston." She looked at him. "I think he's worried about his reputation as well."

"If you were to ask me, I'd say it's the money he's protecting, not his reputation."

She remembered him sitting at her garden table, his face passive, but his fingers tapping as if he wished he were elsewhere. His clothes were immaculate and his grooming impeccable.

"I would never tell anyone…." she said.

"But under the same circumstances, perhaps he would."

She looked at him and narrowed her eyes.

"He's a gentleman."

"He's still human, milady, and a cowardly one at that. He sent someone to do his dirty work, and the blighter mucked it up good." He looked at the house again. "I'll send a cable to London. They can look into this Lord Dudley Winston." He looked into her eyes. "I don't think he'll come back here with everyone out looking form him, but I'll send P.C. Jones to stay here tonight. Will you be all right if I go?"

"The doctor is here, and I have a pistol."

She showed him the small gun.

"You be careful with that lot. Don't go shooting your hand off." He watched her put it back in her pocket. "Then I'll be off. You go inside and lock the door."

"I will, Constable."

She watched him walk to the hill, and then she heard Millie scream. She ran into the house and went to Millie's side.

"What's happened!" she cried.

"Get behind her and wrap your arms around her shoulders,"

Dr. Miller said, and Felicity did as she was told. He pulled the arm while Millie screamed, and Felicity pressed her face against Millie's head and held her tightly. He kept manipulating the arm until he felt the bone slip into place.

"That should set things right," Dr. Miller said. "I'll need strips of cloth and something to use as a sling. And safety pins."

Felicity went into the bedroom and looked through her drawers. She had one spare petticoat. She took it to the kitchen and got the shears from the breakfront drawer, and then laid the petticoat on the table and cut out a large square of cloth. She cut the rest into strips. After she retrieved the safety pins from the drawer, she brought everything to the doctor. He wrapped Millie's arm with the strips of cloth and pinned the ends so it would stay tight. He folded the cloth into a triangle and showed Felicity how to fashion a sling. After Millie's arm was set in the sling, the doctor motioned Felicity to follow him to the kitchen.

As he washed his hands, he looked at Felicity.

"I know you're Lady Armstrong," he said. "I imagine you've been coddled most of your life."

She held up her chin and looked down her nose at him.

"I've been on my own for two years."

"But you've never seen a bone set before."

She relaxed her stance. "No."

"We were lucky. If it had been anywhere else, it would have been harder to set, and much more painful. The arm muscles are more forgiving. They stretch to allow the bone to fall into place." He dried his hands on a dishtowel, and then looked at her. "She has to rest. I'm going to give you a bottle of laudanum. Give her a few drops at a time for pain, but be careful. Only give them if the pain is severe." He looked toward the parlor. "She's young. I don't want her craving laudanum." He looked at Felicity. "Do you understand?"

"I do, but how will I know if I'm giving too much?" she asked.

"Give her three drops at a time. It will dull the pain to a place

where she can handle it. After five days, stop giving it to her."
Felicity's cheeks reddened, and the doctor put his hand on her
shoulder. "You've done well, milady."

His tone was softer, and his eyes kind.

"Thank you," she said.

He went to the parlor and she watched him pick up his bag.
He looked at Millie.

"I've instructed Lady Armstrong that you should rest. I've
given her medicine to help with the pain. You have to keep that
sling in place for several weeks, young lady, and you must listen
to Lady Armstrong. Do you understand?"

Millie nodded, and Dr. Miller handed Felicity a small bottle
with a stopper.

"I'll remember," she said.

"I trust you." He looked into Felicity's eyes. "But she will cry
out in pain, especially if she lies on it in her sleep. You must
adhere to what I've told you."

He went to he door, and then looked at Felicity.

"Will you come outside?" he said.

She followed him out the door and to the edge of the yard.

"I know Millie's mother," he said. "While I doubt she will care,
I'll tell her what's happened."

Felicity was surprised that someone else was aware of Mrs.
O'Malley's indifference. Dr. Miller sighed. He seemed weary, and
she saw a hint of sadness in his eyes.

"I delivered Millie. Her mother was…indifferent toward her
when she was born. I watched Millie grow, tended her brothers
through fevers and broken bones, and I never saw her mother
show any sign of affection or concern for Millie's well-being." He
looked at the meadow. "I was glad to hear she was living with
you. That girl deserves better than what she gets at home." He
looked into her eyes. "I've never said this to a living soul, but I
believe you care about her." He paused. "I think her brothers
have…tampered with her."

Felicity had no idea what he was implying. He saw the look on her face, surmised her innocence, and leaned toward her.

"I think they took advantage of her. I believe they've…known her, as in the Bible."

Now, Felicity's eyes widened.

"Dear Lord."

"Keep her here, Lady Armstrong," he said.

"I will, and…thank you for telling me."

"As I said, I shall return in two weeks to check her arm."

She watched as he went down the hill to his awaiting carriage, and waited until she saw it moving through the dusky meadow as she processed what he had told her. Mrs. O'Malley's attitude made more sense to Felicity, but it also made her angry that the woman would allow her sons to do such a thing to a young and innocent girl. Felicity decided she would never allow Millie to return to that household. She would do whatever she had to do, but she would never allow Millie to be subjected to her brothers' depravity again.

CHAPTER 19

Detective Inspector Ira Grayson

Scotland Yard

*S*cotland Yard, the home of the Metropolitan Police, sat on land that had, at one time, been divided into Great Scotland Yard, Middle Scotland Yard, and Little Scotland Yard. Some believed that Scottish kings had used the land when they came to pay homage to the realm, and others claimed a farmer named Scott had owned the property. Over the years, streets were named for the land divisions and at some point in history, Middle Scotland Yard and Little Scotland Yard were merged to form Whitehall Place, but Great Scotland Yard remained.

In 1829, the newly formed Metropolitan Police needed a home. They chose a building adjacent to the Public Carriage Office, a commission that licensed taxis. The public used the back entrance of the building to reach the commissioners, and they traversed a reception area that became the new police station. Their address was 4 Whitehall Place, but the entrance was on Great Scotland Yard. In time, the "Great" was dropped to form Scotland Yard.

The goal of the Metropolitan Police was to prevent crime in the growing city of London. Sir Robert Peel's Metropolitan Police Act created a trained and organized force, and many of London's citizens viewed them as "government spies." The police were prohibited from looking into their private lives.

This new police force was also tasked with other duties such as lamp lighting and calling out the time, and despite the public's negative view of their presence, they were successful, and crime declined.

Restrictions placed on their ability to look into the private lives of British citizens led to the formation of a secret detective unit, which cane out of hiding in1842, when Queen Victoria became the target of an assassin and the department came under fire. Many believed the attempt could have been prevented, and newspapers blamed the departments' inefficiency for their incompetent handling of the Queen's safety. The papers called for a real "detective department" to be formed within the Metropolitan Police.

Two inspectors and six sergeants were appointed to do the detective work, but following a bribery scandal that led to the imprisonment of three detectives in 1878, new rules of conduct were implemented, and financial dealings between the detectives and the public were forbidden. The newly named "Criminal Investigation Department," or C.I.D. was formed.

Detective Inspector Ira Grayson joined the force as a young lad, barely meeting the five foot eight height requirement. His keen eye and astute perception, however, led to a recommendation from his superior that he be admitted into the investigative services.

In an effort to look older than his twenty-eight years, Ira began sporting a mustache, and long hours of reading the copious notes in each case file necessitated the use of pince-nez glasses.

He had shown an affinity for solving murder cases, and his "gut," the intuition that guided him through each case and indicated which clue he should follow, became legendary among his fellow detectives.

When the C.I.D. received a cable from Whitley regarding the murder of an elderly woman, Ira was assigned the case. He shared a large office with several other detectives. The dark-paneled room had one window, and each man had a lamp on his desk that stayed lit day and night. While Ira would handle the more heinous crimes such as murder, another named Lowell Cranston handled the gentry, including the royal family. Several detective sergeants assisted them with their investigations.

Ira was looking at the poster from Whitley that had arrived in the morning mail. He painted the corners of the poster with tacky glue, put it on his blackboard, and then wrote a name next to it – Rufus Flagg.

Flagg had been identified by Cranston as a "private detective." His clients consisted of titled gentlemen who found themselves in compromising situations such as blackmail by a prostitute, or a pregnant, common girl seeking marriage. Flagg would deliver a bag of money and a train ticket out of town. His methods of intimidation were more cerebral than physical, but they were effective.

"He was arrested a few months ago," Cranston said. "His file should be in the archive."

After retrieving the file from the archive, Ira glanced at it recalled an incident involving Flagg. He had been hired to watch a prostitute named Lil. She had noticed Flagg lurking at the end of the hall near her flat and had summoned her mack, the man she worked for, and he beat Flagg to a bloody pulp before dumping his body in the alley behind Lil's building.

"Is that the file," Cranston asked.

"Yes."

"Did you know that Flagg was a bobbie years ago?"

"It's not in the file," Ira said.

"Got arrested one too many times for public drunkenness. He was dismissed and started working as a private detective. I think he's tussled with some prostitutes, but I can't see Flagg murdering anyone."

"Why is that?" Ira asked.

"He's a coward. The drunkenness was only part of the reason he was sacked. He couldn't confront criminals. He'd back off and turn tail."

"But what if he were pushed too hard?" Ira asked.

"Ira, the victim was an elderly woman. Believe me, if Flagg killed her, it was an accident."

Ira took off his glasses and wiped the lenses with his handkerchief as he contemplated what Cranston had said. He sat back and clasped his hands over his stomach. The letter accompanying the poster said the house had been ransacked and the old woman was lying on the kitchen floor with a gash in her head, an iron skillet by her side.

Flagg had been searching for something. Perhaps the old woman was outside at the privy when he got inside the house. She returned to find him tearing her house apart, screamed, and he hit her over the head with an iron skillet before running away.

Ira read the last entry in the file. Cranston had interviewed Flagg regarding his beating. Flagg said he had been hired to watch Lil and had gone to her building so he could find places to hide as he kept an eye on her. He boasted that he hated sloppy work, and that the only reason he'd been caught that night was that he was "...drunk as a boiled owl."

He took out his pocket notebook and began a list. Flagg was:

1. A drunk;
2. A coward;

3. A private detective who claimed he hated sloppy work, yet drank to excess while on duty;
4. Had ransacked a house looking for (?);
5. Was often employed by nobles who enjoyed the company of prostitutes.

A young officer came to Ira's desk with a piece of paper in his hand.

"Another notice, Inspector."

He gave it to Ira, and then left him alone. Ira saw Rufus Flagg's face on it, only this time he wasn't wearing a bowler hat. He'd been spotted in Tolwich where he'd injured a girl before fleeing from police.

"What have you gotten yourself into, Rufus?" Ira said aloud.

He wrote down the details regarding the crimes in his notebook, and then affixed that poster to the wall beside the first one.

He looked at his own bowler hat on a chair beside his desk. It was a common choice among working men, those who did dirty jobs to support unhappy wives and too many hungry children. Unfortunately, Flagg didn't have a wife to interview, or children, and the address he'd given in his file was marked as "vacated."

The clock on the wall struck twelve, and Ira put the glasses in his vest pocket, his umbrella under his arm and picked up his hat. It was time for lunch, and he felt like taking a walk. He went through the reception area known as "Black Hall," and the young officer who'd brought him the notice watched him put on his hat as he went out the entrance.

It was raining, and he opened his umbrella before walking under the arch to the sidewalk. He walked two blocks to a small public house he frequented on odd days of the week. Upon entering the establishment, he closed the umbrella and placed it in the stand near the door.

The pub was full of men who had taken refuge from the weather and many looked familiar. He found an empty table near the back of the room, sat, and then placed his hat on the chair beside his.

Brody, a slender waiter who stood no more than five foot tall, came to Ira's table with a pint and set it down in front of him.

"Inspector," he said.

"Brody," Ira replied.

"Are you here to eat?"

"Aye."

"It's boiled beef today."

"Bring me a bowl," Ira said. "And biscuits."

As Brody walked away, Ira took out his notebook and the gold-plated pen his father had given him when he joined the force. It had served him well by helping him chronicle the capture of some dastardly criminals. His memory was long, and he had an uncanny ability to see things as they were rather than as someone else wanted them to be.

Ira's gut was talking to him. It told him that the death of the old woman hadn't been Flagg's goal, and now he wanted to know why Flagg had been in Whitley. As luck would have it, another private detective named Roy Hobson had just walked into the pub. Ira waved him over.

Hobson, like Rufus, was a bit shady. His clients were also rich men with bad habits. Roy shuffled up to the table, Ira nodded toward the empty chair across from his, and Roy looked around the room before taking the seat.

"Have you seen Flagg lately?" Ira asked.

"Well, hello to you, too."

"Flagg, have you seen him?"

Hobson shrugged. "Here 'n there."

"Is he working?"

Hobson sat back and looked down his nose.

"Might be."

Ira looked Roy in the eye.

"I read his file," Ira said. "He mentions you. Two years ago you worked a case together and while he was arrested, you avoided capture. He said you absconded with money you'd both earned in a blackmail scheme."

"I done no such thing," Roy said. "And if he says so, he's a bloody liar." Roy pursed his lips.

"The lord in question chose not to prosecute, and we had to let Flagg go. The lord never mentioned you, though." Roy's smug smile irritated Ira. "However, since Flagg is wanted for murder, I could bring you in for questioning."

Roy stiffened and shook his head. He and Flagg were not friends. Though they had worked a couple of jobs together, Roy felt no allegiance toward him, and he didn't want to be involved in a murder investigation. He looked around the room again, and then leaned forward and folded his arms on the table.

"I heard he had a job, a big one. He was talking about leaving London."

"When was that?"

"Few weeks ago."

"Did he say who he was working for?" Rob shook his head. "He didn't give you a name?"

Roy sighed as he weighed whether to tell Ira the name of the nobleman. He didn't know the lord well, but one of his acquaintances had met with him, and he said that what this particular gentleman wanted him to do made Roy's friend run like a frightened rabbit. Flagg got the job after he'd turned it down.

"I don't do that sort of stuff," his friend told him.

"What sort of stuff?" Roy asked.

The man leaned toward Roy and put his hand to the side of his mouth.

"Murder," he said softly.

Roy shook his head. He drew the line at murder, but the man said Flagg had agreed to take on the job.

"He's paying him good, Roy," the man said. "I heard it's over five thousand quid."

"And the hangman's noose if he's caught."

They agreed that neither of them could do such a job, and laughed at the thought that Flagg had accepted it.

"e'll skedaddle before he kills anyone," the man said.

"With his tail between his legs."

Roy looked at Ira with a blank stare as he thought of Flagg being wanted for murder. Ira's patience was wearing thin.

"Did he give you a name?"

Roy twisted his mouth, and then sat back.

"It's one of them nobles on Grosvenor Square. His name is…" He looked around, leaned in as close as he could without standing up, and whispered, "Winston."

The name meant nothing to Ira, and he took out his notebook and wrote it down.

"Thank you, Hobson," Ira said. "I'll remember this."

"I will, too."

Roy got up and went to the bar. Brody bought the bowl of boiled beef, potatoes, and cabbage to the table. The warmth of his lunch took the chill from his bones and he felt the tension leaving his shoulders. A good meal and a pint of ale always made one feel just a little bit better.

CHAPTER 20

*W*hen he returned to the office, Ira saw Cranston at his desk and approached him.

"What do you know about Lord Winston?" he asked.

Cranston pulled a ledger from a shelf above his desk and opened it to the last page.

"The present Lord Winston?" Ira nodded. "His father, Lord Harold died a few months ago. His mother is deceased, and his brother, Roland, died in India." Cranston looked up. "The regimental commander ruled that it was an accidental shooting."

"What were the circumstances?"

Cranston shrugged.

"I asked for information and was turned away. The Queen's Hussars were not inclined to discuss the matter. I took my information from the newspaper." He looked at the ledger. "It did say that his brother found him."

"His brother," Ira said.

"The present Lord Dudley Winston." Cranston looked at the page again. "He's the second son."

"Would any of your acquaintances be willing to talk to me about the family?" Ira asked.

Cranston shut the book and sat back in his chair. He had an odd look on his face, and then twisted his mouth.

"There's a widow in Hampton. She's lonely, and she likes to talk about her friends. I've found that more often than not she tells the truth."

"Do you think she'll talk to me?"

"If I go with you. I'll have to send my calling card first, though. She doesn't abide any breach in etiquette."

Ira smiled.

"When do you think she'll respond?"

"Give it a day or two. I don't want to put her off."

Two days later, Ira and Cranston were waiting in the parlor of Lady Samantha Pence-Jones, a woman in her middle years, who enjoyed the intrigue of talking to the detectives about those she believed were up to no good. They each sat on a not too comfy chair with a low back and a hard seat, and each held his bowler hat on his lap.

Lady Samantha entered the room as if she were entering a ball, extending her arms as if to embrace them, and twirling like a ballerina, the bottom of her black silk skirt billowing like a sail on the wind.

"Gentlemen," she said.

Her actions took Ira aback, and as they rose from their seats, Ira's hat fell, but he waited until she was seated to retrieve it. Cranston smiled broadly and held out his arms, too.

"Lady Pence-Jones!" he cried. "You're a vision to behold."

Ira looked at him as if he'd lost his mind, but she was responding to his flattery. She sat with a flourish in an over-stuffed chair across from them and held her head high. She arranged the drape of her pink silk skirt so that it covered her shoes, and then kept her eyes on Cranston as the men sat.

The lady wore makeup so thick that cracks had formed in the lines on her face. Her lip rouge was a garish red, and Ira wondered if the rest of the ton noticed it, or if they, too, wore their makeup that way.

"My dear Lady Pence-Jones, I read that your dinner party was a smashing success," Cranston said.

"Oh, yes, indeed it was," she said.

She produced a hand fan and touched the edge of it with her fingers, indicating that she wanted to talk. Ira had no idea what was happening between her and Cranston, and as usual, his patience was wearing thin. He looked at Cranston, who had a silly grin on his face, and bristled.

"We have some questions…" he said, but Cranston reached over and put his hand on Ira.

"In due time, Inspector," he said. He looked at Lady Pence-Jones. "Your guest list was impressive."

"We were all so shocked at the death of dear Prince Leopold. I wasn't sure anyone would come, but I told them all that by coming together to mourn him, we would be honoring his memory."

"You are so wise," Cranston said. Ira was grasping the edge of his hat so tightly that it nearly popped out of his hand. "Milady, if you would be so kind, we have some questions regarding the late Lord Winston."

She smiled like the cat that ate the cream, and then sighed.

"I knew him well, a lovely man, and his son, Roland, such a dear boy." She leaned toward him. "He died in India. It was a terrible thing, just terrible. He was so young."

"Did you ever speak to Lord Harold about Roland?" Ira asked.

She was holding her fan in the left hand and changed it to the right. Cranston put a hand on Ira.

"It was a devastating loss," Cranston said.

"Simply devastating, and Lord Harold was inconsolable. His mourning never ceased." She bit her lower lip. "He was the heir. He would have been Lord Winston, not his other son, Dudley."

Ira noted the change in her voice when she said, "Dudley."

"I take it you don't like Lord Dudley," Ira said.

She glared at him, and again, Cranston reached over and put a hand on Ira's arm.

"You must forgive my associate, Lady Pence-Jones. He's never been in the presence of such a grand lady."

She lifted the fan and let it slide over her left cheek. Cranston feigned shock.

"My dear Lady Pence-Jones!"

She smiled and winked at him.

"I wonder if you could tell me something about Lord Dudley," Cranston said.

She held her head up and pursed her lips.

"There's little to tell. He attended one of my dinners with Lord Huntley, but I did not converse with him."

"I have the impression that you weren't very fond of Lord Winston," Cranston said.

She put her hands on her lap and straightened her back.

"It is not that I wasn't fond of him," she said. "He seemed preoccupied, and I find that rude. When one is invited to a dinner party, one is obliged to pay heed to the host or hostess."

She tilted her head back, and Cranston raised his eyebrows.

"Oh, Lady Pence-Jones!"

Now, she hung her head, and then she looked up, and Ira noticed a twinkle in her eye.

"Since you've been so kind, I must confess that I haven't been completely honest with you." Her seductive smile made Ira cringe, but Cranston responded by leaning forward. She looked at Cranston and held the fan in front of her mouth, a not so subtle invitation to kiss her, and then removed it. "He was intro-duced to me at Lady Marsdale's ball last season. He was an impu-dent boy, and when he looked at me, a shiver went up my spine." She tilted her head. "He leered at me! Well, I moved away from him as quickly as I could." She leaned forward. "I also heard that he had attended Lady Campbell's dinner party not one month after his father died! It was scandalous, but he is young, so those in attendance felt that with no one to guide him, they would simply ignore his misstep."

Ira leaned toward Cranston and whispered.

"How old is Lord Dudley?" Cranston asked.

"Lady Marsdale told me he had just passed his twenty-fifth birthday."

Cranston looked at Ira, who looked frustrated. Lady Pence-Jones was holding her fan to her mouth again, so Cranston decided it was time to go.

"I thank you for seeing me, Lady Pence-Jones."

He and Ira stood.

"Will I see you again, Inspector Cranston?" she asked.

"I'm sure you will." She extended her hand, and he took it. "How could I stay away?"

She giggled, and Ira looked at Cranston, who seemed unaware of her obvious infatuation. Then, as if her false façade had become too heavy to bear, her face grew serious, and Ira thought he was seeing the true face of Lady Pence-Jones.

"Lord Harold was a lovely man," she said again. Cranston let go of her hand and returned to his seat. Ira sat, too. "I found him charming. I often thought he might…well, one day, he called on me, and over tea, confided that he was unsatisfied with the explanation given him regarding the death of his son."

"Unsatisfied," Cranston said.

He seemed as surprised by the change in her demeanor as Ira. She was no longer acting like a besotted schoolgirl. She looked older, and sad.

"Roland had been a soldier for many years, and the explanation for his…accident didn't make sense." She sighed and seemed to drift a bit. "So many things are passing away," she said. "Sacred things that were once held in high esteem." She sighed again. "But when I heard Lord Harold had…passed away, I, it was too much." She looked at Cranston. "He was a good man."

"I'm sure he was," Cranston said.

She ran her hand over her skirt.

"I've been in mourning for my husband for ten years, but I also wear these clothes to honor Lord Harold." She clasped her hands on her lap. "He told me that when Roland was cleaning his pistol, it went off and he shot himself." A single tear rolled down her cheek. "He was angry. He said his son would never be so careless. He wanted an inquiry, but no one would listen to him." She looked at Cranston. "He did not say, but I felt he was unsure of the circumstances."

"In what way, Lady Pence-Jones?" Cranston asked.

She closed her fan and held it with both hands.

"Dudley was there. Lord Harold said that Dudley would often grumble about being the second son. While Lord Harold was loath to say it outright, I believe he thought..."

"Dudley shot his brother," Ira said.

She ignored his impudence this time, but looked at Cranston.

"Is that what he thought, Lady Pence-Jones?" Cranston said.

She nodded her head and then put her hand to her mouth.

"So many of my friends are gone," she said softly. "It feels disloyal to Lord Harold to talk about his son." She ran her hand over her skirt again. "But I didn't lie about the way he made me feel." She looked at Cranston. "He is not a gentleman."

"Did he do something to you?" Cranston asked.

"No, but he was disrespectful toward his father, and it hurt Lord Harold. He was so disappointed in Dudley."

Cranston looked at Ira, and then they stood.

"You've been most helpful, Lady Pence-Jones," he said. "Thank you for seeing us."

She looked up at Cranston and Ira now could see rings under her eyes.

"Do you think it is unusual for a soldier to have such an accident?" she said.

"I do," Cranston said.

"Dudley told Harold that he ran for help, but…Harold questioned his version of the event."

"Is there anything else you want to tell me?"

She looked around the room as she pondered his question.

"Sometimes when I'm dining with friends, Dudley is mentioned. It is said he is a poor manager of his father's estate."

"Is Dudley the only heir to his father's fortune?"

Now she offered a sly smile, and the coquette returned.

"I wouldn't know, Inspector, as the will was never made public."

The will had not been filed. It was highly unusual, especially for the members of the ton, not to probate a will.

"Is Lord Dudley in financial difficulties?" Cranston asked.

"The estate was large," she said. "But I've heard he owes money, and until the will is filed, he will not have access to it."

"Thank you again, milady," Cranston said. "I promise the next time I come to see you, I'll stay a bit longer."

"I look forward to your next visit, Inspector."

She never acknowledged Ira, but he didn't mind. Cranston had worked his charm on her, and had given him the lead he was looking for.

CHAPTER 21

*A*s they walked to the rail station, Ira mulled over what had happened with Lady Pence-Jones.

"You knew how to handle her," he said.

Cranston smiled. "I knew something was amiss when she didn't offer us tea."

"I must admit I was a bit put off by her behavior."

"That's because you don't understand the language of the fan, Grayson."

"You mean all that business with the fan meant something?"

"Of course, old chap. She was telling me how much she liked me, and she thought you were impudent."

"I was no such thing."

"This is why I handle the royal family, Grayson. I know how they are, how they think, and how they communicate."

"I'm just glad she knew something about Dudley." Ira kept his eyes on the sidewalk as they walked. "Do you think he killed his brother?"

"It is odd that a soldier would shoot himself while cleaning his weapon."

"You said no one would talk to you about it."

"No one would see me. I think the whole incident was an embarrassment to the Queen's Hussars." Cranston was also looking at the ground. "You have to remember something, Grayson, these people are not like us. If the regimental commander thought Dudley shot his brother, he'd have kept it to himself."

"Why?"

"Because Dudley is a nobleman. His father was a lord. If they had no witness, they had to assume Dudley was telling the truth. They couldn't question his integrity."

"That's bollocks," Ira said.

"To you and me, yes, but to them it is perfectly acceptable."

"Not to Lady Pence-Jones, and certainly not to Lord Harold."

"I agree, but she would never talk about this to any of her friends," Cranston said. "She wouldn't sully Lord Harold's name that way."

"We should have asked her how Lord Harold died."

"I'm afraid she would have swooned before answering that question."

"Then how do we find out?" Ira asked.

"We wait and see if the will is filed, and then we can ask his solicitor."

"Why not ask him now?"

Cranston stopped and smiled at Ira.

"Solicitors don't like talking to the police. However, if we could find out the name of his physician, we might persuade him to tell us how Harold died."

"And how are we to find out who he is?"

"Therein, my dear Grayson, lies the rub."

* * *

THEY SPENT the rest of the afternoon discussing the Winstons. Ira made a list of important facts he'd gleaned from Cranston's ledger, and Cranston remembered a few more things about Dudley.

"What happened to his mother?" Ira asked.

"She died twenty years ago. Shortly thereafter, Lord Harold and the boys moved from the country to London and into one of the older, wooden townhouses. At some point, it burned to the ground, and was rebuilt."

"I want to talk to him," Ira said.

"Just send a calling card first."

"But I'd rather he not know I'm coming."

"Suit yourself, but he'll probably leave you standing on the stoop."

The following day, Ira boarded the train to Whitley. As the scenery passed unnoticed, Ira looked at his list. He had added questions regarding Lord Harold's will, and the first one read, "Why hadn't the will been filed?"

The picture of Lord Dudley forming in his mind was that of a spoiled, jealous boy who might have manipulated events to enrich himself, events that might have included fratricide. If that was the case, then why wait to file a will that gave him the entire estate?

As he stepped off the train and saw the quaint village of Whitley, he wondered how he would connect Lord Dudley to Rufus Flagg, and Flagg to Hedda Muir. He took out his notebook and made small columns with "HM," "RF," and "DW" above each, and dedicated a page in his notebook to each of them.

He was deep in thought as he walked through the market and past the pub. Soon he was standing in front of the police station and looking at the old stone walls, barred windows, wooden door, and a sign reading "Police" hung from a post near the road.

When he entered the building, he told P.C. Woolsey his reason for being in Whitley, and the man went to fetch P.C. Leary. Ira watched him walk to a door beside the last cell of three located behind the counter. Leary came through that door, gave him a cursory glance, and then he narrowed his eyes, prompting Ira to extract his identification from his pocket.

"I am D.I. Grayson with Scotland Yard." He took the folded wanted poster from his other pocket. "I was wondering if I could ask you some questions about Hedda Muir, and have a look at her house."

Leary looked at Ira's identification papers and sniffed.

"I did a thorough investigation," he said. "Like the poster says, that man was seen lurking about. A neighbor gave a description."

"Perhaps we can talk while we walk there," Ira said.

"I've got photographs of the scene."

"And I will want to see them when we return."

Leary looked at Woolsey, whose cheeky smile irritated him. He muttered to himself as he went to a row of hooks on the wall and retrieved the key to Hedda Muir's house, and then he walked past Ira to the road outside. Ira quickened his pace to keep up with Leary's long strides.

"She was lying on the kitchen floor with a big gash on the back of her head," Leary said. "Blighter hit her from behind with an iron skillet."

"You didn't specify in your report that the iron skillet had been identified as the murder weapon."

Leary looked down at Ira.

"It was lying next to her."

"Was blood found on the skillet?"

Leary stopped. "I did a proper investigation."

"Yes, well, I'm sure you followed proper procedures, Constable." Ira moved ahead of him. "I just find it useful to inspect a crime scene with my own eyes."

"There's nothing to see!" Leary cried. "The vicar had some ladies clean it up."

Ira's calm demeanor was annoying Leary. He didn't like being second-guessed by some know-it-all detective from Scotland

Yard as if he didn't know what he was doing. After all, he'd been twenty years on the force.

As they approached the cul-de-sac, Leary took Hedda's house key from his pocket.

"It's the white one on the left. T'other belongs to Roger. He's the one who gave a description of the assailant."

"Well, then I'll have to talk to Roger, too."

They walked into the semi-circle and Ira looked at the three houses. He saw an old man sitting in front of the one on the right, and watched as Leary walked over to him.

"Roger," Leary said. "This gentleman would like a word." Roger didn't move. Leary looked at Ira. "You'll have to speak up. He don't hear so well."

Leary waited while Ira walked across Roger's yard. The man looked Ira up and down before setting his gaze on the inspector's face.

"I'm Detective Inspector Grayson from Scotland Yard. I wondered if I could ask you a few questions."

"What's that you say?"

"I said I'd like to ask you a few questions!" Ira shouted, and Leary started laughing. Roger's eyes twinkled.

"On with ya, Roger," Leary shouted. "He's asking about Hedda Muir."

Ira pulled the poster from his jacket pocket.

"Constable Leary said you gave him a description of the man who killed Hedda Muir."

"That's right. I saw him lurking about."

"What was he doing when he was 'lurking about'?" Ira asked.

"He was kneeling under the window. I yelled at him, and he took off down the road."

"When was that?" Ira asked.

"I'm not sure. It was before she died."

"Did you see him the morning Hedda Muir died?"

Roger shook his head. "But I seen Hedda. She was in the garden."

Ira looked at Hedda's house and saw a large garden on the left side of the house near the back.

"How long was she in the garden?"

"Don't know. She was out there when I went in to make coffee."

"Thank you, Roger," Ira said.

He tipped his hat and turned to rejoin Leary.

"You should talk to the girl," Roger shouted.

Ira stopped and looked at Roger.

"What girl?"

"Lady Armstrong. She was staying with Hedda when it happened."

Ira looked at Leary.

"There was no mention of her in your report."

He took out his notebook and wrote down her name.

"A pretty little thing she was." Roger nodded. "The constable talked to her. He'd know."

"Yes, I'm sure he would." Ira looked at Leary and held out his hand. "May I have the key, Constable?"

"I'll open the door," Leary said.

They walked to the front door of Hedda's house. The sun was at the back of the house and the parlor was illuminated by the late afternoon sky. The place smelled of lye soap.

"She was in the kitchen," Leary said pointing to the doorway in front of them. "Facedown, blood coming from the gash in her head."

"Which rooms were ransacked?"

"In here. He'd pulled out drawers and whatever was in them. He broke a table lamp."

"Why wasn't Lady Armstrong mentioned in your report?"

Leary blushed. He was still ashamed. He had promised to watch over the ladies and he felt responsible for Hedda's death.

He kept Lady Armstrong out of the report because she was a lady, a noblewoman, and he decided that she couldn't have killed her dear friend. Besides, the jury at the inquest hadn't looked upon her as a suspect, either.

Ira stared at him as he waited for Leary's answer. When it was clear there was none forthcoming, he continued.

"Did Lady Armstrong know what he was looking for?"

Leary shook his head.

"Why had Lady Armstrong come to Whitley?"

Leary took a deep breath.

"She said she'd come to visit Hedda because she'd been Lady Armstrong's housekeeper. She lives in Tolwich."

Lady Armstrong had been her employer. Ira took out his notebook and pencil to add this information to his notes. Was this the connection between Hedda Muir and Lord Dudley?

"She sent Roger to the police station before the funeral to ask us to send a cable to Tolwich."

"For what purpose?"

"She thought the man might be looking for her and she was worried about her maid alone at her house in Tolwich."

"Did she say why she thought the man might be after her?"

Leary rubbed his chin.

"He didn't mention it."

"And you didn't think to ask *her* why before she left Whitley?" Ira said, his voice rising as his face turned red.

"No need to shout at me," Leary said. He puffed out his chest. "I done a proper investigation."

The man's attitude was infuriating, and it seemed he was determined to drive Ira mad. Ira went to the kitchen and Leary followed.

"Roger said she was in the garden," Ira said. He looked down and saw the pink stain on the floor. "And she was here." He looked at the table. "How was she lying?"

Leary pointed to the pink stain. "Her head was there and her feet, there." He pointed to a spot away from the door.

"So she might have been trying to go out the kitchen door." Ira walked around the table, and bent over to look under the edge of the breakfront. He saw something and took out his pen. He used it to move the object closer. It was a shard of glass.

"Did she bring something with her from the garden?"

"There was a basket of herbs on the table. You can see it in the photographs."

Ira got up, took out his notes, wrote that down, and then stood near the pink stain.

"So, she would have put the basket down, and then she heard something." He turned his head. "She saw him and tried to run out the kitchen door, but he was too quick." Ira looked at the table and then at the stove. "Where was the skillet?"

"Near her head."

"On which side of the body?" Ira asked.

Leary looked down. "The right."

Ira went to the stove.

"He would have had to run here, grab it, and then come around the table to hit her from behind. It would have taken too long."

Ira studied the scene and imagined her coming inside with the basket. She placed it on the table. Perhaps she was going to cook something and brought the skillet to the table.

"Was there any food on the table?" he asked.

"No, nothing but the basket and the base of a lamp."

"Was there oil in the skillet?"

"Don't remember," Leary said.

Ira's irritation with the man grew, but he didn't have time to think about his incompetence. He had to figure out how Flagg had managed to kill Hedda Muir.

"And you believe he used the skillet. I ask you again, P.C. Leary, did you find blood on the skillet?"

"It was on the floor next to her head."

"That is not what I asked."

"She had a gash and it was right next to her head!" Leary cried.

"Yes, but if she was holding it, she could have dropped it when he hit her." Ira imagined her lying on the floor. "Perhaps she had tried to defend herself using the skillet." Ira put his hand on the table. "And why was the lamp here?"

"Don't know." Leary looked at the floor as he thought about something. He hadn't understood why the lamp was there, but now, as he recalled the broken glass around Hedda's head, he blushed. The detective saw it and took a deep breath.

"P.C. Leary."

"The chimney was smashed. There were pieces of glass around her head."

"But that wasn't in your report," Ira said loudly. Leary glared at him. "Didn't you think it was relevant, Constable?"

"I wrote the report when I got back to the station. It might have slipped my mind."

"You didn't take notes while you were here?"

Ira was infuriated. The broken glass gave another version of the crime, but if he hadn't seen the house and questioned Leary so closely, he'd have gone back to London with the wrong hypothesis. To him, Leary's lack of professionalism was unforgivable.

Ira went to the parlor and looked around. He found a lamp on the end table with a brass base missing its chimney, and when he picked it up, he felt its weight. A man could cause a fatal injury with it if he chose to. Ira returned to the kitchen where Leary was rocking back and forth on his heels.

"I suggest you update your report, Constable, and have it reflect that Hedda Muir was most likely hit with a brass lamp and not the skillet. The killer heard her come in and grabbed the lamp, hit her, and probably left it on the table when he ran from the house."

Leary remembered the lamp being on the table, and it made his blood boil. Why hadn't he seen it that way? He hated being made a fool by a detective from London, and now he would have to memorialize his shame in the report.

"Where was Lady Armstrong when Hedda Muir was killed?" Ira asked.

"She said she was in bed. She found Hedda and sent Roger to fetch us straight away."

"And you questioned her thoroughly."

Leary looked down his nose at Ira.

"I did. She was in her bedroom when she heard a noise."

"That was her alibi, that she was in the bedroom. Did you ever suspect that *she* might have killed Mrs. Muir?"

Leary's anger flared.

"The lady had come to the station with Hedda Muir the day before. They told me a man was following them. I walked them home and watched them walking arm-in-arm." He came closer to Ira. "That girl wouldn't have harmed a hair on Hedda Muir's head."

He was so close Ira could see the hairs in his nose, so Ira backed away. Leary, like Lady Pence-Jones, was reluctant to believe that a gentlewoman could commit such a crime. It had colored his judgment and might have allowed a murderer to escape justice.

Another thought entered Ira's mind. What if Lady Armstrong had hired Flagg to kill Hedda Muir? Servants and their masters didn't mix socially, and the lady wasn't just visiting, she was *staying* at Hedda Muir's house. Why not take a room at the inn?

His gut was surprisingly silent, but he took out his notebook and added this theory to his notes. He took a look around the house before leaving and didn't talk to Leary on the way to the police station. When they got there, Leary gave him the file and he looked at the photos. From the position of her body, and the brass lamp on its side, Ira was sure his version of events was correct.

He returned the file to Leary, but he was still fuming. The man was a fool, and Ira hated wasting time.

"You must remember to detail your reports," Ira said. "I cannot ignore this gross negligence on your part."

Leary stood and towered over Ira, his nostrils flaring, his lips quivering.

"I done a proper investigation."

His tone was fueled by anger and envy, a lethal combination, and Ira understood that if he pushed him too far, the man might lash out, and Ira could end up in hospital. He backed away, muttering to himself as he gathered his things, and then headed out the doorway to the lobby.

Leary followed him, and when Ira reached the door, he tried in vain to hold his temper, but the sheer ineptitude of Leary's investigation galled him. He put his hand on the doorknob, and then looked behind him.

"I have never seen such absolute incompetence displayed by a police officer."

Leary walked toward him.

"Missing details, false conclusions, and witnesses released before they have been properly questioned. This, PC Leary, is precisely why the CID was formed. Incompetent fools like you who botch investigations that lead to the perversion of justice. Do you understand that your actions might have allowed a murderer to escape justice?"

P.C. Woolsey's eyes were so wide that it looked as if his eyeballs would pop out of his head.

"Get out of my station," Leary said.

"He's been seen in Tolwich," Woolsey said. Ira and Leary looked at Woolsey. "We got a cable. The man in the poster – he's hurt the girl living with Lady Armstrong."

CHAPTER 22

*M*illie watched Felicity hang her petticoat on the line behind the cottage. The girl was pulling weeds from the garden with her good arm, but she was dismayed over her disability. She should have been hanging that petticoat.

"I'm sorry, miss."

Felicity looked at her.

"For what?"

"Because I should be doing that for you."

"Oh, Millie, you've nothing to be sorry about." She came to Millie and got on her knees beside her. "This wasn't your fault."

"I should have hurt him."

"How? He was bigger than you, and he surprised you." She put her arm around Millie's shoulders. "I'm just so grateful he didn't…"

"I know, miss, but I still wish I had hurt him. I wish I had broken his arm, and his leg, and his neck."

Felicity squeezed Millie's shoulder with her hand.

"No, you don't wish that, because if you had… killed him, you'd have to live with that for the rest of your life."

"But I want him to pay for what he did."

Felicity put her head next to Millie's. She had been having these very same thoughts.

"Well, I think it's nearly time for lunch."

Felicity went to the back door, and paused to look at Millie before going inside. She saw Millie turn her head away and wished she could take away her pain.

Despite her bravado, the attack haunted Millie. At night, she lay on her pallet, and if she heard a sound, or a squirrel would jump on the roof of the cottage, beads of sweat would cover her forehead. She'd lie stone still as she waited for the next sound, believing that the man had returned to kill her because she'd seen his face.

Her arm would throb, and she'd use her good hand to pull the blankets to her chin. Her heart would pound and her hands would shake. It was just like when her brothers lay next to her, running their hands up and down her body, while threatening to tell their mum it was Millie that told them to do it, that it was she, the Jezebel, that made them do those things to her.

Millie pulled another weed from the garden, but her hand was shaking. Why wouldn't those memories go away? She had never encouraged them, had never wanted them to touch her, but when their mum discovered one of them with Millie, she'd blamed the girl, and locked her out of the house for days.

As anger replaced fear, Millie ripped the weeds from the ground, and pounded them with her fist. Tears burned her eyes, her mouth quivered, and she swore to herself that if she had to kill to protect both her and Felicity, she would.

Inside the house, Felicity took the loaf of bread she'd made from the pantry. It had not risen as she'd hoped it would, but Millie assured her that the next time, they'd let it sit near the stove longer. The lack of height hadn't affected the taste, though. It just made smaller sandwiches.

As Felicity cut into the bread, someone knocked on the front door. She held the knife and went to look out the window. The constable who had been there during the night was nowhere in sight, but she saw a small gentleman at the door. He had a thin mustache and was wearing a bowler hat. He carried an umbrella and wore a long, black overcoat.

"Hello," she said though the window.

"Are you Lady Armstrong?" he asked.

"I am."

"I am Detective Inspector Grayson of Scotland Yard. I've just come from Whitley and was hoping I could speak with you regarding the death of Hedda Muir."

"How do I know you are from Scotland Yard?" she asked.

Ira took out his badge, held it up, and she went to the door to let him in.

"Did you see a constable heading to town on your way here?" she asked.

"I didn't, milady."

"He was supposed to stay, or send someone to keep an eye on us." She had no idea how long she and Millie had been alone. She looked at the inspector. He had kind eyes. "Would you like some tea, Inspector?"

"I would, thank you, milady."

She had a soft voice and, in contrast to Lady Pence-Jones, wore an air of meekness. No wonder Leary had taken her at her word.

He looked around the cottage and noted the shabby furniture. The decorations were remnants of her noble past, but they did little to hide the impoverished reality of Lady Armstrong's situation.

Lady Armstrong, though, seemed oblivious to her surroundings. He didn't see her remove the knife from the folds of her skirt and return it to the counter as he followed her into the small kitchen, which was dominated by a large stove.He followed her into the small kitchen, which was dominated by a large stove. *The wall between the kitchen and parlor should be knocked down,* he thought, as he sat at the kitchen table, for the heat was suffocating despite the open window over the sink.

Millie came in from outside and saw him sitting at the table. She put her hand on her pocket, and Felicity went to stand between her and Ira.

"Millie, this is Detective Inspector Grayson. He is from Scotland Yard."

Millie looked around Felicity. He looked at her pale face. He couldn't tell her age, but she looked young, and as if she hadn't enjoyed a good meal in quite some time. The edge of the sleeves on her worn, brown dress didn't reach her wrist, and the hem was too short. He also took note of the sling holding her right arm.

He watched her go to the sink to wash her hand, and Felicity pumped water for her. The girl kept looking at him as Felicity washed the dirt away. She didn't smile as she sat in the chair across from his, and kept a wary eye on him as Felicity checked the wood in the stove. She opened the damper and set the kettle on to boil.

"I'm afraid we're out of biscuits," she said. "Would you like a sandwich?"

"No, thank you," he said. "Do you mind opening the door?"

"It is a bit warm in here," she said.

She opened the door and the fresh breeze felt heavenly. Ira watched as Felicity took cups and saucers from the breakfront and filled each cup with tea from a small tin on the windowsill. He noted that she wore an apron and that some of her hairpins had loosened and hung at odd angles. He was struck again by how well she had adapted to her poverty.

"I'm afraid we're all out of cream, Inspector, but we do have sugar."

Her voice still had the edge of nobility, but far less than Lady Pence-Jones.

"I don't need sugar."

As they waited for the kettle to boil, she sat in the chair next to Ira. He took out his notebook, glanced at his notes, and then looked at Felicity.

"Do you mind if we begin our interview?"

"Is this to be a formal interview?" she asked.

She looked confused.

"It is, Lady Armstrong. I have questions the constable in Whitley was unable to answer.

She clasped her hands on the table and held her head high, and Millie glared at him.

"According to Constable Leary, you came to visit Hedda Muir."

"Yes, I did."

"According to his records, you were there when the suspected murderer entered the house."

She stared at her hands and her lower lip trembled as she remembered finding Mrs. Muir on the kitchen floor.

"Yes," Felicity said softly.

"It was horrible for her," Millie said.

Ira looked at the girl and was struck by her vehemence. He looked at his notes and continued.

"How would you describe your relationship with Hedda Muir?"

"We were very close. She was like a mother to me."

He made a note in his book.

"What prompted your visit to Whitley?" he asked.

Felicity stretched her fingers and then clasped her hands again.

"There were things I wanted to ask that only she could answer."

Ira noted the way her shoulders slumped and the slight change in her demeanor as she searched the memory of her visit. Her expression was similar to those worn by mourners at a funeral.

"Constable Leary told me you and Hedda Muir came to the police station the day before she died to report a man who'd been following you, is that correct?"

She nodded.

"Constable Leary walked us home. Mrs. Muir told him she had seen the man standing outside the cottage and again at the market. It made her, us, uneasy."

"You said your reason for visiting her was to ask her some questions. May I ask what sort of questions?"

Felicity squirmed in her seat. Millie saw her discomfort and then looked at Ira.

"He knocked me down and broke my arm," Millie said.

Defiance exuded from her and Ira felt it across the table. He had no doubt that if she chose to she could knock him out of his seat, notwithstanding her broken arm. He returned her gaze and didn't blink.

"And how do you know it was the same man?" Ira asked.

"Because he looked mean," Millie said.

Ira took the folded poster from his pocket and showed it to Millie.

"Is this the man?"

"That's him," she said.

He looked at Felicity.

"According to Constable Leary, you didn't see the man in Hedda Muir's house."

"No. He was gone when I found her."

"He wore a bowler hat," Millie said. She looked at Ira's hat on the chair beside her. "Just like that one."

"So you have no way of knowing who was in the house at the time," Ira said.

Felicity looked at him.

"The man was lurking outside the house. He was peeking in the window the night I arrived in Whitley. Mrs. Muir's neighbor saw him."

"But he didn't see the man that morning."

He saw fear in her eyes, as she understood what he was intimating.

"I would never harm her." She straightened her back. "I was asleep, Inspector, I promise you that had I been awake, he would not have had the chance to hurt her. I would have done anything for her." Tears rolled down her cheeks. "She was more dear to me than my own life."

He watched her, looking for signs of hubris, but saw none. He believed her.

"But you do see my problem, don't you, Lady Armstrong? You didn't see him. No one saw him that morning."

"I saw him," Millie said. "When he came in here, I saw him."

"Yes, but that was here in Tolwich," Ira said. "Were you in Whitley?"

She didn't like his tone. Millie wanted to punch him in the nose.

"She stayed here," Felicity said. She remembered the cables that were sent. "Constable Leary sent a cable here to warn them that the man might come here, to the cottage."

"He told me that, and he also said you thought the man might be looking for you. Why would he be looking for you, Miss Armstrong?"

Felicity looked at Millie.

"Millie, please go and see if the clothes have dried." Millie glared at Ira, pursed her lips, and then went out the back door. She looked at Felicity. "It's all right. Please go and check the clothes."

Millie gave him another defiant look, and then walked outside.

CHAPTER 23

elicity sighed, and then looked him in the eye.

"Someone I'd known a long time ago came to visit me. It was quite unexpected and though he told me his reason for coming, it left me curious."

"Who was it?"

"Lord Dudley Winston."

Ira's gut responded, and he reached for the pen in his vest pocket.

"Why did his visit leave you curious?"

"Because I hadn't seen him since I was twelve, and he hadn't sent word that he was coming."

"What reason did he give for the visit?"

"He said he thought I might need company, and then he talked about his visit to Rosendale. That was the name of my home. Dudley and I had walked in the garden."

"But you didn't believe him."

The teakettle whistle blew and she went to pour the tea. She recalled her uneasy feelings when Dudley arrived at the door.

"He came without warning." She poured the water into the

cups, brought them to the table, and sat. "He should have sent word that he was coming."

Ira recalled Cranston's insistence upon sending a calling card to Lady Pence-Jones.

"If I were still living in Rosendale, it would have been an egregious breach of etiquette." She put her hands around her cup. "He knows better than to do something like that. I think he only did it because of my present circumstances."

"And that made you angry."

She looked at him.

"Yes, it did. I felt as if he had come to mock me so he would have something to gossip about when he returned to London." She looked at Ira. "Why else would he claim he wanted to offer me company? It made no sense." She sat back. "He is a gentleman. He didn't strike me as the sort of man who would offer solace to anyone, let alone someone he hardly knew, unless…"

"Unless he wanted something." Ira looked at his notebook. "And you have no idea what that might be."

"Not at the time." She inhaled loudly. "That's why I went to see Mrs. Muir. I was hoping she would remember him, or could tell me something about the Winston family."

"Did she remember them?"

Felicity nodded her head.

"She remembered the day they came to Rosendale." She looked at Ira and he saw tears forming in her eyes. "She had kept a secret from me all my life."

Ira waited for her to continue, but he feared she wouldn't reveal the secret to him. How would he compel her to do so?

"Will you share it with me?" he asked.

She got up and went to the kitchen window. She crossed her arms and sighed.

"My mother died when I was born. She wrote letters. They were more like pages in a diary."

"Letters."

She turned to face him.

"They were bound in a red ribbon. She had never sent them to...you must promise me you will keep this is strictest confidence."

"I cannot promise before I know what it is you want to tell me, but I can tell you that no one will know unless it is relevant to solving Hedda Muir's death."

She looked sad. Surely Inspector Grayson would understand the importance of hiding her bastardy.

"The letters were about a relationship between my mother and his father." She blushed a deep red and her voice was barely audible. "I am Dudley Winston's half-sister."

Now he understood why she was so reluctant to talk. She was a bastard, and if news of her illegitimacy became public knowledge, she would suffer untold abuse. The shameful history of bastardy had been argued in parliament for years, and had yet to be resolved.

Earlier in his career, Ira had raided "baby farms," and seen the bodies of murdered infants, whose parents, rich and poor, had abandoned their newborns to people who promised to find them homes, and when they failed, they would murder the unwanted children.

"I see." He also understood why Lord Winston might be eager to have her disappear off the face of the Earth. "And this is what you discovered when you visited Hedda Muir?"

She nodded.

"I asked her about that day, the day Dudley came to Rosendale. There were things about that day I couldn't remember, and I felt as if I had to, as if it might explain why Dudley came to see me.

"She remembered their visit, but said she hadn't heard them talking. Later, our butler, Mr. Conway, told her what had happened. Lord Harold drank too much, and he spoke about my mother, and about me. Mr. Conway saw my father's face change when he saw the way Lord Harold looked at me."

"He knew," Ira said.

She nodded.

"After their visit, my father was cordial, but he had changed. He usually spent his time at home with me, walking near the river, or reading in the library, but after Lord Harold's visit, he would walk alone. Shortly afterward, he remarried and left me alone with my stepmother while he traveled. He would stay away for months at a time and I missed him terribly."

"Lord Harold died a few months ago," Ira said. "He might have told his son about you, a dying confession of his sins if you will. Or, perhaps, Lord Harold remembered you in his will and Dudley wanted to know why."

She looked at him and narrowed her eyes.

"But he would know I'd never tell a living soul. He would know we could never bear the shame."

"In my experience, young men are more concerned about their inheritance than their reputations."

"That's not true. Dudley would be shunned."

"For a time, perhaps, but he's an eligible, titled bachelor with a fortune. There's not a mother in London who wouldn't overlook your existence to land him as a son-in-law."

She stared at him, her eyes wide, and her heart aching. She knew he was right. Dudley wouldn't suffer as she would, so he had little reason to hide her secret.

"But if he had to share his fortune," Ira said, "now that might provoke him into taking a train to Tolwich to see how his dear old friend is faring."

"But he understands the rules of society. He should have written he was coming."

Ira leaned toward her.

"He didn't want you to know."

She understood, and her heart began to pound. She struggled to remain calm, but she remembered the way Dudley came to the house on foot, unaccompanied, with no footman, valet, or groomsman, and walking across the meadow so late in the afternoon.

"I know the man who is accused of killing Hedda Muir," Ira said. "His name is Rufus Flagg. He fancies himself a private detective, but his main occupation is handling problems for nobles who find themselves in sticky situations, usually involving women." He leaned toward her. "I know Flagg, and I know he's not a killer."

"But he killed Mrs. Muir, and he hurt Millie."

"If he did, it was most likely an accident." He looked out the window, and then at her. "The report said the house was ransacked as if he was looking for something."

"The man had been near the house. Perhaps he heard us talking about the letters."

"The evidence you would need to make a claim on his fortune."

She sat back. Never in a lifetime would Felicity do such a thing!

"I'd never take him to court. The scandal would be too horrible."

"But you'd have evidence, Lady Armstrong, and even though you know you'd never risk your reputation by making a claim, he couldn't take that chance." He paused. "Flagg must have told Lord Dudley about the letters, and then he sent Flagg to handle his sticky situation."

She shook her head.

"That can't be. Dudley came here before I knew about the letters."

"Yes, because as I said before, he discovered your secret, came to see you hoping to find you alone and vulnerable, but for some reason, failed to follow through. He then hired Flagg, who upon

186

hearing about the letters, hoped he'd make a few quid more if he brought them to Lord Dudley."

Sadness and revulsion left her speechless.

"But he's a gentleman," she said softly.

"I assure you, they are not immune to such thoughts."

"He came here alone."

"And if he came here to murder you, something stopped him, and now we must find Flagg." ." He finished his tea in one gulp, stood, pocketed his notebook and pen, and then picked up his hat and umbrella. "I'm going to stop by the police station on my way to the train. I'll tell the constable that he must have a man here at all times until we catch Flagg."

When she looked up at him, her eyes were red, and the circles under her eyes were darker than when he'd arrived.

"You're sure it's him."

"As sure as I can be. Don't you worry, milady. We will find him."

She looked in his eyes.

"Why did he run away after hurting Millie? Why didn't he kill us?"

"That I cannot answer, but I can say that if he knows Flagg failed, Lord Winston might send someone else." He sighed. "You and the girl should leave here. Is there somewhere else you can go?"

She shook her head and sat back in her chair.

"I have a pistol my father gave me."

"Be careful, milady. If you shoot and you miss, he might get the gun away from you."

Constable O'Toole came through the back door and saw Ira.

"I'm sorry, milady," O'Toole said. "Someone was supposed to be here. I've given him a good tongue lashing." He looked at Ira. "And you are?"

"D.I. Grayson of Scotland Yard. I apologize for not stopping at the police station before coming here."

O'Toole glared at the high and mighty detective.

"Walk outside with me," Ira said to O'Toole. He looked at Felicity. "Thank you for the tea, Lady Armstrong. I will let P.C. O'Toole know as soon as we have him."

"Thank you, Inspector."

The men walked outside where their horses waited.

"Constable, it's imperative that you or one of your men is here at all times."

"I know how to handle things well enough."

"I don't doubt that you do, but she and the girl were unprotected when I arrived. It's imperative that you have a man stationed here day and night."

"If he tries to come by here again, we'll catch the bloke."

"Very well, I'm on my way back to London. And if you don't catch him, I'll cable you when *we* have him in custody." As he began to walk the horse downhill, he remembered Flagg, and looked at O'Toole. "The man in the poster, his name is Rufus Flagg. He fancies himself a private detective."

Ira disappeared down the hill, and O'Toole watched until he saw Ira heading to town. He had promised to look after Lady Armstrong and Millie, but as he stood there, his eyes roaming the expanse between the cottage and town, he wondered if his promise to protect them was just an idle boast.

CHAPTER 24

*I*ra finished his tea as he stared at the notes in his notebook. He was mulling over his interview with Lady Armstrong and thinking about Lord Dudley Winston. He found her naiveté charming, but he feared it would be her undoing if she still had any doubts about Winston's intentions. Ira's gut knew that Winston was the precipitator of all that had taken place in the last few weeks, but he had no *evidence* to prove his theory. Now he had to search for real evidence against Lord Dudley Winston.

He looked at Cranston, who was reading a newspaper, got up, and went to his desk.

"May I disturb you?"

"You may. I was just reading the death notice for Prince Leopold. I knew him and I liked him. Such a shame him going that way."

"He was still a young man."

"Yes, he was."

"I interviewed Lady Felicity Armstrong. She was acquainted with Lord Winston. Do you know who responded to the house when his father died?"

Cranston shook his head.

"It was deemed a natural death."

"So no one was interviewed."

"There was no need for an inquest," Cranston said.

"Whose decision was that?"

Cranston took a deep breath.

"The doctor said he'd been ill for a long time. His death was not a surprise, and therefore, it was not necessary to investigate it further."

Ira sat in the chair beside Cranston's desk. He looked at the ceiling and sighed.

"Do you know the name of his butler?"

Cranston shook his head again. Ira frowned and sighed.

"Do you think Winston will talk to me?" he said.

Cranston sat back in his chair and now he looked at the ceiling.

"If he is involved, he might be willing to talk, especially if he thinks he can manipulate the situation. Right now he feels safe. He's rich, he's titled, and he has no history of consorting with the likes of Rufus Flagg."

"And if he had anything to do with his brother's death, or his father's, he's confident."

Ira walked back to his desk. He thought about the will and thought he now understood why it hadn't been filed. Dudley was waiting until Felicity was no longer an issue. As he looked at the blackboard, Cranston came to his desk with his ledger.

"Why don't you keep this while your investigating him," he said.

Ira ran his hand over it as if it were the Holy Grail. He began by looking up the Armstrong line, which included Lady Felicia Armstrong's scandalous death at the hands of her Spanish lover. Her will had been filed two days later. She had left Lady Felicity Armstrong a mere two hundred pounds a year.

Lord Harold Winston had two sons, one who died of an accidental gunshot wound in India, and Dudley, the current Lord Winston. There was no mention of Lord Dudley entering the military. The entire account of Roland Winston's death was taken from a newspaper article in the Times that had been affixed to the family page.

Why was Dudley in India? He wasn't in the military, and India was not the sort of place you'd expect to find a spoiled gentleman, unless the family had an estate there. There was no mention of one, so what was his purpose in being there?

Felicity was Dudley's half-sister. Had his father, in a moment of weakness or remorse, left her money?

"His other rival died in India," Ira said.

Sometimes the truth just rose out of nowhere and came out of Ira's mouth. At that moment, Ira knew that whatever had happened to Roland Winston had not been an accident. If so, it meant that Dudley was not afraid to do whatever was necessary to get what he wanted. But why, then, hadn't he killed Felicity when he had the chance?

Ira thought of Millie. She wasn't a soft creature to be dismissed. Perhaps she had intimidated him, or he suddenly thought someone might have seen him in town. Whatever the reason, Ira was thankful for it.

He looked at his pocket watch. It was twelve-thirty and his stomach was grumbling. It was an even day, so he took his lunch pail out of the bottom file drawer and ate his lunch while forming a list of those he wished to interview.

Number one on that list was Lord Winston's butler. He wanted to find out what Dudley had told him when he went to Tolwich. Number two on the list was the lord himself. He wrote down questions for each and memorized them as he ate, and decided that if the lord could eschew the rules of society, then so could he. He wouldn't send notice – he'd simply appear on his doorstep.

* * *

THE DIGNIFIED RED brick façade of the Winston townhouse typi-
fied the homes of the gentry, but the topiary on each side of the
doorway was cut to resemble giraffes and added a touch of
whimsy. Ira glanced at them, shook his head, and frowned as he
approached the front door. Unlike the topiary, Ira wasn't
whimsical.

A tall, sedate man with thinning gray hair answered his
knock. He wore a butler's uniform and had a silver tray, which he
held out to Ira. Ira held out his identification, the man read it,
and then he stepped to one side so Ira could come in. He didn't
ask for Ira's hat.

"Wait here," he said, and left Ira in the foyer.

Ira put his umbrella in the stand beside the front door and
looked at the foyer. The floors were tiled in black and white
squares. There was a round table in front of him with a vase of
long-stemmed yellow roses at its center. Beyond that, Ira saw a
large staircase going to the second floor. It was wider than his at
home, but not as wide as some he'd seen. There were double
doors on the left and right side of the room, but they were closed,
so he didn't know what sort of rooms were behind them.

Ira wandered to the doors on the right and opened them. The
room looked like a lady's parlor. It had a small fireplace with a
wing chair on each side. The décor was decidedly feminine,
which lead Ira to assume it had been Lady Winston's favorite
room, but then he recalled that she had died before Lord Harold
moved to London. Who had it been decorated for? The room
reminded Ira of his grandmother's parlor.

When the butler returned, Ira shut the doors.

"Might I ask you your name?" Ira said.

"It's Oliver, sir."

Oliver held out his hand for Ira's hat, and Ira gave it to him.
Oliver laid it on the table before leading Ira to the second floor.

"I'd like to speak to you before I leave," Ira said as they ascended the stairs.

"You'll have to ask Lord Dudley if I have permission to speak, sir."

Ira bristled at the idea of asking Dudley's permission, but he respected the man's concern. He would come back when Dudley wasn't there.

When they reached the top of the stairs, Oliver opened a door on the right side of the wide hallway. Two large windows at the end of the hall lit the area and made it feel bigger than it was. Ira followed Oliver into the library and looked at the trophies hung on the walls indicating that either the late lord or his sons had gone on safari in Africa or India.

"Detective Inspector Grayson, milord," Oliver said, and he was gone before Ira could ask him his last name.

Lord Dudley sat behind a mahogany desk embellished with detailed carvings. He wore a red silk smoking jacket, had a shock of curly dark blonde hair over one eye, an impertinent smile, and nails buffed to a high shine. He stood when Ira came in and extended his hand over the desk, but didn't come around to greet his guest.

The room was dark but for the light given by a fire in the massive stone fireplace that filled one wall. It was hot, but Dudley appeared not to notice, while beads of sweat dotted Ira's forehead.

The man is positively reptilian, Ira thought.

"Won't you sit down, Inspector?"

Dudley returned to his seat and put his feet on the desk, crossing one over the other. Ira saw the casual pose as Dudley's attempt to show Ira he wasn't the least intimidated by the diminutive detective. Ira sat and placed his arms on the arms of the chair, his hands resting on the ends carved to look like the heads of snakes. He flicked his fingers over the pronged tongues.

"So, what brings you here today, *Inspector*?"

His mocking smile irritated Ira, but he suppressed his anger. Nobles often felt above the law, and Dudley was no exception. Ira crossed his legs to show he was at ease.

"I'm pursuing the investigation of a murder that took place in Whitley. Your name was mentioned, and I'm simply here to confirm your whereabouts when the crime was committed."

Ira watched Dudley's eyes for any sign of agitation, but Dudley remained calm.

"I can assure you, Inspector, I have never been to what was it, Whitley? Why, I've never even heard of it."

"Are you acquainted with Felicity Armstrong?"

A slight rosy hue tinged Dudley's cheeks.

"You mean *Lady* Armstrong," he said. "Yes, I am. In fact, I recently visited her at her home."

He was telling the truth. Ira pressed him.

"Is it true that you arrived at her door unannounced?"

Dudley's eyes narrowed, he put his feet down, and clasped his hands on the desk.

"I'm afraid it is. It was a whim, you see." Dudley hesitated as if trying to remember what he'd said to Felicity, and then he smiled. "I thought she might be in need of some company. I had lost my father and knew what it was like to be left alone." He sat back. "Of course, I should have written her first, but, as I said, it was a whim."

"How do you know Lady Armstrong?"

"We were neighbors when I was young. After we moved to London, we didn't see them, but one day, my father decided to visit Rosendale and I went with him. I was seventeen at the time and I kept her company while our fathers talked."

"Did you see her after that visit?"

"No, not until that day in, what was the name of that town?" He paused. "Tolwich. That was it. Tolwich. I took the train and arrived sometime in the afternoon."

"She said you walked across the meadow rather than coming on a horse or in a carriage."

"I asked at the livery but they didn't have a horse to hire."

Ira took out his notebook and wrote this down. He'd ask O'Toole to see if anyone at the livery remembered Lord Dudley.

"Besides, it felt good to walk. The weather that day was wonderful."

"How long did you stay in Tolwich?"

"I took the train back to London that evening."

"Lady Armstrong said you didn't stay long. That's a long way to go for such a short visit."

"I could see Lady Armstrong was uncomfortable. I knew my breach of etiquette bothered her and decided to go before she asked me to leave." He looked at Ira. "Pardon me, Inspector, but what has this to do with a murder?"

"Lady Armstrong was visiting a woman named Hedda Muir. She lived in Whitley, and she was murdered."

"I've never heard of a Hedda Muir," Dudley said.

"She was the housekeeper at Rosendale when Lady Armstrong was a child." Ira paused. "Do you know a man named Rufus Flagg?"

Ira saw a flicker of recognition in Dudley's eyes, and then the lord pretended to dust lint off his trousers.

"I've never heard of him either."

"He's a private detective, the sort of man who will do just about anything for the right price. I've been told by a reliable source that he has been working for you."

Dudley smiled. "Well, they were mistaken. I have no such person in my employ."

Ira stared into Dudley's eyes.

"So you have no knowledge of his whereabouts?"

"None whatsoever."

Ira uncrossed his legs and took a folded piece of paper from an inside pocket in his suit jacket.

"Scotland Yard received this poster from Whitley." He held it up, and watched Dudley's face. "This man is a suspect in the murder of Hedda Muir. Her neighbor saw him and gave a description."

Dudley shook his head slowly.

"Lady Armstrong also saw him when he was following her and Hedda Muir through town and lurking outside Mrs. Muir's home. When I stopped in Tolwich the day before yesterday, Lady Armstrong told me she'd seen him again. He'd ransacked her house and assaulted her young ward."

The muscle in Dudley's jaw twitched.

"What a terrible man, and that girl is not her ward; she's her scullery maid."

Dudley didn't try to hide his contempt for the girl. Perhaps she *had*, as Ira suspected, seen through his façade and said something that had upset him.

Good girl, Millie.

"But it looked to me as if they were rather close, like sisters," Ira said.

Ira watched for a reaction to the word "sister," but Dudley's face remained passive. Perhaps he didn't know about Lady Armstrong.

"So you have no idea why this man would be following them?"

"Inspector, I've told you I don't know him, so how could I possibly know why he was following them?"

Ira hated his smug attitude, but he saw no point in trying to get him to admit he knew Flagg until he had further proof. He stood so he could look down on Dudley.

"Very well, then. Thank you for seeing me."

"I'm sorry I was unable to help you, Inspector."

Dudley stood and tugged at the bell pull. Within seconds, Oliver returned.

Ira's mind was filled with doubt. As sure as he was that Dudley had something to do with what was happening to Felicity

Armstrong, Dudley seemed confident and unperturbed by Ira's questioning.

He followed Oliver down the steps and to the door where Oliver handed Ira his hat as he waited for Ira to retrieve his umbrella. He put on his hat and went out the door Oliver held open, and it shut as another question entered Ira's mind. He knocked, and Oliver reopened it.

"Have you had any unsavory visitors within the last month?"

"No, sir."

"I see."

"Will that be all, sir?"

Ira nodded, and Oliver shut the door. It wasn't until Ira was back at his desk that he remembered he hadn't gotten Oliver's last name.

In the library, Dudley stood at the window facing the street and looked down at the sidewalk. The inspector was walking away, and Dudley felt a sense of relief. The man was clever, but it was obvious he had no evidence of Dudley's association with Rufus Flagg.

No, Dudley had been careful, and he smiled as he watched the inspector disappear down the street.

CHAPTER 25

Rufus Flagg

*R*ufus was angry. He hadn't meant to hurt the girl; he hadn't meant to hurt anyone but Lady Armstrong. For the last week, he'd been too far away from home, and now all he wanted was a hot meal and a pint.

Why had he agreed to such a foolish plan? The money. He had heard what the lord was offering and it blinded him.

Now, as he ran from the cottage in Tolwich, he knew he'd have to go back to London. He'd have to return the lord's blood money.

As Rufus entered the rail station, he saw the poster with a drawing of him in his bowler hat. He was wanted for murder. The old woman had died.

He took off his hat hoping it would work as a disguise, and hid behind a column until the train arrived. He went to the seat farthest from the entrance, left a quid note in his pocket for the conductor, put the hat over his face, and stayed that way until he got to London.

It was dark when he reached London. He walked with his

head down and stopped off at a pub, drank two pints, and then he noticed a young man staring at him. He left, and the young man followed him until Rufus dodged him by slipping down an alley.

He didn't want to face the lord, but he had taken two thousand quid in advance. The lord was rich; he could tell the coppers the money had been stolen, and what could Rufus say? The judges would believe the lord, and Rufus would end up in jail, or hanged for the murder of the old woman. He hoped that if he gave the money back...he hoped the lord would just forget his name.

He knew where the lord lived; he'd followed Winston home the night he offered Rufus the job. He didn't like Winston, but he did like the idea of having five thousand quid.

He stood outside the townhouse and shuffled his feet as he tried to come up with an excuse for his failure, and decided to tell Winston the truth. Nothing he'd planned had gone right, and the rural towns had confused him. People had seen him, and he kept falling asleep when he was supposed to be keeping watch.

After the first night, Rufus knew he couldn't kill Felicity. He heard the ladies talking about the letters, and he got it into his head that if he gave them to Winston, it might be enough to call them even. He never found the letters, and now, with half the country looking for him, all he wanted was to board a ship heading for America. Maybe Winston would let him keep the fare.

He wiggled his toes and felt the banknotes, which he kept in his boots. Rufus took the money out of his boots before he knocked on the front door.

"I'm here to see Lord Winston," he told Oliver.

Oliver looked him up and down, asked his name, and then told him to wait on the stoop. Rufus wasn't insulted; he knew that's the way "they" treated people like him. A few moments passed and the old man returned, let him inside, took his hat, and led Rufus up to the library on the second floor.

* * *

D.I. Ira Grayson

P.C. Palmer was sitting at Ira's desk and looking at the poster.

"I'm sure it were him," Palmer said. "He was wearing a bowler hat and downing a pint when I come in."

"You're sure it was Flagg?" Ira asked.

"Aye, because I kept me eye on him and he kept hiding his face. When I moved closer to him, he left in a hurry. I lost him when he went down an alley."

"Where is this pub?"

Palmer gave Ira the address, and accompanied the detective to the pub, which was near Palmer's flat. The place was empty at noonday, and the barkeep recognized Palmer right off and nodded at him.

"Aye, what brings you in so early?" the barkeep asked.

"Looking for a bloke I saw in here last night," Palmer said.

Ira took out the photograph of Flagg from his police file and held it up. The barkeep nodded.

"Aye, he was here. Don't know his name though."

"Has he been here before?" Ira asked.

"Could've been. He looks like any other working bloke."

"Could you look at it again, please," Ira said as he laid the photograph on the bar.

"It's important, Ted," Palmer said. "He's killed someone in Whitley."

Ted looked again, but shook his head.

"Sorry, Ken. I don't know his name."

They left the pub in dismay for it was the only lead Ira had had since finding out that Flagg was in Tolwich. He looked at

Palmer and then at the street. He had asked the patrolling officers to keep a lookout for him, but so far, Palmer was the only one to come forward. Time was passing and if he didn't catch up with Flagg soon, his trail would grow cold, and Hedda Muir's murder would go unpunished.

Ira took out his notebook and looked for the address he'd written down when he'd looked up Flagg's file.

"Let's go and see if we can find someone who knows where he lives," Ira said.

Palmer followed him, reducing the length of his strides to match those of Inspector Grayson's. He was so excited to be part of the investigation that he could barely contain his smile. Ira looked up at the lad, who had just passed his twentieth birthday, and saw his enthusiastic grin. He liked the boy and was happy to have someone with a desire to learn by his side.

A canvas of the building where Flagg had lived until a few months before was of little help as none of the residents had befriended Flagg. Only one remembered him and he said he hadn't seen him since Christmas. That gave them a timeline, but nothing else. Not even the landlord could tell them what had happened to Rufus Flagg.

"Took off without a word," the man said. "Owes me for December. If you find him, let him know I don't forget."

They walked a few blocks and asked passersby if they knew him or had seen him, but no one claimed to recognize him, and it seemed to Ira that they were either accomplished liars or that Flagg had been a ghost.

It was almost four when they returned to the Yard and Palmer was relieved of duty for the day. Ira went to his desk and made notes regarding their progress. He recalled Cranston saying that Rufus wasn't a killer, but, Hedda Muir was dead, and witnesses described him as the assailant.

Lady Armstrong was a credible witness, she had a connection to Lord Dudley Armstrong, and she had seen Flagg. The interview with Lord Dudley had proved less than enlightening, or had it? Ira's gut had been bothering him ever since he left the townhouse and now he thought of Dudley Winston again.

Ira recalled the library in the Winston townhouse and noticed the lack of any family portraits or photographs of Lord Harold or Roland Winston, and Dudley seemed far too, well, happy for a man who had recently lost his father. The picture developing in Ira's mind was not a pretty one, but rather a sinister effigy, riddled with scars.

After days of mulling over all he'd learned, Ira firmly believed that it was Lord Dudley Winston who hired Flagg to harm Lady Armstrong. Until he found Flagg, his thoughts would remain a theory, and his supervisor wouldn't agree to let him search the Winston townhouse.

Ira went to the window and looked at the wet street. Pedestrians huddled under umbrellas as they walked by. It was just another day to them, but in Tolwich, two young women waited to hear that he had caught their attacker.

He left the window, took his jacket from the chair behind his desk, grabbed his topcoat from the coat rack, and took his umbrella from the stand. His wife would be delighted to see him home early and would, perhaps, have made him his favorite – Shepherd's Pie.

CHAPTER 26

Kingston on the Thames

*L*ittle Mary Farmer clutched her favorite rag doll to her chest.

"No," she said.

Her older brothers, Tommy and Jimmy, were circling her, and grabbing at the doll's legs. They smiled at each other, nodded, and then each took a leg and pried the doll out of little Mary's arms.

"Giver her back!" Mary cried.

"Come and get her," Tommy, the eldest, said.

Despite their mother's warning to stay away from the riverbank, the boys had gone there to catch toads, and Mary followed them. Mary knew she shouldn't be there, and she kept looking behind her to see if her mother was walking toward her.

Now, though, as they twisted Nellie, ripping her seams and spilling her stuffing, Mary wished she'd obeyed her mother. She began to cry, and Tommy smirked.

"You're nothing but a big baby," he said as he twirled Nellie around his head by her half torn leg.

Mary's fear turned to anger, and she ran to him and kicked Tommy in the leg.

"Give her back!"

Tommy dropped the doll and rubbed his shin.

"Why, you little…," he said, and then pushed Mary, picked up Nellie, and hurled her through the air.

The doll landed near the tall grass at the edge of the river-bank. Mary went to retrieve her and was dismayed to find that Nellie had landed facedown in the muck. She picked up the doll, and then saw what lie underneath. Nellie had landed in the palm of a hand, and as Mary followed the length of the arm attached, she backed away with widened eyes and screamed.

"Shut your pie hole," Tommy said, but Mary kept screaming.

"Something's wrong," Jimmy said.

He ran to his sister, hoping to find a large, ugly toad he could chase her with. He smiled broadly as he came alongside her and looked behind the tall grass. Like his sister, he, too, backed away and yelled at the top of his lungs.

"Bloody hell," Tommy said.

He walked to them shaking his head.

"Just a couple of babies, that's what you lot are."

He followed their fearful eyes and saw the hand. His bluster vanished as fear rose up his spine. He looked at the arm, shoulder, and head of the corpse and held his breath as the gag reflex kicked in, warning him to look away.

The head was at a slight angle, the lips blue, and the skin gray. The eyes were gone, leaving empty, black holes. A stench rose from it that became more intense with each second they stood there, and Jimmy was the first to tear himself away from the sight and run toward home.

Tommy, however, didn't scream, but as his stomach turned over, he turned to little Mary, and vomited all over her pinafore.

* * *

IRA'S GUT was turning cartwheels as he read the newspaper while sipping his breakfast tea. The small article in the Times about three children finding a body on the banks of the Thames in Kingston spoke to Ira. The inquest had been held the day the body was found, and the jury had agreed upon the cause of death – murder. The victim had yet to be identified, and all inquiries were to be addressed to the coroner.

Ira stood, kissed his wife on the cheek, put on his hat, grabbed his umbrella, and went to Scotland Yard. He didn't know if Supervisor Kent would approve his trip to Kingston, but he might give Ira permission to go if he paid his own train fare.

Supervisor Kent was a gruff, bewhiskered man who'd been policing the city for two decades. His girth had increased since becoming supervisor, but his mind was keen, and he always sided with his officers when it came to investigations. For that, he won the undying loyalty of his men. Ira knocked on Kent's door and waited for permission to enter.

"Come in," Kent said.

The office was small, with one window looking out onto the courtyard. The desk was made of pine and stained to look like mahogany. It faced the door. A newspaper was on the desk and a line of smoke rose from a pipe resting in an ashtray. The odor of cherry tobacco was pleasing, and the supervisor looked calm. It was a good time to make a request.

"Sir," Ira said. "A body has been found in Kingston."

"I'm aware," Kent said.

"I'd like to go to Kingston and talk to the coroner. Perhaps he took a photograph, and if it's Flagg, I could identify him."

Kent sat back and put his hands on his stomach.

"Now why do you think it's Flagg? The description reads that it's a male with a balding head. That's half the men in London."

"I feel it in my gut, sir."

Ira's gut was not to be dismissed lightly. Kent looked up at him and shook his head.

"Your gut, eh, well, I can give you permission, but not the fare."

"I'll pay it myself."

Kent sighed. "If it turns out to be Flagg, I might be able to reimburse you, but I can't promise you anything."

"I'm happy to do it, sir."

Kent smiled, and Ira thought he looked like a satisfied walrus.

"And if it is Flagg, what will that tell you?"

Ira looked out the window at the rain.

"I've been to Whitley and Towich. I've spoken to witnesses, and I've determined that Lord Dudley Winston might have hired Flagg to harm Lady Felicity Armstrong."

"*Might* have hired him."

Ira felt his face flush.

"Yes."

"Based on what *evidence?*" Kent asked.

Ira swallowed.

"My interviews, and the witnesses."

Kent sighed, looked toward heaven, and shook his head again.

"Grayson, you are one of my best detectives, but you know as well as I that we need more than your gut when it comes to investigating a lord of the realm."

"I do, sir."

Kent looked at Ira. He liked the man, but proving the guilt of a member of the ton was difficult, and that was when there was irrefutable evidence of a crime. They had solicitors and more money than God, and the Crown Court was loath to prosecute a person whose character was embedded in their title.

"Go and find some hard evidence," Kent said.

"Thank you, sir."

* * *

IRA DISEMBARKED from the train in Kingston and went straight to the police station. Ira asked the P.C. in reception where he could find the coroner, and was given an address about a quarter of a mile away. The building was two stories high, and the coroner's office was found on the first floor. The foyer was empty, but the doors were clearly marked.

Ira walked into an office on the left side of the foyer and saw a man sitting at his desk. He was as wide as he was tall. He, like Kent, had a walrus mustache, but no other visible hair, except his eyebrows.

"Yes," the man said without looking up.

"I'm D.I. Grayson from Scotland Yard. Did you oversee the inquest of the body found on the riverbank?"

"Nasty business that," the man said. "Bloomfield."

"Bloomfield?" Ira said.

"I'm Bloomfield."

"Yes, indeed. Are you the coroner?"

"Aye, and I supervised the inquest. I suppose you want to see the body?"

A tingle went up Ira's spine.

"Do you still have the body?"

Bloomfield shook his head.

"I have the photographs."

Ira's disappointment was hard to hide, but when Bloomfield took the photographs out of a file on his desk, Ira perked up. He sat in the chair in front of the desk.

The first photograph was of the full body. It was partially clothed in a shirt and pants, but was missing shoes and socks. The next photograph showed his face and the black holes where the victim's eyes had been were startling. Ira looked at the scruffy beard, the nose that had been broken and badly set, and hair that was usually covered with a bowler hat, and knew it was Rufus Flagg.

Ira looked at the scruffy beard, the nose that had been broken and badly set, and hair that was usually covered with a bowler hat, and knew it was Rufus Flagg.

"It's Rufus Flagg," he said.

"Someone you know?" Bloomfield asked.

"Someone I've been looking for." He looked at the full body photograph again. "What was the cause of death?"

"Doc said he was strangled."

"Were you able to determine how he got there?"

"The water rolls south, Inspector."

"I see," Ira said.

"We buried him in an unmarked grave behind St. Mary's," Bloomfield said. "Did he have any family?"

"None that I know of," Ira said.

"Well, he's there if anyone wants him."

Ira took a long look at the photograph of Flagg's head, and then stood.

"Thank you, Mr. Bloomfield. You've been most helpful."

"I'd like to know what happened to the bloke," Bloomfield said.

"I'll write you as soon as I know."

Ira walked to the rail station and waited for the next train to London. He thought about Flagg's eyes. The report said fish ate the eyes, and as he thought about that, Ira's stomach turned, and he ran to a nearby trash bin.

CHAPTER 27

Felicity woke before dawn, went outside, and looked toward the pastel horizon. Her thoughts went to Captain Fowler, for she had not heard from Mr. Benjamin, and she felt the need to move on with her life. As she gazed at the beautiful colors in the sky, she knew that her dream of entrepreneurship was over. The decision to abandon hope had not come with a resounding boom, but with a whimper as it drifted away, and she felt sad, yet eager to make a new plan for her future.

A horse was tied to a tree next to the house, and she saw that the man, a fisherman who had volunteered to keep watch, was sitting against the house sound asleep. He had chosen not to sleep in the chair so he could remain vigilant. The fact that he hadn't heard her open the cottage door and walk past him did little to calm her anxiety.

She went inside, cleaned the ashes from the stove, placed fresh logs in the bin, and then lit a fire under them. It would take a while for them to heat, so she went to the garden and picked some apples from the tree. It would be a nice day, and she decided it was time for her and Millie to take a walk to town.

The laudanum helped Millie, but it made her sleep longer.

When Millie woke up, she looked for Felicity, saw her out the window, and then started a pot of oats. She also put on the teakettle. She was able to do it all with one arm, and smiled broadly when Felicity came inside.

"We're going to town today," Felicity said. She put the apples on the table. "I want to make a pie and we need flour."

The pain in Millie's arm had subsided and she was eager to get out of the house for a while. She loved looking at the books on Mr. Tompkins' shelf and finding one she hadn't read. He kept them at the back of the store and lent them to his customers.

After they ate their breakfast, they dressed and walked outside. The man was still asleep, and Felicity hesitated before waking him.

"Hello," she said.

He rubbed his nose and opened his eyes.

"Oh, milady. I didn't hear you."

"It's quite all right. Millie and I are walking to town."

"I'll come with you," he said. He looked at the horse. "I'll ride slow."

Felicity held Millie's hand as they walked down the hill. The man tipped his hat and went ahead of them, but was true to his word and was never more than a few yards away. They didn't talk while they walked, for each was thinking about the man in the bowler hat.

It had been a few days since they'd heard anything about him, and Constable O'Toole hadn't come by with any news. They looked from side to side as they made their way across the meadow and were happy to see the old Roman road turn to the cobblestones that lined the town streets.

They went past the police station and the man waved good-bye. Someone would take his place and would be there when they went home.

The owner of the pub was sweeping the slab outside his front door when they walked by and he waved.

"Aye, it's a grand day," he said. "You look lovely today, Miss Millie."

She smiled and put her nose in the air, and Felicity touched her arm.

"Oh, Millie, you have an admirer."

"Oh, that's just Mr. Calloway. He's just being nice because of my arm."

"Still, you should thank him for the compliment."

Millie stopped and looked at Mr. Calloway.

"Thank you," she said.

He winked and continued to sweep.

Mr. Tompkins' Mercantile was across the street from the market stalls, and he often complained that they were stealing his business, but since they weren't there year round, the mayor refused to make them move. It was a bone of contention between Mr. Tompkins and the mayor, and their feud had gone on for twenty years.

Felicity and Millie walked up the steps and into the store, which had several aisles, each arranged by Mrs. Tompkins. Millie went straight to the back of the store while Felicity went to the sidewall where bolts of fabric were lined up by color on a shelf.

She wanted to buy a yard to make a new sling for Millie. Her eyes went to a hunter green with bright pink daisies.

"Millie," Felicity said. "Can you come here?"

Millie followed the sound of her voice to the fabrics and saw her holding up the fabric.

"It's lovely, miss."

Felicity held it against the soiled sling.

"I want to make you a new sling," she said. Millie's eyes lit up. "I guess this will do."

Millie returned to the bookshelf and Felicity took the fabric to the counter where Mrs. Tompkins had a yardstick.

"Oh, it's lovely," she said when Felicity laid the fabric on the counter.

"It's for a new sling," Felicity said.

"Oh, poor dear. When I heard about what happened, it near broke my heart."

"She's feeling much better."

"She's such a little soldier. Carrying on after all she's been through."

"I must say I admire her," Felicity said. "I don't know how I would have acted had it happened to me. She never complains."

"We're all tested, milady."

"Yes, we are." Felicity ran her hand over the fabric. "Half a yard should do." She watched Mrs. Tompkins measure the fabric. "Mrs. Tompkins, I've decided I'd rather be called miss from now on."

Mrs. Tompkins looked up from her cutting.

"Do you mean it, milady?"

"I do."

Mrs. Tompkins looked as if she had something else to say, but chose not to.

"Very well, miss."

Felicity knew Mrs. Tompkins would tell anyone who came in that she was calling herself miss now, but she didn't mind. It would save her having to explain it to everyone herself.

Millie came to the counter, but she didn't have a book.

"No book?" Felicity asked.

"I've read them all."

"Then perhaps we should take the train to Colton and look in the bookstore there."

Millie looked at her as if she'd gone mad.

"A real bookstore, miss?"

"Yes, a real bookstore."

Mrs. Tompkins folded the fabric into a square and Felicity put it into her basket.

"Oh, Millie, we need flour."

Millie fetched the flour and Felicity paid Mrs. Tompkins. When they got outside, Millie sniffed the air.

"I smell cinnamon buns."

"Isn't that heavenly?" Felicity said.

The bakery was in an old building a few yards away. The man who owned it had added a large, modern oven, but continued to use the oven built into the fireplace for it sent the aroma of his baked goods into the air, luring hungry customers from all over town.

There was a large window in front and tables for those who wanted to eat their purchases while they were still warm. The place was always full of customers, but it was later in the day and there were tables available.

"Can we go in, miss?"

Felicity had received her monthly allowance, and decided to splurge even if it meant they only had fish once a week.

"Yes, and we'll have a cup of tea, too."

They went inside and Millie went to a table while Felicity ordered the buns and a loaf of bread. She brought them to the table and Millie held hers to her nose and sighed with delight.

"These are better than anything else I can think of," she said.

"They are delicious. They remind me of the hot cross buns cook would make for Good Friday. Mrs. Muir and I would have them with tea in the garden."

Felicity's expression changed for a moment as the sad memory of Mrs. Muir's death filled her mind.

No, she thought. *She'd want me to enjoy this moment.*

"Thank you, miss," Millie said.

"You're most welcome."

The man was watching them as they ate their cinnamon buns. They were sitting in the center of the window and from the outside it looked as if they were in a picture frame. Felicity looked happy. The girl looked too thin, but seemed to be enjoying the pastry. It was a sweet scene, and as he watched them chatting away, he wondered if she would ever give him the time of day.

"There you are," Constable O'Toole said. "Tompkins is looking for you."

The man glanced at O'Toole and smiled.

"Then I best be going back to work."

The man hobbled away from O'Toole, who pitied him. Sam was new in town and often looked sad. He told those who asked that he'd lost his leg while serving in the army. Mr. Tompkins had a compassionate heart and had given Sam a job and a room at the back of his store, and so far, Sam had proved to be an honest and willing employee.

O'Toole watched Sam go into the mercantile and then went into the bakery. Mrs. Tompkins had told him not to call her lady anymore, so when he saw Miss Armstrong through the window, he was eager to share a bit of news he'd received that morning. He went inside and straight to the table where she and Millie were savoring their cinnamon buns. Felicity looked up at him and smiled.

"They do look tempting," he said. He patted his belly. "My wife says no more or she'll leave me." He smiled, and the ladies laughed. "So, I've good news for you both. That man won't be bothering you anymore."

Felicity's eyes widened.

"He's dead. They found him in Kingston on the riverbank."

Felicity put her bun down and looked sad, but Millie looked triumphant.

"Good," she said. "He deserved to die."

"Millie!" Felicity cried. "No one deserves to die."

Millie blushed. "I'm sorry."

But she wasn't sorry at all. She was glad for now she wouldn't have to think about him coming into their house at night.

"Do they know who he is?" Felicity asked.

"Man's name was Flagg."

"Do they know why he killed Mrs. Muir?"

"That detective is still looking into that, mil…miss." He looked at the hot rolls in a basket on the counter. "Well, I'd best be going. I'll leave you now to your cinnamon buns."

"Thank you, Constable O'Toole."

He tipped his hat and left them to finish their treats, and despite her admonition to Millie, she, too, was glad he wouldn't be bothering them anymore. She was also glad to hear O'Toole say *miss*.

When they left the bakery, Millie noticed when Felicity didn't stop at the market for potatoes, and felt the pennies in her pocket.

"I think I'll buy some potatoes," she said, and before Felicity could stop her, she was off to the stall a few yards away. She returned with two large spuds and put them into the basket.

The walk home was easy and they both felt relieved of a terrible burden. The sun was bright and the sea blue, and for the first time in a long time, Felicity felt like going to the beach.

"I'm think I'll go to the beach when we get home," she said. "Why don't you come with me?"

Millie looked up at Felicity and smiled broadly.

"It will be just like a holiday," she said.

"We'll take a picnic."

"And put our feet in the water."

They climbed the hill fast for they were both eager to change their clothes and make their picnic lunch. When they got inside, Felicity took her purchases out of the basket and put a tablecloth in it, along with bread, jam, and two apples. She changed out of her blouse and skirt and into a shift and apron, and before leaving the house, she made Millie a new sling.

CHAPTER 28

Oliver

Oliver sat at the kitchen table while Mrs. Green kneaded a loaf of bread. Her actions stirred memories of another he had worked with many years ago, and for a moment, his heart ached. Mrs. Green had retained a youthful appearance despite her years of service, and had been blessed with her mother's, golden hair. She looked at the bread as she worked it, and then cast her blue eyes on Oliver.

"It's odd him going off like that," Mrs. Green said.

"He's an odd one," Oliver said.

"But he left Chester here. What's he plan to do, dress himself?"

"It's none of our business what he plans to do."

Mrs. Green stopped kneading and looked at Oliver. Her expression telegraphed her thoughts, and Oliver smiled.

"I know you prefer it when he tells us everything he's up to," Oliver said, "but it's up to him what he'll share, and what he'll withhold."

"Well, I still don't like it."

"So, what are your plans for the day?" he said.

She picked up the dough and turned it over.

"Haven't had time to think about it," she said.

"The staff was overjoyed when I let them go for the day," Oliver said.

"They was out that door so fast it made me head spin."

She laughed out loud, and then looked at Oliver's face.

"What's wrong, dearie?"

"Oh, nothing to worry about. I'm just thinking of something I read in the paper."

She kept her eyes on him as she pummeled the dough.

"Why don't we go to the concert in the park this afternoon?" she asked. "I can leave the bread to rise."

"I'm afraid I wouldn't be very good company, Flora."

She put her hands on her hips and shook her head.

"I wish you'd share it with me."

"Share what?"

"Whatever it is that's got you all tied up in knots."

He smiled at her, but it was half-hearted, and Mrs. Green felt it was wrong to nag at him. She continued to knead the bread, and then put it in a bowl and placed a towel over it to let it rise.

"Are you sure you don't want to go out? We could have some tea in the garden café. They have such nice dainties, and we wouldn't have to rush."

"You go along, Flora, and go to the concert, too."

"T'wouldn't be any fun going alone."

"But I insist."

He took out his wallet and put a pound note on the table.

"If I recall, you had a birthday not long ago. Go and have a day off all to yourself."

"If I didn't know you so well, I'd be insulted," she said as she picked up the note. "But I can see that you're determined to get us all out of the house, so I'll go, but I won't enjoy one minute of it."

She hung her apron on a hook in the pantry and then went

upstairs to change her clothes. Oliver allowed the quiet, warm kitchen to settle his nerves, but something had been working on him for a long time, and this was the first opportunity he'd had to think on it properly. Twenty minutes passed before he heard Mrs. Green come down the stairs and he heard each "click" of her footsteps on the tiled floor as she came toward him.

"I'll wait if you've changed your mind," she said.

She was wearing her favorite broad-brimmed straw hat decorated with ribbons, feathers, and one large ostrich plume stuck in the ribbon around the brim. Her gown was a hand-me-down from her last mistress, who often gave her day clothes to the women on staff. It was navy blue with white pinstripes, straight sleeves, a peplum over a ruffled skirt that covered her feet, and a bustle that added a few inches to her generous bottom. It was odd to see her dressed in her street clothes, and for a moment, he couldn't take his eyes off her.

"Oliver," she said. "Are you sure you want to stay here alone?"

"Quite sure."

"Then I'll be off."

She looked at him as if she were trying to decide whether to go, but chose to leave, and he waited until he heard the door close before rising from the table.

Oliver climbed the stairs to the second floor and glanced at the library. In all his years of service, he had been loyal to his employers, but recent events had placed a burden on his devotion to the Winston family. He would never admit it to anyone, least of all another member of staff, but he detested the young lord, and had been contemplating in earnest the idea of leaving his household. He'd sent letters in answer to ads in the Times, and had received a reply from one, a manor in Dorchester, but he had yet to reply.

It was during his perusal of the ads in the Times that Oliver had seen an article regarding a body found in Kingston. A drawing of the victim had caught his eye, and a trickle of fear rose up his spine. He tore the article from the paper and had placed it in his bureau drawer.

Oliver stood on the second floor landing and wondered what to do. Should he ignore his conscience and continue on as he had for years, tending his duties, earning his pay until the day he chose to retire, or should he honor his conscience and tell what he knew?

His indecision was interrupted by the doorbell, and he looked down the stairs as if whoever was there would simply walk inside. He could ignore it; everyone was gone for the day. Minutes passed as he wavered at the top stair, and the bell rang again. Whoever it was, they were not going away. He went downstairs, picked up the silver card tray as if Lord Dudley was in residence, and opened the door.

The small, intrusive detective had returned, and Oliver held the silver tray behind him.

"Oliver, isn't it?" Ira asked.

"Yes, sir. Lord Dudley is away, sir."

"I'm not here to talk to Lord Dudley. I'm here to talk to you."

* * *

IRA NOTICED that Oliver was dressed in street clothes. He also noticed a slight twitch in the butler's jaw as they stood at the door.

"May I come in?" Ira asked.

Oliver moved aside. Ira passed him and waited near the table for direction from Oliver. The old man seemed vexed, as indicated by the expression on his face, and Ira's gut began speaking to him.

This man knows something. It's disturbing, and he isn't sure what to do.

"Has he gone to his club?" Ira asked.

"No, sir. He told me he'd be gone for a few days and nothing more."

"Then we won't be interrupted."

"No, sir. Would you like some tea?"

"If you have it made."

"Do you mind sitting in the kitchen?"

"Not at all."

Oliver led him down the hallway to the last room on the left. The kitchen was long but not wide, and the table filled the center and had a chair for each servant in residence. Ira sat at the head while Oliver put the kettle on to boil. Ira took out his notebook and waited for Oliver to take his seat.

Oliver took out the teacups and would glance at Ira from time to time. He was wondering if it was divine providence that had sent the detective, or happenstance. Whatever the reason, he was glad that the decision to talk to the police had been taken out of his hands.

When he had finished preparing the teacups, he sat. The lines in his face were deep, and his hair was almost pure white. He began to speak before Ira could ask him a question.

"I'm a good servant," Oliver said.

Oliver kept his eyes lowered, and Ira saw his lips tremble as he waited for Oliver to continue. Oliver felt the tear form and was powerless to stop it from rolling down his cheek.

"I've earned my position. I've kept silent." Ira put his hands on his legs, sat back, and listened. "I've saved money, and I never complained."

"How long have you worked for Lord Dudley?" Ira asked.

"Two years."

"Where were you before you joined this household?"

Oliver took a handkerchief from his pocket and wiped his eyes. He sat up straight and looked Ira in the eye.

"I was the head butler at Rosendale."

Rosendale. Ira remembered the name, but couldn't settle on

the context. He began swiping the pages of his notebook and found the name. Felicity Armstrong had mentioned it when he interviewed her.

"You worked for the Armstrong family," Ira said. Oliver nodded. "You came here when Lady Armstrong lost the manor house."

Oliver held his head up. "Lord Harold asked me to come here." He looked into Ira's eyes again. "*He* was a good man."

"You liked Lord Harold."

"Aye, I did like him. He and Lord Michael had been friends long ago, so I knew him. When he offered me the post, I took it, and I served him well."

"And Lord Dudley? Do you serve him well?"

Ira watched Oliver's face as he thought of Dudley. He tried to mask his anger, but his lack of success made Ira happy. It was easy to coax the truth from an angry man.

"What do you think of Lord Dudley, Oliver?"

"He's not his father."

"What was his relationship with his father?" Ira asked.

"I wasn't here when his brother died, but those who were, told me that Lord Harold was never the same again. He loved that boy."

"But not so Lord Dudley."

Oliver shook his head.

"He's more interested in his social calendar than his duties here."

Ira looked at his notebook.

"How do you feel about Lady Armstrong?"

Oliver smiled and grew tender.

"She was a sweet lass, that one." Then Oliver's face fell. "Hedda and I raised her."

"So you would say she was like a daughter to you."

"Aye. I loved her dearly." Oliver looked into Ira's eyes. "No one else seemed to care about her. Hedda and I…"

Now tears rolled freely, and he turned his face away from Ira.

"I'm sorry for your loss," Ira said.

"She was a good woman. I should have gone with her. I should have married her."

Ira was quiet while Oliver collected himself.

"I've spoken with Lady Armstrong. She told me something in confidence."

"She told you Lord Harold was her father."

"Did anyone besides you and Hedda know?"

He shrugged.

"Perhaps the others servants knew, but Lady Phillipa was a good mistress. I don't think any one of them would have wanted to hurt her, or Lady Felicity."

"Do you think Lord Harold hired you to keep his secret?"

Oliver shook his head.

"He hired me because he trusted me." Oliver closed his eyes as a painful memory arose in his mind. "He confided in me."

"What did he tell you, Oliver?"

Oliver sighed as the whistle on the teakettle blew. He got up and filled the teacups, and then brought them to the table.

"Cream?" he said.

"No, thank you."

Oliver returned to his seat and put his hands around the warm teacup.

"He told me he had made a new will. He knew Lord Dudley would be angry if he found out, and told me what it said in the event..." His lips quivered. "He wanted someone to know in case something happened to him."

"Did something happen to him?"

Oliver looked at the wall.

"He summoned me to the library after his solicitor left. He told me how much he'd wished Roland were alive." Oliver took a deep breath. "He said he had left Lady Felicity some money. He'd put her in his will as his goddaughter. She was to inherit twenty thousand pounds."

Ira gasped. It was the motive he'd been searching for.

"Did Dudley find out?"

Oliver closed his eyes and nodded his head.

"He was outside the door when Lord Harold told me. I found him there when I opened the door to leave, and I saw his eyes. He was so angry."

Ira got up and began to pace. His gut was twisting and he could not sit still.

"Did Dudley kill his father?"

"A few weeks later, Lord Harold became ill. Dudley went to his room and closed the door, but I stood outside." He stopped and looked into his teacup. "The inquest said it was natural." He looked at Ira. "I was there, inspector, I heard them."

"What did you hear?"

"I heard Lord Dudley smother the life out of him."

"Why didn't you tell me when I was here?"

Oliver shook his head. His red rimmed eyes and slumped shoulders told Ira all he needed to know. Oliver was no one. He was just a servant. He had heard, but not seen, what happened, and after the inquest declared it a natural death, who would believe him?

"You could have told me," Ira said. "I would have listened to you."

"When I came here, one of the under butlers told me to keep away from Lord Dudley. They believed he had killed his brother." Oliver looked into Ira's eyes. "He would have killed me."

Ira looked at Oliver. He had reason to fear Dudley.

"The will hasn't been filed," Ira said. "Has anyone talked about that?"

Oliver shook his head.

Ira's gut was talking. Now he was sure that Dudley didn't

want it known that his father had left Felicity money, and that he wanted her dead before the will entered probate.

"The bills haven't been paid this month," Oliver said. "I handle the accounts. I know he doesn't have enough to pay us."

Dudley must be desperate, Ira thought.

He's got to get rid of Lady Armstrong so he can file the will and inherit his fortune. Whatever had stopped him from killing her before might not be enough to stop him now.

"Do you have any idea where Lord Dudley might have gone?"

"No." Oliver sighed. "He didn't take his valet, either. And he left his horse and carriage, too."

"His horse?"

"Lord Dudley always takes his horse. He travels by carriage, and when he arrives at his destination, he rides his horse."

"And he didn't take either this time?"

Oliver shook his head, and then his eyes narrowed.

"There was one other time when he left his horse home." Ira's pulse quickened. "But that time, he came home that night. I didn't think much of it then, it being only one night, but it was odd."

"When was this?" Ira asked.

"A few weeks ago."

"Did he leave the house on foot?"

Oliver nodded. "Aye, both times. I assume he walked to the train."

And he would walk across the meadow in Tolwich.

"When did he leave?" Ira asked.

"Early this morning. He told me to give the staff the day off. He didn't know when he'd be returning."

"I have to go." Ira stood. "You've been very helpful."

"Before you go, I have something for you," Oliver said.

Ira followed Oliver to the foyer and watched him open a closet in the hallway.

"We had a visitor one evening not long ago, a scruffy man whom I'd never seen before. Lord Dudley saw him in the library, and told me I was no longer needed. I left them alone, and the next morning, I found this on the table in the foyer."

Oliver reached up to the top and pulled something down. Ira's mouth was agape as he looked at the bowler hat in Oliver's hand.

"He never returned to retrieve it, and the day before yesterday, I saw his picture in the Times." Oliver held up the hat to show Ira the inside. "His name is inscribed on the inside band." It read Rufus Flagg.

CHAPTER 29

*S*upervisor Kent looked at him and shook his head.

"The butler said he didn't know where Lord Dudley was going," Kent said.

"No, but I know he's going after Lady Armstrong."

The older man shook his head again, folded his hands over his ample stomach, and looked out his window.

"But you have no proof."

"I have Flagg's hat, the one he always wore. It has his name inscribed on the inside band!" Ira stood and pounded his fist on the desk. "I have to go to Tolwich now. If I wait another day, it might be too late."

Kent took a deep breath.

"We're talking about a nobleman," Kent said.

"A nobleman who might have killed his father and his brother, and I know he killed Flagg."

"But you see my problem, don't you, Ira? You have no proof." Ira's mouth twitched and he sat. "It's your gut, isn't it? Your bloody gut."

"Please, sir, just let me go to Tolwich."

"Aye, go, but be careful. Don't arrest him unless...just be careful, and send a cable to Tolwich. Tell them to send someone to her house."

"Yes, sir."

Ira went to his desk to get his hat and umbrella before catching the train. He told the man in the cable office to send a dispatch to Tolwich right away telling them not to take their eyes off Felicity Armstrong's cottage.

The last train stopping at Tolwich was about to leave the station when Ira ran and climbed aboard. He settled into a seat near the front so he could be the first off when it reached its destination.

* * *

IT WAS dusk when he arrived in Tolwich, and Ira headed toward the police station. He passed the pub where a raucous party was underway, and then went to the police station a few yards away. The station was empty. Had they received the cable?

"Bloody hell," he said.

He didn't have time to search for them and imagined Felicity and Millie lying on the cottage floor dead by a madman's hands. He went to the livery and hired the only horse in the stable – an old dray horse named Sid.

"He's a good old horse," the owner said, "but he's used to the carriage. I don't know how he'd be with you on his back."

"Then we shall find out," Ira said.

The man put a saddle on Sid as Ira paced, his hands swinging and clapping, and then the man helped Ira into the saddle.

"e's big," the man said.

He was indeed, and Ira held onto the reins tightly for he knew if he fell off, he'd never get back on by himself.

"Follow the road, and keep to it when you get to the meadow. He knows the way."

"The horse?" Ira asked.

"Aye. Tompkins uses him to make his deliveries."

Sid's slow progress through town was maddening, but no matter how hard he urged the horse on, it trotted along as if it had nary a care in the world. An ominous foreboding grew in Ira's gut as the evening shadows hid the wildflowers in the meadow, making it look like a vast, black ocean. The horse was unperturbed, but Ira couldn't sit still. He kept squirming in his seat, and wishing he could fly.

The roar of the distant sea and the chirps of crickets couldn't draw his attention from thoughts of the bowler hat in Oliver's hand, or the realization that Rufus had most likely met his death in that house. Rufus could have forgotten his hat, but as a man who wore a hat everyday without fail, Ira knew that habits formed were hard to deny, and that hat had been labeled. It was important to Rufus, and Ira didn't believe he would have left the townhouse without it.

Had Dudley murdered Rufus in a fit of rage, or had his death been an accident? Was it a calculated act that gave Dudley a pleasurable release as in the act of making love?

Ira touched the Bulldog revolver holstered on his left side under his jacket. It was his police issued weapon, and he had never fired it in the line of duty. He did practice, and his aim was good, but he hoped he would not have to fire it this night.

He saw the lights of Bee's Nest cottage looming ahead and tried to measure the distance. Without a landscape to help him, it was hard to determine whether it was one mile or two, but he had been riding for quite some time. He encouraged himself by saying it was no more than a half-mile, and then felt an ache in his back. What if Dudley had a pistol?

He kicked the sides of the horse and it grunted, but it would move no faster. He would have made better time on foot, but he recalled the pitted landscape from his last visit and didn't want to turn an ankle. Instead, he worked on a plan of what he would do when he arrived at the cottage.

Felicity was Dudley's main target. Would she believe the lord was there to kill her? Had she been told that Flagg was dead, and if so, would her guard be down knowing that Flagg was no longer a threat? He wondered if one of the constable's men was still there. Maybe Felicity asked them to keep him there. Hadn't they talked about Lord Dudley when he interviewed her? Yes, but she had her doubts that Dudley could do such a thing.

But what about Millie? he thought.

The girl wasn't as soft as Felicity. He saw steeliness in her that reminded him of some of the prostitutes he'd encountered when he was a bobbie; women hardened by life and itching to hurt others, as they'd been hurt. Despite her broken arm, Millie would not sit still and let him hurt her lady.

* * *

FELICITY SMILED as she wiped the supper plates with a towel for she had a surprise to share with Millie. A letter had come from Mr. Benjamin saying he had gone to America and would be returning to England soon with news for her.

"That's why I haven't heard from him," she said.

Millie was at the table playing with a deck of cards, and when Felicity put the last plate on the breakfront, she put the kettle on to boil, and Millie dealt the cards. Felicity filled their cups with Mrs. Muir's soothing lavender tea, and they played Old Maid while they waited for the kettle's whistle.

"Millie," she said. "Do you remember when we talked about moving to another town?"

Millie's eyes lit up. "Yes."

"I think it would be better to live closer to other people."

Millie shuffled the cards as she thought about moving away.

"Where would we go?" she asked.

"Somewhere near the sea, but without the memories." Felicity watched Millie deal the cards with her good hand. "I would have to ask your mother for permission to take you."

Millie looked at her and Felicity was taken aback by the anger she saw in Millie's eyes.

"She'll want money."

"Well, if I sell this cottage, I will have a bit more money," Felicity said. "Still, she might want to keep you here."

"No, she won't." Millie stopped dealing the cards and stared at the table. "My mother doesn't love me. She told me I should have died when I was born."

Felicity's shocked expression made Millie blush.

"How could she say such a thing?" Felicity asked.

"She thinks it's my fault." Dr. Miller's words came back to Felicity as Millie twisted a thread on the edge of her new sling. "She says I…"

When she saw tears roll down Millie's cheeks, Felicity reached across the table and put her hand on Millie's arm.

"My brothers touched me. They'd…do things, and Mum said it was my fault. She told me she doesn't want me anymore."

Felicity's stomach clenched as Millie confirmed what Dr. Miller had said. She swallowed, and then gripped Millie's good arm.

"You're never going back there," she said. "You will always have a home with me."

"Really, miss?"

"Really, and from now on, you must call me Felicity."

Millie smiled, but it faded when she heard something, and looked toward the parlor.

"Did you hear that?" she whispered.

Felicity listened, but heard nothing save the roar of the sea.

"It's just the wind," Felicity said.

There was a knock on the door and Millie put her hand on her pocket. When they heard the man was no longer a threat, Felicity wanted to put it back in the bedroom drawer, but Millie asked if she could keep it a little while longer. Felicity gave in to her wishes, and now looked at the girl's hand.

"It's all right," Felicity said. "I won't open it until I know who's out there."

Felicity went to the window and saw young Constable Edward Jones at the door.

"Hello, miss," he said.

She opened the door and he smiled broadly.

"P.C. O'Toole got a cable from London asking us to watch your house."

"Did it say why?" she asked.

"Not sure, miss, he just said that fancy detective wanted someone to stand watch, and then he sent me." P.C. Jones smiled again. "He said I'm to stay outside so I don't fall asleep."

"Would you like some tea?" she asked.

"No, miss."

"Very well. Just give us a holler if you need anything."

She closed the door and wondered why the detective wanted someone at the cottage. They had found the man in the bowler hat. She felt a chill go up her spine, and then shrugged it off as foolishness before returning to the kitchen table.

CHAPTER 30

*L*ong before she had her arm broken, Millie had learned to use Felicity's derringer pistol. Mr. Brewer taught her how to clean it, load it, and how to take aim. She loved taking shots at the old stump near his farm. Felicity worried that the old pistol might go off accidentally, but Millie wasn't the least bit intimidated by the weapon and, in fact, rather enjoyed the sense of power it gave her.

Felicity had been reluctant to let her keep the gun in her pocket, but she understood that Millie felt vulnerable with her arm in a sling. The pistol alleviated some of Millie's fears, and since she had learned how to use it, Felicity relented and allowed her to keep it near her.

Felicity returned to the table, saw that the teacups were empty, and she felt tired. She took the cups to the sink and rinsed them out while Millie went to the parlor window. The lamp on the end table had been moved to the one beside the chair, which made it harder to see outside, so Millie moved it back. She then looked out the window again and was able to see the black outline of P.C. Jones sitting near the door. She opened the door a crack and peeked outside.

"Why are you here?" she asked.

"I was told to come and watch the house," he said.

Millie went back to the kitchen. Felicity was putting the cups and saucers away. She had heard Millie talking to Eddie and now the girl was staring at her.

"I didn't want you to worry," Felicity said.

"Why is he here?"

"I don't know. He said that detective from London sent them a cable."

"But the man is dead."

"I know, Millie."

"Then why do we need him here?"

Felicity saw the fear in Millie's eyes and her hand on her pocket.

"I'm sure it's nothing, just a precaution."

"A precaution from what?" Millie put her hand in her pocket. "What's going on?"

"Please be careful with that, Millie," Felicity said. "It's getting late. It's time for bed."

"I don't think I can sleep."

"Then rest. I'll see you in the morning."

Millie looked toward the parlor, and then went to her pallet. She didn't take off her shoes or her dress, but she did lie down.

Felicity made sure the back door was bolted, turned down the lamp over the kitchen table, and then went into the parlor. She rubbed her neck as she thought about the young constable sitting against the front door, and again wondered why he was there. What had the detective said while he was there? He'd intimated that it was Dudley who was behind Mrs. Muir's death and Millie's attack, but it was still hard for her to believe that a gentleman would go to such lengths. Surely he knew he could talk to her about his concerns.

She sat on the settee and tried to remember the day he came to the cottage. Their conversation had consisted of inconsequential tidbits of gossip, and he had made her feel self-conscious. He had said nothing about his father other than he had passed away. She had been so upset by his sudden appearance that she had failed to pay attention to his words.

She was lost in thought when a knock on the door startled her.

"Yes, Constable Jones," she shouted. She looked at the door and saw that she had forgotten to bolt it before sitting. "You may come in."

She stood and began to walk to the door. The door moved as it opened, and she saw Jones, but his face looked odd, and then she saw a dark stain on the front of his uniform. He fell face first onto the floor and she screamed.

"Why Felicity, is that any way to greet a guest?"

* * *

LORD DUDLEY HAD a grin on his face. He dragged Jones out the door, and then looked at the blood on the floor.

"So sorry," he said. "This is why I prefer strangling, or smothering, but I didn't see the constable in time to grab his throat." He came closer and Felicity backed away. He leaned toward her and adopted a cheeky tone. "I think he fell asleep. I thought it best to do it quick and be done with it." He took a small, folded knife from his pocket. "I keep it sharp." He opened it and put his hand in the air. "That way, I can get the job done in one stroke." He slashed it through the air as if to cut her throat.

Felicity's eyes were wide in horror. He was grinning as he put the knife back into his pocket. He looked around the room and shook his head.

"Ghastly," he said. "Rather like that tea you gave me during our little chat."

Millie heard Dudley's voice and got up. She felt her stomach clench as it had when supper was done and her mother told her to go to bed. That's when one of *them* would come to her bed. She went to the wall that separated the kitchen from the parlor, pressed herself against it, and held the gun close to her chest.

Dudley took off his coat.

"It's a lovely night," he said. "But I do think we should close the door."

He went to the door, but kept his feet away from Jones' blood. Felicity was screaming inside, trying to get herself to move, but she was frozen, just as she had been when one of Felicia's lovers cornered her in the hallway near her bedroom door. She watched him shut the door, and then he looked at her over his shoulder.

"You know it's hard for me to believe you and I are related." He knew. He turned and folded his arms. "You have no wit or charm, and you smell like a scullery maid in July."

"What do you want?" she said softly.

"What do I want?" He came closer, and wrinkled his nose. He took a handkerchief from his pocket and placed it near his mouth. He looked around the cottage again. "This truly is a hovel. "How can you abide living like this?"

She was speechless, and the numbing darkness that had always protected her fell on her mind like a shroud. She watched him as if he were in a play, on a stage alone, performing a soliloquy for an audience of one. She willed her foot to move, but it wouldn't obey her.

"Please don't do this," she whispered.

He walked across the floor and looked inside the kitchen door. Felicity held her breath, but he didn't go in. He went to the window and looked into the darkness, and then over his shoulder at her.

"Why are you here?" she said.

"Do you recall our visit a few weeks ago where I told you that Father had passed away?"

"Yes."

"Well, just before he died, I discovered he had a secret." He glared at her. "Something he'd kept hidden for years." He knew. "Something he wanted to set right." He turned and looked into her eyes. "He made a gesture, a small bequest to his *goddaughter*."

"His goddaughter?" she said.

She was vexed. Why would Mrs. Muir tell her she was his daughter?

"I overheard him talking to his solicitor." He came closer. "He wanted to add a codicil to his will leaving her a great deal of money. Funny he'd never mentioned her before, don't you agree?"

He glared at her and she cringed.

"Well, you can just imagine how I felt." He sneered at her. "So after we were told that Father had little time left, I went to his desk drawer and jimmied the lock. I found the new will." He sat in the chair by the hearth. "I went to his room and confronted him. I told him I would fight it, that no whore of his would get a farthing of his money, and that's when he told me you weren't his whore." He leaned forward. "You were his bastard daughter."

She looked away and bit her lips. He loved seeing her fear.

"You know, dear Felicity, I was not a happy child. I didn't like sharing my toys." He flicked an imaginary piece of lint from his trousers. "I didn't like being the second son, so I visited my brother Roland one day, and when I returned home, I was the *only* son."

She kept her eyes away as she understood his meaning. He was confessing he had killed his brother, and she knew that nothing would stop him from killing her, too.

She had never been so frightened, nor felt so helpless, and she shook her head. She realized she would die that night. She couldn't stop him, not if he wanted her dead, and this knowledge awakened something in her. She looked at him now and put her arms at her sides.

"You've come here to kill me," she said.

"Yes!" he cried. He was delighted. "Oh, I'm so happy you

understand." He stood. "What do you have to live for anyway? You have nothing, and no man would choose to marry you. Truly, Felicity, what do you have to live for?"

She was going to cry, but swallowed hard against the tears.

"How dare you decide what my life will be?" she said.

"I had nothing to do with it. It was your whore of a mother when she dropped her bloomers." Now he saw rage on her face. "Oh, dear, dear, look at you. You'd like to see me dead now, wouldn't you?"

She didn't have the pistol or she would have shot him. She hated his face, and his fancy clothes, and his arrogance. Every slight she'd ever endured came to the surface, and she was unaware that she had thrown herself at him until she felt his hands on her arms.

* * *

IRA AWOKE WITH A START. He was still holding the reins, but the horse had stopped moving. He collected his thoughts and looked in the direction of the cottage, but it wasn't there. He looked to his right and saw a wall of darkness.

As they adjusted to the darkness, he ran his eyes up the wall and saw the stars. He slipped off the horse and walked toward that wall, and then found himself walking upward.

The old horse *had* known where to go, and had stopped right next to the hill the cottage was built on. Ira climbed it slowly and felt the ache in his legs. He was used to walking on flat surfaces. The roar of the wind and sea muffled all other sounds. He was climbing against the wind and had to stop to catch his breath a couple of times, but soon he saw the lights of the cottage as he neared the top of the hill.

The light from the window illuminated the yard, and he inched his way to the door.

* * *

"POOR FELICITY. Doomed to die a spinster, her chastity untarnished by a man's touch." Felicity was struggling to hit his face, and he tightened his grip and pulled her closer. "I remember you following me about the garden like a lovesick puppy." He bent over and whispered in her ear. "Have you been dreaming of me?" He stood. "You want me to touch you, don't you? You want me to do nasty things to you."

He laughed hard when he pushed her to the floor.

"Of course, you'll have to wash first." He took off his coat. "But I shall be gentle." He took off his vest and his ascot. "Get up."

She was near the kitchen doorway. She slid toward it and he grew angry.

"Get up!" he cried. He went to her and grabbed her hair. "Get up!" He pulled her up by her hair and threw her on the settee. "Stupid little whore."

In the kitchen, Millie heard him, his words echoing what her brothers had called her.

"Stupid little whore."

She closed her eyes and shook her head. She felt their hands as they moved over her body, her arms pinned under theirs, and powerless to fight them off, only now she had a gun.

"Why are you doing this?" Felicity cried.

She looked into his eyes and saw blind hatred.

"Because he loved you more than he loved me."

He threw her to the ground and was unbuckling his belt when they heard a gunshot.

CHAPTER 31

*M*illie was sobbing, and Felicity saw a red stain appear on Dudley's shirt. He fell on her, and Felicity tried to push him away. Neither of them saw Ira when he ran in with his revolver drawn.

He went to Felicity and pulled Dudley away so she could get up. Ira turned him over and used the sleeve of Dudley's shirt to try and stop the bleeding, but he knew it was too late. He felt his neck for a pulse, but there was none.

Millie was sobbing so hard that she fell to her knees. Felicity went to her, knelt beside her, took the gun from Millie's hand, and then she hugged the girl as tightly as she could.

"It's all right now, my darling girl," Felicity said softly. "It's all over."

Ira knew what had happened, but his duty called for him to ask Felicity what had had transpired.

"Miss Armstrong, was Lord Dudley threatening you?" he asked.

"Yes," she said.

"Did you fear for your life?"

"Yes."

He sat back on his heels and contemplated his next move. He didn't want to leave the scene until it could be photographed.

"Where is your nearest neighbor?" he asked.

"Mr. Brewer's farm isn't far," Felicity said.

"In which direction?"

She looked to the east.

"It's too dark," she said. "You'll have to wait until morning." She looked at Dudley. "Can we cover him?"

"Do you have an extra bed sheet?"

"You can take the one from my bed."

He went to the bedroom, and then brought the sheet back to the parlor.

"Are you going to hang me?" Millie asked.

Ira covered the body, and then looked at Millie.

"It's not for me to decide, Millie."

"Oh," she said.

Felicity was still beside Millie and with her arm around the girl's shoulders. She held her close and Millie put her head on Felicity's shoulder.

"They can't hang her," Felicity said. "She didn't know what she was doing."

"It's not up to me, Lady Armstrong."

Felicity was crying now, and embraced Millie. Ira looked out the door.

"Who was that lad?"

"Constable Jones."

"I think I'll move him away from the door."

Ira went outside and pulled Jones' body to the side of the house. He was angry. They should have sent an older policeman, someone who would have known how to take Winston down, and none of this would have happened. In the morning, he would give O'Toole a piece of his mind.

* * *

THE FOLLOWING DAY, an inquest was held at the pub. Each man on the panel had known Millie all her life, and after Felicity testified that Dudley had killed young Edward Jones, it didn't take them long to declare that the murder had been "accidental."

Inspector Grayson wanted it known that P.C. O'Toole had sent P.C. Jones, a boy not three months on the force, to stand guard at Miss Armstrong's house when he should have done it himself. He had, instead, been at the pub to "keep the peace" during a party. O'Toole protested his remarks, and that, too, was duly noted in the record.

The decision of the panel would be on the record, but it would be up to a judge to decide Millie's fate. Most agreed, however, that the judge would respect the decision of twelve honest citizens performing their civic duty.

Dudley's body was placed in a plain wooden coffin and sent to London on the next train. After he was taken away, the pub opened for business, and the jurors lined up for a free pint in gratitude for their service.

As Felicity and Millie left the pub, Dr. Miller ran after them to offer them a ride, but they declined.

"We'd like to walk," Felicity said.

Dr. Miller had been to the cottage that morning to declare the deaths of Winston and Jones. He thought of the cottage floor, where blood had stained the floor near the settee and the front door. He had cleaned up the blood before leaving the cottage, but pink stains remained.

"Are you sure you want to go home?" he asked.

Felicity looked at him, and then toward the meadow.

"I'm quite sure."

Events of the night before had sealed her decision to move. She was going to tell Millie that they would be moving out of the cottage as soon as she spoke to Mr. Benjamin. In the meantime, she would cover the stains with a small rug when they got home.

CHAPTER 32

*I*n the days that followed, Millie's arm mended, but her spirits were low. Felicity, too, felt the enticing pull of numbing melancholia, and each day was a battle against its call. She and Millie spent more time walking along the shore while the warmth of the sun and salty air healed their aching hearts.

"I've placed an ad in the London Times," Felicity said one day as they sipped their morning tea. "One for each house."

"Have you decided where we'll go?" Millie asked.

"Not as yet, but we have time to make a decision."

She looked at Millie and remembered the little girl she'd been. Now, she was more cautious with her words, and wasn't keen on walking to town. Millie had always believed she could take care of herself, but never thought it would mean taking another person's life. The anger that had led to Dudley's death still frightened her, but one day when she went to Mr. Brewer's farm for eggs, he put his hand on her shoulder and looked her in the eye.

"You were angry, girl, and you'd been angry for a long time. Don't let it take you to such a terrible place. The next time you feel that way, yell, scream, and carry on like a banshee."

Millie had thrown her arms around him, but he was not

accustomed to displays of affection, and blushed as he patted the back of her head.

Felicity, too, had changed. She came to see her father as the villain in this play, for he had left her mother, an innocent girl who longed for love, alone and at the mercy of Lord Winston. He had also abandoned her to Felicia's care.

Lord Michael, like many noblemen, felt they had the right to live as they chose, while the women in their lives were imprisoned by archaic rules invented to keep them enslaved. As far as Felicity was concerned, her father was responsible for everything that had happened, and she wanted to exorcise his ghost from her life.

The bookcase in her bedroom held books from Rosendale that she had selected based on the memories they invoked. Millie and she had read them together, and now Millie, too, associated them with warm memories of her first year with Felicity.

As she looked out the kitchen window during breakfast, Felicity saw the rain watering her garden, and made a decision that would alter the course of their lives.

"I'm going to give Mr. Tompkins the books," she said.

"What books?"

"The books in my room. I don't want them anymore."

Millie was vexed.

"Are you sure?" Millie asked.

"Yes, I'm sure." Felicity drained her cup. "We'll go to town tomorrow and ask Mr. Tompkins to come and collect them with his wagon."

Millie looked sad. Every day, Felicity chose another piece of furniture, or picture on the wall to sell or discard. To Millie, those items were part of her home, and she couldn't understand how Felicity could be so insensitive about them, but the books were not like a worn settee. They were like living, breathing parts of her soul.

Millie pushed her chair away from the table and took her cup to the sink. She stood with her back to Felicity, who felt a change in her demeanor.

"What's wrong, Millie?"

"Nothing is wrong, miss."

Felicity got up and went to her.

"You're upset because I've chosen to give the books away."

"I don't understand why we can't keep them."

How could she explain her decision? How would Millie ever understand the convoluted feelings associated with the leather-bound tomes?

"We shall buy new books. We'll have plenty of money when we've sold both houses, and you can choose them."

"Yes, miss."

Her voice was above a whisper. She rinsed out her cup, and then left Felicity for the comfort of her pallet.

Felicity spent the rest of the afternoon cleaning the kitchen, and then sweeping and dusting the parlor. By four, Millie had not come out of the pantry, and the rain had stopped. The sun was high in the sky, and the wind blew over the meadow. Felicity went to the pantry and saw Millie, who was just waking up.

"Let's go to town now," Felicity said.

"May I stay here?"

"No, I want you to come with me."

Felicity remembered how Mrs. Muir would force her to rouse herself and go for walks near the stream that ran along the edge of Rosendale. She resented those intrusions for her desire was to hide from the world, but now understood why Mrs. Muir had been so insistent. It was too easy to give up; one had to fight if one was to survive.

She watched Millie get up using her good arm, and then Felicity got her market basket. She put on her hat, and they left the cottage. Millie lagged behind, and Felicity would glance at her from time to time to see if she was still moving. By the time they got to town, Felicity was glad to see the bakery.

"They'll be closing soon," she said.

"It's late. We should have waited until tomorrow."

"Aye, but then we wouldn't have biscuits for Sunday breakfast."

"But it's only Friday."

Felicity frowned.

"I didn't want to wait until tomorrow. I don't want to come to town when the market stalls are here and it's so crowded you can't move." Millie looked at the ground. "Why don't you go and tell Mr. Tompkins about the books and ask him if he can fetch them for me?"

Millie didn't say a word; she walked away, leaving Felicity in front of the bakery. When she went into the mercantile, Mr. Tompkins was taking an inventory of the store.

"Hello," she said.

"Aye, it's Miss Millie come to see me. How are you, Miss Millie?"

"My arm is almost healed."

"Now that is good news." He saw her frown and narrowed his eyes. "Why do you look so sad?"

"Miss Armstrong wants to give you her books."

"More good news. We can always use more for the shelf."

"She asked if you can come and fetch them in your wagon."

Mr. Tompkins saw how sad Millie was and put down his pencil and paper on a barrel near the end of the aisle.

"What's this all about then?" he asked. "You look like you lost your best friend."

Millie's lower lip quivered and she began to cry.

"I love the books. I don't want her to give them away."

"Well, I'm sure she has a good reason."

"She said we'll buy new ones," she said softly. "But I'll still miss them."

"Aye. There, there, don't be carrying on so." He went behind the counter and took a small bag from under the counter, filled it with raspberry drops, and brought it to her.

"Here, now have one. It will make you feel better."

She looked at the bag, and then took out a drop and popped it into her mouth.

"You know, Miss Millie, things change when you grow up. It's not easy when they do. You keep wanting them to stay the same."

Mr. Tompkins was right; she didn't want things to change. She had loved her life with Felicity before Lord Dudley came along, and she was angry that everything good in her life had been tainted by his arrival in their lives. She popped another drop into her mouth and managed a small smile.

"These are good," she said.

"It's good to see you smiling," he said. "Why don't you share them with Miss Armstrong?"

"I will." She sighed. "Will you come and fetch the books?"

"First thing Monday morning."

She smiled again.

"I'll let her know," she said.

After she left, Mr. Tompkins picked up his paper and pencil to finish his inventory, and he saw Sam stocking shelves. Mr. Tompkins had heard him come in late last night, and he worried that the lad was drinking too much ale. Sam had something to drink about, having lost his leg, but there was nothing wrong with the rest of him, so why couldn't he be happy?

Mr. Tompkins, who, with his wife, had decided that Miss Armstrong needed a good man to take care of her, believed that Sam was the perfect man to woo her. They had been conspiring to bring them together, and as he thought about Miss Armstrong's books, Mr. Tompkins walked over to Sam and put his hand on the man's shoulder.

"Miss Armstrong wants to give us her books," he said. "I told Millie you'd fetch them on Monday morning." Sam broke out in a cold sweat. His hands began to shake and Mr. Tompkins felt a shudder as he held Sam's shoulder. "Are you all right?" Sam nodded, but Mr. Tompkins saw that the color had drained from his face. "Well, you don't look good, lad."

"I'm fine, truly, I'm fine."

Mr. Tompkins completed his inventory while Sam tried to finish stocking the shelves. He thought about Miss Armstrong and her lovely hair, and felt his stomach clench. Whenever she came in, he could hide in the back room, or leave the store out the back door, but if he had to go to her cottage, how would he avoid seeing her?

Mr. Tompkins watched Sam from behind the counter. The man was a nervous wreck! Perhaps he was smitten with Miss Armstrong and couldn't overcome his shyness, or maybe he thought she would reject him because of his wooden leg.

Mr. Tompkins pursed his lips and shook his head again. He thought it was foolishness. Sam was a good man, and Tompkins couldn't believe that Miss Armstrong would look down on him because he was crippled. He had to build the man up and push him into her arms. That way, Sam would have to confront his fear, and perhaps, find a partner with whom he could share his life.

He had asked Sam to fetch the books, and Sam *would* fetch the books.

* * *

SATURDAY MORNING, Mr. Tompkins heard the bell and looked over the shelves, but couldn't see who had come in. He walked to the front of the store and saw a man no more than five feet high. He wore a business suit, a bowler hat, had dark eyes, a mustache and goatee, and wore gold wire spectacles. He also carried a briefcase.

"Good afternoon," the man said.

"To you, too," Mr. Tompkins said.

"I wonder if you could tell me how to get to Bee's Nest cottage."

Mr. Tompkins rubbed his chin. No one outside of Tolwich called it that, and since the terrible events that had transpired there were still fresh in his mind, he was reluctant to give the man directions.

"I might, if you tell me what business it is of yours."

"My name is Noah Benjamin. I'm Lady Armstrong's solicitor. I've come from London and I need to speak with her regarding a delicate matter."

Delicate matters. What he really meant was that it was none of Mr. Tompkins' business. Mr. Tompkins bristled over the man's attitude, but he looked harmless. Still, after what had happened to her, he didn't want to send another man to her door unless he was absolutely sure she would come to no harm.

"Constable O'Toole can take you there," he said. "Turn right and you'll see the police station on the left hand side of the road."

"Thank you."

As he watched the little man leave, Mr. Tompkins wished he could have taken him to the cottage so he could find out what "delicate matter" the little man had to discuss with Miss Armstrong, but since he couldn't leave the store unattended, he frowned, and went back to straightening his shelves.

CHAPTER 33

*A*s he walked toward the police station, Noah Benjamin recalled something he'd read in the newspaper about Lord Dudley Winston and stopped. He hit himself on the head with palm of his hand.

"You fool. She is probably under duress."

No wonder the man wouldn't tell him where she lived.

He went into the police station and asked for Constable O'Toole. In no time at all, they were riding toward Bee's Nest cottage in a hired carriage Noah paid for. As they rode across the meadow, Noah shared what he could about his reason for the visit, and O'Toole got a measure of the man. When they arrived at the foot of the hill, O'Toole told him he'd have to park his carriage at the foot of the hill.

"Too steep," he said.

Noah looked up and inhaled, and then exhaled before starting the climb up the hill. He was smaller than O'Toole, but the big man was faster. He made it to the top well before Noah appeared at the ridge.

O'Toole had already knocked on the door and had been greeted by Felicity when Mr. Benjamin reached the door. He took out his handkerchief, wiped the sweat off his brow, and then smiled at Felicity.

"Mr. Benjamin!" she cried. "I'm so happy to see you. Please come in."

She stepped aside and let him into the cottage, but he turned to O'Toole and put out his hand as the large officer came through the door.

"I must insist upon talking to her in private," Noah said.

O'Toole looked at Felicity, who nodded her head. He frowned as he stepped back so she could close the door.

Millie was in the kitchen and came to the doorway. Noah saw her as he took off his hat. He smiled, but she didn't, and went back into the kitchen without a word.

"She's been ill," Felicity said. "Do you mind sitting in the kitchen?"

"Not at all."

She looked at his briefcase.

"Would you like some tea?"

"Yes, please."

Noah looked around the parlor as he followed her into the kitchen. He went to the table, laid down his case, and then sat while Felicity prepared the teacups.

Mr. Benjamin! She glowed with excitement as she filled the kettle with water. She couldn't wait to hear what he had to say.

"I hope you will forgive me for coming without notice," he said. "I have some wonderful news and I simply forgot everything in my haste to get here."

She sat as they waited for the kettle to boil and looked at the folder he was taking out of his case.

"I know you've been to America. Did you receive the papers from Vicar Stephens?"

"Yes, indeed. Oh, I have so much to tell you that I'm unsure where to start." He opened the file. "The money from the bequest has been added to your trust. You will see it reflected in your allowance next month." He took another folder from his case.

Noah had returned from America with good news. He had invested the fifty pounds he'd promised Lady Armstrong in Mr. Alexander Graham Bell's "American Bell Telephone Company," and had the stocks made out in her name. Bell's company was doing very well, and Noah knew he had made a wise decision.

"Do you recall the fifty pounds I offered to invest in your name?"

"Yes, very well."

"Well, I met a man in America who told me to invest in Alexander Graham Bell's telephone company. He even introduced me to Mr. Bell himself, and I after talking to him, I knew it was the right place to invest your money."

"Why Mr. Bell's telephone company? Don't we have one in England?"

"Yes, we do, but I was so impressed with his machine, and with him, that I simply had to invest with him." He leaned toward her. "I truly believe it will make you a rich woman someday."

As she looked at the stocks he purchased in her name, he took another file from his case.

"Lady Armstrong, I have something else to tell you."

"You needn't call me Lady Armstrong, Mr. Benjamin. I've renounced my title."

He stared at her in disbelief.

"But it's your birthright. Why would you renounce your birthright?"

"It became more of a burden than a blessing. I'm very happy without it, I assure you. Now, what else have you to tell me?"

"Have you told anyone else of your decision?"

"Just the people here in town."

He shuffled through some papers and then looked at her with a smile.

"Very well. So, the firm of McKenzie, McKenzie, and

McKenzie has informed me that you are a beneficiary of a bequest from Lord Harold Winston."

She sat back in her chair and glared at him. He saw the look on her face and was surprised.

"But this is good news, Lady Armstrong. His estate is large, and you will be able to lift yourself out of this poverty and regain your position in society, which is why you should consider your decision to renounce your title."

"I don't want his money. I don't want anything from him."

Mr. Benjamin's face fell.

"Of course, that's understandable considering…"

"Give it to charity," she said. "Burn it. I don't care."

"Yes, Lady…Miss Armstrong, as you wish, or course, but if we invest some of it, you could live off the interest and still have a comfortable life."

"I don't want it. Not a farthing."

"Whatever you wish. I will find some worthy charities and let you choose which you'd like to support."

She was solemn and her hands were clasped in front of her. Mr. Benjamin hesitated while she absorbed the news of Lord Harold's bequest.

"And what of Captain Fowler?" she asked.

He took a sip of tea, and then took a deep breath.

"After making inquiries, I found your ship." Her eyes lit up. "There is some confusion, however, regarding what happened to the good captain."

"He wasn't with the ship?" she asked.

"I'm sorry, Miss Armstrong. I could find no one who remembered him."

When the kettle whistled, Millie, who had been listening from the pantry, came and turned off the flame. She poured water over the tea and brought the cups to the table. He smiled at her, but Felicity just stared at his case.

"I hope you don't mind, but I've arranged for the sale of your ship. It will add ten thousand pounds to your trust."

Her last hope, the one dream she'd had left to hang onto, could finally be put to rest. The ache in her chest grew, and she feared it would never go away. Tears formed and fell, and Noah looked away while she wept.

Mr. Benjamin looked to Millie, who stood against the counter, and then shifted his papers.

"If you are agreeable, I will need your signature on these papers," he said.

She looked at the papers, took the fountain pen he had laid on the table, and signed them. She looked at him and thought he had the kindest face she'd ever seen. She was glad she had met him and that he was handling her affairs.

Felicity signed all the documents, stopping once to look at the amount in Lord Winston's estate. It would indeed lift her out of her poverty, but the thought of using his money was abhorrent to her, so she signed and pushed it toward Mr. Benjamin.

"The money from your ship will be placed in your trust within the next month, and as I said, I will return so you can choose which charity you wish to endow." He stood and put on his hat. "I look forward to seeing you again soon."

"Mr. Benjamin," Felicity said. "There is something else."

"Yes, Miss Armstrong."

"I've placed an ad in the Times to sell my cottage. I also want to sell the one in Whitley."

"Both of them?"

She nodded.

"I wish to move away from here."

"I'm sure that can be arranged," he said.

"I will use the money to buy another home, but Millie and I haven't decided yet where we want to go."

"Very well. Perhaps I can find some available homes for your consideration."

"That would be wonderful, and there is something else." She looked at Millie. "I want to adopt Millie."

He looked at the girl and saw her cheeks redden.

"Truly?" Millie asked.

"Yes, truly. I want to keep you safe." She looked at Noah. "But her mother might want money. Can you handle that as well?"

"Of course, I'd be delighted."

Felicity and Millie walked him to the door, and O'Toole backed away from the window when Noah went outside. They both tipped their hats to the ladies before descending the hill, and Millie put her arm around Felicity's waist.

"Do you mean it, Felicity?" Millie asked again.

"Yes, I mean it. I love you and I want you to have a good life." Felicity threw her arms around Millie and hugged her tightly. "And when we find our new home, you shall have a proper bed."

CHAPTER 34

*S*am stood on the platform with a ticket to London in his hand. He'd thrown his things in a sack before leaving the mercantile before dawn and left a note for Mr. Tompkins.

Sam hated his cowardice, but his feelings for Felicity were strong, and he couldn't imagine she would want half a man. His wooden leg was showing wear, and even with the sheepskin Mr. Tompkins had given him to cushion it, his stump hurt at the end of the day. When he lost his leg, he wasn't sure what sort of work he could do that would support a wife and children. Stocking goods at the mercantile barely fed Sam. He'd make a sad excuse for a husband indeed.

He'd gone out the back door after Millie came to the mercantile that Friday, and he'd followed her so he could catch a glimpse of Miss Armstrong. Even without her title, she was still too good for the likes of him. He saw Millie walk through the market, and when she met Miss Armstrong, he stopped breathing. The longing to hold her, to hear her voice, was breaking his heart.

He went back to the store knowing he could never be with her. That's when he made the decision to go, and now, three days later, he was still pining, and knew the ache in his chest would remain until the day he died.

* * *

"BLASTED, FOOLISH MAN," Mr. Tompkins said.

He found the note on the counter, and then went upstairs to show it to his wife. She was in the kitchen finishing the breakfast dishes when he showed her the note. She sighed, but he was livid.

"I gave him a job, and a place to sleep, and all I wanted was for him to be happy."

"Oh, my darling, don't you see?"

"See what?"

She smiled as she placed her hands on his chest.

"What was Sam going to do today?"

Mr. Tompkins eyebrows met as he thought.

"He was to go and fetch Miss Armstrong's books."

She raised her eyebrows, and then he understood.

"Has he ever spoken to her? No. He's run into the back room, or left the store every time she comes in. If you ask me, he's so smitten he can't bear the thought of being near her."

"And I was sending him into the lion's den," Mr. Tompkins said.

"I haven't heard the whistle this morning. Go and see if he's still there."

Mr. Tompkins walked as fast as he could to the rail station. He felt like a fool. He'd worked with the man for months now, but he never understood how shy he was, or how deep his feelings for Miss Armstrong. When he got to the platform, he saw Sam waiting on a bench with a sack near his feet. He went to him and sat beside him.

"So, you want to leave me," he said.

"It's time. I've got to be off on my own."

"So you leave me high and dry to run the mercantile all on my own. That's a fine how-do-you-do."

Sam glanced at him and took a deep breath.

"I am grateful for what you've done for me, I truly am, but it's time. I need…I need to know I can take care of myself."

"Bollocks," Mr. Tompkins said. "This has nothing to do with you taking care of yourself, or some such foolishness. This has to do with Miss Armstrong, and you know it." Sam's cheeks reddened and Mr. Tompkins nodded. "Aye, you have feelings for the lass, but you're too shy even to talk to her."

"That has nothing to do with it."

"You're a terrible liar, Sam." Sam looked at him. "You care for her." Mr. Tompkins looked at Sam's peg leg. "And you don't think she can care for you because you lost your leg. Now that there is bollocks, and you know it."

A train whistle blew and they both looked down the tracks. Sam leaned forward to grab his sack, and Mr. Tompkins grabbed Sam's arm.

"Don't do this, lad. Don't go because you're scared. If you do, you'll keep running anytime something gets hard, and you'll be running all your life."

Sam's lip trembled and he shook his head.

"I can't," he said softly.

They felt the vibrations as the train drew closer, and Mr. Tompkins searched his mind for something that would change Sam's mind. He still had his hand on Sam's arm, and wouldn't let go.

What can I say to him? he prayed. And then he knew what to say.

"You can't leave me, lad. I've no children, and now, we've become accustomed to having a son we can rely on. If you leave, Mrs. Tompkins will wail, and I'll spend all my time consoling her." He stood. "Come. We're going home."

"Please let me go."

"I can't do it, lad. I can't live with Mrs. Tompkins alone anymore. I need you, and you owe me for being such a generous soul."

Mr. Tompkins waited for Sam to get up, and he felt Sam's movements as he pushed himself up and onto his legs as if he felt them himself. Sam looked at the train, and then at Mr. Tompkins, and then at his sack.

"She'll never want such a coward," he said.

"You're not a coward, lad, you're a survivor, and you'll survive this, too."

Mr. Tompkins took Sam's sack from his hands and started walking away, and he could hear the peg leg hit the platform floor as Sam followed him home.

* * *

MILLIE WOKE UP FEELING WONDERFUL. When Dr. Miller had checked her arm, he'd said she'd have to wear the sling for two more weeks. Today was the last day, and she thought of leaving it off, but Felicity would remember what he'd said. Millie was cooking their breakfast when Felicity came into the kitchen.

"Mr. Tompkins is coming for the books today," Millie said.

Millie didn't want to give the books away, and she'd been moping around for two days while Felicity pulled them from the bookcase and stacked them in the parlor.

"You're really going to give them away," Millie said.

"They remind me of things that make me feel bad," Felicity said. "I want to move away from those thoughts, but we will buy new ones we haven't read."

As she said it, she heard it – she wasn't thinking of Millie, she was thinking only of herself. The selfish desire to rid herself of the past was hurting the girl, who loved the books as Felicity had when she was young. If Felicia had taken them from her, she would have been devastated.

She went to Millie and put her hands on Millie's shoulders.

"I didn't understand what they meant to you. I think we should tie them in bundles so we can take them with us to our new home."

Millie looked at her and smiled broadly.

"Do you mean it?"

"I do, and what's more, you will have a bookcase in your room for them."

"I can have them in my room?"

Felicity nodded, and Millie hugged her as she thanked her over and over, and then looked up at Felicity.

"What about Mr. Tompkins?"

"I'm sure he'll understand."

"But he's coming with the wagon."

Felicity pursed her lips.

"We could try to meet him in the meadow."

"Shall we leave our breakfast?"

Felicity looked in the skillet at the scrambled eggs.

"They won't last. We'll eat now. Sid's an old horse and I'm sure Mr. Tompkins won't arrive before we're done."

* * *

FELICITY HUMMED as they walked over the ancient stones. She often imagined how it must have been two thousand years ago when the Romans occupied Britain. Did they know how long their legacy would last?

"There he is," Millie said.

They could see a wagon in the distance, but something about it was odd.

"That's not Mr. Tompkins," Felicity said.

"It must be Sam."

"Who's Sam?"

"He works for Mr. Tompkins."

"I've never seen him before."

Millie smiled.

"He's handsome and he has a wooden leg."

It was the first time Millie had shown an interest in someone of the opposite gender, and it warmed Felicity's heart, but by the way she said "wooden leg," Felicity feared it was that more than his handsomeness that Millie found appealing.

"Oh, he's handsome, is he? And how old do you think he is?"

"He's old," she said. "Like Mr. Brewer's son."

Mr. Brewer had a son who had recently turned thirty-five.

"That's not old, Millie, though he would be too old for you."

Millie wrinkled her nose.

"Oh, Felicity, I would never. I was thinking about you."

"Me!" Felicity cried.

"It's not too late for you to find a husband, is it?"

"Well, perhaps if I wanted one, no, but...why are we talking about this?"

"I don't want you to get lonely if I go away when I grow up."

Felicity felt a tug at her heart.

"You mustn't worry about me, Millie. I'll be all right. In fact, I've grown rather fond of being on my own. If you decide you want to go away one day, I'll be right as rain."

They were getting closer to the wagon and Millie started running toward it. Now, Felicity could see the beardless man and thought that from this distance, he was handsome. She smiled as she watched Millie running toward him and shook her head. Was *she* ever that young?

The wagon stopped as Millie came to its side and said something to Sam. Felicity caught up to it and smiled when Sam looked at her. When she got close, she looked at Millie, and the girl smiled.

"Sam, this is Miss Felicity Armstrong."

"Hello, Sam," Felicity said.

Sam took off his cap.

"Miss Armstrong."

His heart was beating so hard it was pounding in his ears. Sweat broke out on his forehead, and he tightened his grip on the reins.

Felicity came up to Sid and stopped to pet his mane.

"How are you, Sid?" she said, and then looked up at Sam. "Has Millie told you?"

"I told him we're keeping the books," Millie said.

"So I'm afraid you've made this trip for nothing," Felicity said.

She came closer and was by the side of the wagon across from Millie. Sam was looking at her, but he didn't speak. Felicity smiled at him, and then something flickered in her eyes.

He had no beard, nor captain's cap, nor a blue pea coat, but she knew his eyes. She backed away.

"Felicity," he said.

He thought of the day he woke up in the hospital.

"It can't be," she said.

He thought of the nuns teaching him how to care for his leg.

"Aye, it is."

He thought of the day he left the hospital in Liverpool without telling anyone when all he had was a picture and an address.

Disbelief washed over her as she looked at his hair, his nose, his mouth, and she felt as if she was falling backward in time, to the place they had met the last time she saw him.

"Oh, my Lord," she said.

Sam stood and came down off the wagon. His peg leg shifted a bit, and he almost stumbled, but held onto the side of the wagon. When he righted himself, he looked at her, his eyes pleading for mercy.

"I couldn't remember my name, or where I came from. All I had was this."

He took the tattered piece of paper from his pocket and handed it to her. She saw the drawing he'd made.

"It got me through the voyage to China, but on the way back, I cut my leg and it festered. The fever affected my memory. I didn't even know I'd been taken to the hospital." She kept shaking her head. "When I was well enough, I came here because of this address, but I didn't remember who you were until I saw you in town."

Millie came around the wagon, her eyes wide and her mouth agape, but Felicity just stared at him. She should be crying for joy, and throwing herself into his arms, but she felt numb.

"When I remembered you, I remembered how I loved you, and I couldn't bear for you to see me this way."

A tear rolled down her cheek as his voice brought back fond memories of their time together. She wanted to trust him, to drop her guard, and wrap her arms around his neck and pull him to her, but she could not. She was not the same naïve girl whose need for love outweighed her good judgment. She was a woman who had lost everything and survived.

"I believed too easily in the past." She looked at him. "I kept watching the sea for your ship, and hoping so hard that I could barely breathe." Tears flowed freely now. "I loved you so…" She began to sob. She was afraid to be overwhelmed again, out of her own control, and losing the liberty she'd worked so hard to obtain.

"Please, Felicity," he said.

She shook her head. "No, I can't."

She began to run toward home, and Millie was still staring at him.

"You're Captain Fowler," she said.

"I didn't know, Millie. I swear to you, I didn't know."

"You don't have to convince me," Millie said.

She turned and ran after Felicity, leaving him alone in the meadow.

CHAPTER 35

M r. Tompkins came to her door later that afternoon. It was his fault that Sam had come to fetch the books, and the lad turned up drunk and empty-handed four hours later and wouldn't say a word.

"You have to go and talk to her," Mrs. Tompkins said. "Please, Jonah."

Millie answered the door and smiled when she saw him.

"Hello," she said, and then she frowned. "She's not feeling well."

"I've come a long way, Miss Millie, and I want to see her."

Millie opened the door wider and he saw Felicity sitting on the settee. She was looking at her hands, and he noticed she was twisting a hanky.

He came inside and took off his hat. He went to the chair by the hearth and sat, and she knew he would not go until he found out what had happened that morning.

"Mr. Tompkins," she said.

"Would you like some tea?" Millie asked.

"Aye, I would." He looked at Felicity and she at him. "So, what's this all about? I sent my clerk to fetch your books and he returns four hours later drunk as a boiled owl with an empty wagon."

She looked so unhappy, and worse than she had after the terrible event when the lord was murdered right in front of her. She seemed unable to form words, and he felt he would have to move the conversation along.

"Sam is a good lad, Miss Armstrong, and I know he has feelings for you. I'd be very disappointed to find you had hurt him when all he wanted to do was get to know you. Sam…"

"His name isn't Sam," she said. "His name is Henry Fowler. I… hired him to command my ship."

Tompkins narrowed his eyes, and then raised his eyebrows.

"I didn't know you had a ship, miss."

"It was a long time ago when I first came here. I'd hoped he would bring back goods we could sell." She looked at him. "I hoped to increase my income."

"Then why didn't he tell me this himself?"

"He claims when he injured his leg, he became ill with fever. It affected his memory. He came to Tolwich because of the address on an old piece of paper he had in his pocket."

"Blasted man," Tompkins said. "Oh, sorry, miss, it's just that he tried to run away this morning and I talked him into staying. Why, if I'd known he's been lying to me all this time, I would have put him on that train myself and good riddance."

Millie came out of the kitchen and glared at him.

"Sam is not useless," she said. "He works hard."

"And why are you defending him, lassie, when he went and took advantage of poor Miss Armstrong that way?"

Millie folded her arms across her chest.

"He was hurt. He didn't do it on purpose."

Felicity twisted the hanky again.

"I had tender feelings toward him."

Tompkins sighed. "Aye, and he stomped all over your heart."

"But he didn't know!" Millie cried. "What's wrong with you?

He was hurt, and I saw his face." She looked at Felicity. "He loves you."

Her words roused something in Felicity. She remembered how Henry had tried to dissuade her from investing her money with him, and how she felt safe when she was with him.

"You don't know that, Millie," she said.

"Aye, miss, you tell her. What does a lass her age know of love?"

"I've read your books," Millie said. "The hero always looks forlorn when he's in love, and Sam looked forlorn as anyone I've ever seen."

"Henry," Felicity said. "His name is Henry."

"He had me fooled," Mr. Tompkins said. "I thought he was a good man."

"He was a good man, Mr. Tompkins."

"Aye, perhaps, but he's been through a lot, he has, and when a man suffers, all sorts of things happen to him. It changes his heart."

"I don't believe that," Millie said. "I don't believe...Henry has a bad heart."

Felicity thought of Henry drinking. She had seen her father drunk once – the day Lord Winston and Dudley came to Rosendale, just before her world was turned upside down. Lord Michael's inebriation followed a traumatic revelation. Had her rejection had the same affect on Henry?

She struggled with her emotions as she tried in vain to protect herself from the strong feelings she still had for him. Could she withstand another crushing disappointment by letting all those feelings destroy her hard won independence?

"He hurt me," she said. "I don't think I could handle being hurt again."

Tompkins curled his lip. Despite his anger at Sam, he couldn't forget the how hard Sam had worked for him, or how grateful he had been when Tompkins hired him. In his heart, Tompkins knew Sam was a good man, and that circumstances could force a good man to make poor decisions. He looked at Felicity and weighed his next words.

"Maybe we're judging him too harshly," he said. "I've seen him work till he can't bear the pain. I've left him with the till and he's never taken so much as a farthing. Until today, I believed he was an honest man."

Millie came to her and knelt near Felicity's feet.

"He's not like Dudley, Felicity."

She wrapped her arms around Millie and tried not to cry. Her emotions were jumbled. She wanted to run to him, but fear kept her frozen in place.

"I know," Felicity whispered.

"Then what's holding you back?" Mr. Tompkins asked.

"I need some time, Mr. Tompkins." She heard the kettle whistle and got up. "I'll get the tea."

"Never mind, miss," he said. "I've got to get back. Mrs. Tompkins will want to know how you are."

"Will you tell him I'm sorry?" Felicity asked.

"Aye, miss, I'll tell him." He put on his hat. "But I think he'd rather hear it from you."

She closed the door and then looked at Millie.

"Have I been a fool?"

"No, miss, you're just afraid."

"I'm sick of being afraid."

"Then maybe you should do what he said. You should go and see him yourself."

Felicity sighed, and then went to turn off the kettle. She and Millie had tea, and then Felicity went to the garden to pick fresh peaches as she recalled a sea captain's kiss.

CHAPTER 36

*F*elicity thought about Henry as she dug into the soft soil in the garden. It had been five days since she'd seen him, and she had avoided the mercantile when she and Millie went to town.

Millie, though, had gone into Mr. Tompkins' store, and had seen Henry's sad face. He hadn't shaved, and looked as if he'd forgotten to comb his hair.

She was hanging the sheets on the clothesline while Felicity worked in the garden and wondered how she could persuade Felicity to give him another chance. She knew the difference between a good man, like Dr. Miller, and a bad man, and she knew Henry was a good man.

After Millie pinned the last sheet to the line, she came over to Felicity and got on her knees. Her sling was gone, and she had been using her arm more and more, but it still ached at night when she tried to sleep. She used it now to pull a weed in the carrot patch, and then looked at Felicity.

"Have you decided to see him again?" she asked.

"I'm still thinking about whether I should."

Felicity stopped and straightened her back. She had done

nothing *but* think about him since that day in the meadow. Her feelings were as raw as the day his ship left the harbor and she longed to go to him, but something held her back. She had been an innocent girl when he went away. Now she was a woman who'd survived, who'd won her independence, and didn't want to lose it. If she went to Henry, could he accept her as she was now?

"I'm not the same," she said. "I've changed."

Millie's eyebrows met as she pondered this, but she couldn't understand why it would make a difference.

"I shot a man, and you still love me."

Felicity heard the sadness in her voice and blushed. At her age, Millie understood that true love was unconditional, and yet Felicity was allowing her fear to keep her from the one man she had ever loved.

"Perhaps I should see him," she said.

Millie glowed with excitement.

"Yes, yes you should. Oh, Felicity, let's go to town right now and see him."

Felicity looked at her soiled skirt and blouse.

"I can't go looking like this," she said.

"Put on your traveling gown," Millie said. "And wash your face and hands."

Millie stood, grabbed Felicity's arm, and helped her to her feet. As they were about to go inside, Mr. Tompkins appeared at the right side of the house.

"'Morning, miss," he said. "Millie."

"Good morning," Felicity said. She saw the look on his face. "What is it, Mr. Tompkins?"

"I come to tell you that Henry is leaving us. He's taking the train to London in one hour." He took a deep breath. "He thinks it would be better if he left you alone."

"No, no it wouldn't be better." She came to him. "I want to see him."

"Then you'd better hurry."

"Come, Felicity," Millie said.

"Did you bring your wagon?" Felicity asked.

"Aye, miss, I did." He smiled. "And I asked for a faster horse."

"Wait for us."

Millie took Felicity's hand and pulled her to the kitchen door.

"We must hurry," Millie said.

"But what if we miss him? What if he boards the train and is gone forever?"

"He won't. He loves you."

Millie took the gown out of the armoire and Felicity began taking her skirt and blouse off. Millie took the pins out of Felicity's hair while she put on the new skirt and blouse, and then she sat so Millie could wrap her hair. When they were done, Felicity looked beautiful.

"He's going to fall to his knees and beg you to marry him," Millie said.

"Millie!"

"Let's go."

Millie again took her hand and led her out the door and down the hill. They almost stumbled in their haste, and went to the wagon at the bottom of the hill. Mr. Tompkins was holding the reins, and as soon as they climbed onto the wagon, he urged the new horse on, and the wagon lurched forward so fast they nearly fell off.

"That's definitely not Sid," Millie said.

As they neared town, Felicity began to worry that he might reject her, or tell her it had all been a mistake, that he didn't love her, had never loved her, and had used her to get himself a ship, but Millie took her hand as if reading her thoughts.

"He loves you, Felicity," Millie said.

The wagon rumbled to town with only minutes to spare. Mr. Tompkins parked in front of the station and helped her out of the wagon.

"Run," Millie said.

Felicity ran to the platform and found him sitting on a bench with a sack at his feet. He saw her and stood, his face a mask of uncertainty. She came to him and looked him in the eye.

"Mr. Tompkins told me you were leaving," she said.

He was afraid to speak lest she vanish before his eyes. Her lower lip trembled, and her cheeks were pale, and she knew she couldn't let him go without telling him the truth.

"These last few days have been unbearable. I couldn't stop thinking about you, and the way we were when we bought the ship."

Tears rolled down her cheeks, and Henry took the handkerchief from his pocket, and wiped them away.

"There, there, it's all right."

"I never stopped loving you. I never stopped looking for you." She heard the train whistle and took his hand. "Please don't go."

He looked into her eyes and smiled, and then leaned toward her and placed a gentle kiss on her lips. It was as though they had never been apart, and she let herself be lost in the moment. She wanted to feel good; to feel whole and so close to him that nothing else mattered. She wanted to be loved, and in that kiss, was her answer.

CHAPTER 37

1890

*F*elicity placed a vase of wildflowers at the center of the kitchen table, and then wandered to the window overlooking her back yard to watch five-year-old Jack playing fetch with Bigsby, a terrier he had found shivering in the barn one cold November morning. He had begged to keep it, and of course, Felicity and Henry surrendered to his pleas.

Jack was a handsome boy with blue eyes like his father's. His life in Cornwall was comfortable and Felicity was grateful that he would never know poverty. Mr. Benjamin had created a trust in his name and would add to it from dividends earned from the stock investments he made for Felicity. Jack would be able to do anything he wanted, and knowing that always brought a smile to Felicity's lips.

She went to the parlor and lay on the divan Henry made her for Christmas. She put on her reading spectacles and opened the letter sent to her from London.

Dear Felicity,

*This is just a short note to advise you that Tom and I have made plans
to see you during the summer holiday. We have some news and wish to
share it with you in person. I can hardly wait to see my baby brother
and his new dog.*

*I am on my way to a meeting now and I must be off. Please hug and kiss
Henry and Jack for me.*

With much love,

Daisy

Millie O'Malley had become Daisy Armstrong when they
moved to Cornwall and her adoption was finalized. Felicity laid
her head back and sighed. Oh, how she missed Daisy!

It had been two years since Daisy married Tom, a decent,
hard-working young man with dreams of changing the world.
Felicity had been worried Tom might not understand Daisy's
past and encouraged the girl to keep it from him, but Daisy was a
modern woman and didn't believe in keeping things from her
husband. Tom heard what Daisy had to say, and then told her
that what had happened in the past was of no importance to
him now.

The wedding had been a small affair with Felicity, Henry, and
Jack in attendance. Felicity had asked if she wanted to invite her
mother, but Daisy said no, that Felicity was her mother now.

She had also received a letter from the hospital in Liverpool
telling her that the new wing would be dedicated in three weeks,
and they would like her and Henry to be there for the occasion.
The money Lord Harold Winston left her had gone to build a
children's wing, and to buy much needed instruments for the
surgical theater.

Felicity stretched her arms above her head, and then ran her
hand over her stomach. She hoped this child would be a girl, but

she'd be grateful for a healthy baby no matter the gender. She always felt exhausted, though, and hoped that Henry would come home soon so she could close her eyes and take a good, long nap.

She got up and went to the kitchen window. Jack was digging a hole and Bigsby was lying next to him. He was a good child, not a wanderer, and she had to keep reminding herself that she still needed to keep an eye on him. She went outside and sat on one of the deck chairs Henry had made so she could go out in the late afternoon and look at the sea.

Their home was built on a hill, just like Bee's Nest cottage, but the view was partially obstructed by trees. She'd christened the house Sailor's Rest in honor of Henry's past, and filled it with comfortable furniture and love.

It had been built for them to their specifications, and resembled a small Queen Anne styled mansion. They had three bedrooms, two water closets, a parlor, a dining room, kitchen, and library, which Felicity and Daisy had filled with new books they bought in London. Daisy took the books from Rosendale with her when she married Tom.

Henry had a workshop in the stable and he had learned how to make furniture. His artistic touch lent itself to strange, modern pieces that appealed to London aristocrats, especially the younger lords and ladies. During the week, he would fill the wagon with orders and, along with a boy from the village, would deliver them to their new owners. He hoped one day that Jack would want to learn how to make furniture, too.

Felicity had formally renounced her title, much to the dismay of Mr. Benjamin. He thought she should keep it for "one never knows when it will come in handy," but Felicity had made up her mind. She was Mrs. Henry Fowler now, and that was the only title she wanted.

* * *

As THE YEARS rolled by and Felicity's family grew, she would often take them to the beach where they would take off their shoes and stockings and run along the shore. Henry fashioned a new leg out of wood that was more practical and fit well, so he didn't mind hobbling through the sand.

As the children grew, two sons and three daughters, they would leave Sailor's Rest as their parents waved goodbye. When Felicity kissed her youngest daughter at the girl's wedding, she cried, and her tears went on for days. Henry held her and wept, too.

"We could move to London," Henry said one evening as they sat outside and watched the stars appear. "We can afford two houses now."

"I prefer the country," she said and squeezed his hand.

"We'd be closer to our grandchildren."

She looked at him and smiled. Henry was always trying to please her, and she always tried not to take him for granted. She brought his hand to her lips and kissed it.

"You are so dear to me, my love," she said.

"What would you like to do then?" he asked. "Would you like to travel?"

"Do you think it's safe to travel?"

He frowned. The war to end all wars had taken a terrible toll on England, and he tried to imagine what Europe looked like now.

"Perhaps we could go to America," he said.

"We wouldn't have wine with our dinner there," she said.

"I've heard there are places called speakeasys where they sell alcohol."

"They also arrest patrons from time to time." She smiled. "Who would bail us out of jail?"

"Well, then, I suppose we could stay right here."

She leaned over the arm of her chair and looked him in the eye.

"We can always invite the children to spend the summer."

He held her hand and rubbed his thumb over the smooth skin. He felt old, as if the wind had been knocked out of him. The truth was, all he wanted to do was sit with her every evening until the Lord called him home, but if she wanted to see the children, she would see the children. Unlike him, she never seemed to age.

"That suits me," he said.

She smiled.

"Well, then it's settled. I'll write to each of them tomorrow."

Henry kissed her hand, and then held it to his chest. He remembered staring up at the stars as her ship sailed toward China, and dreaming of the life he now had.

Felicity still had the spyglass she'd used to watch for the ship, and kept it in her dresser drawer, a symbol of the hope that had held her in its arms while she waited for her life to begin.

The End

THANK YOU

Readers, I hope you enjoyed *A Lethal Legacy*. If you enjoyed the story, then perhaps you can help others enjoy it too.

Recommend it: Just a few words to friends, your book clubs, and your social networks would be wonderful.

Review it: Please tell your fellow readers what you liked about my book by reviewing *A Lethal Legacy* on Amazon. This link will take you to the *A Lethal Legacy* page on Amazon if you'd like to leave a review.

ABOUT THE AUTHOR

A.L. Jambor lives in Florida with her husband, Hans. Amy began writing at the tender age of fifty-eight when she was inspired by a photo of her granddaughter. The result was But the Children Survived, an apocalyptic story about how a pharmaceutical company's greed led to the destruction of North America. From there, Amy began writing fantasy mysteries that incorporated both her love of puzzles and her humor. Nick Dandino and Lord Percival Plep are two of her protagonists – the first a PI in heaven, the second an English lord reincarnated as a pudgy terrier named Libby. She has also written an historical time travel series and a dark crime thriller. You can find all her books on Amazon.com.

For more information go to:
www.aljambor.com

Novels

But the Children Survived

Dangerous Stranger

Their Best Dreams

Where's Audrey?

A Tender Heart

Don't Look Back

What She Deserved

Novellas

The Room in Grandma's House

Kevin Chandler and The Case of the Missing Dogs

The House on the Shore

The Christmas Cottage

Divine Detective Agency Mystery Shorts:

The Body in the Bungalow

The Kid at the Candy Counter

Libby the Psychic Dog in:

My First Christmas

Mystery in the Mansion

Quandary on the Quay

The Nefarious Neighbor